GRAVES

Quentin S. Crisp was born in 1972, in North Devon, U.K. He studied Japanese at Durham University and graduated in 2000. He has had fiction published by Tartarus Press, PS Publishing, Eibonvale Press and others. He currently resides in Bexleyheath, and is editor for Chômu Press.

QUENTIN S. CRISP

GRAVES

THIS IS A SNUGGLY BOOK

Copyright © 2019 by Quentin S. Crisp
All rights reserved.

ISBN: 978-1-943813-92-6

Contents

Sentimental Prolegomenon

HOW can I explain?

There is the world out there and it has immediate, scientific, browbeating claims to being everything, and in that world—also known as 'this world'—you must fight, fight and lose, and you are a weakling to be despised if you suppose there is anything else.

But I came away from my desk today and from all the trouble of everything. Not even from my desk—just came away, as if pulling my face out of a cave into the sweet twilight air whose unboundedness was draggled, as a ruined temple is draggled, with the rust-amber vines of imagination. And I remembered the world had never been anything to me but an unwanted intrusion, a slavery of forgetfulness haunted by unexplained patches of familiarity; only creepers of ivy across crumbling walls at its quiet edges formed any dependable reminder of what it was— what blessed thing—that had been intruded *upon*.

I walked down the hill to Hall Place and the diorama of tranquil ghosts in my mind seemed projected onto the world around me, marbling the trees and buildings with enchantment. The authority of solid matter was dissolved and the primacy of phantasmagoria re-established with cherubic lightness. A question surfaced in my mind: by what deception had I been so long persuaded to repress all that is most important and most natural to me? It was this deception that I had come away from.

I would like to name and thereby to unmask it, but deception is, by its nature, a shape-shifter, and I cannot point my finger without injustice until I have first tracked down the switch deception has made, of one thing for another, in my heart. But since I must defend myself, I shall point even with injustice, and make my defence my confession.

These masks might be empty now, but deception has worn them to defeat me, and might do so again:

Buddhists for whom the word 'ego' is as frequent and indispensable in conversation as the word 'God' is for atheists. Techno-hipsters, suspicious as U.S. border control, who gloat and bray with inexplicable vindictiveness that the ascendancy of machines over humans is nigh. Those on the two sides that both sides insist on, who say, "If you're not with us, you're against us." Those who decree the personal is political, thereby disallowing you *your* personal feelings unaccompanied by *their* political interpretation, while imposing *their* personal feelings as political orthodoxy. *Guardian*-readers who cannot disguise the brittle conceitedness behind the threats they make with Pavlovian readiness to any who question the precarious hauteur of their shrieking scientism. Strategists of political correctness and their eunuch camp-followers who corrode the very fibres of the muscles of the heart of truth.

I believe I know what all of these have in common, though to assert what I believe confronts me with a loneliness like lunacy. Whether they only accept winners or whether they only accept losers, all of the above agree that there is nothing but this in the world. There is only this world, so you have no excuse to spend a second of your time doing anything but winning. Or, for those with the photo-negative version of this creed, there is only this world, so you're deluded—and therefore a loser?—if you spend a second of your time doing anything but losing.

Somehow I feel we're as intimate as mutual blackmailers, you and I. So let's have a moment's amnesty—I'm an old-fashioned madman and you're a hateful vandal. I can tell by your sneer that you already know my prejudices and my failings. I won't tire you with more detail. You're right. I deserve to be alone. I will embrace my loneliness and my failure—that you mock my failure with your own is proof of your hatefulness—and with them I will embrace my right to continue loathing whomsoever I loathe. And with my madness I will embrace the right to go on prizing the impossible that is death-in-life.

And now I must explain this necessary but misleading phrase, 'death-in-life'.

On the 24th of March, 2014, I made a telephone call to the Samaritans. After I had given the relevant background information, the woman to whom I spoke asked the following interesting question:

"What do you feel when you think about ending your life?"

I acknowledged that this was a good question. Strangely, I do not think I had ever been asked precisely this question before, and so I had never in my life been able to speak aloud, until then, the following answer:

"I think I need to have an end in sight, even if it moves. Without an end there's only trouble stretching to the horizon, with no relief, and I can't bear the weight of it. But if I think about killing myself, even start to plan it, there's an end in sight, and the burden is no longer as heavy. I need to feel I could escape at any time. It doesn't have to be immediate, as long as it's in sight. Two years away, maybe, or three. Or I might bring it forward when the sky is especially heavy. So, thinking about killing myself is what's kept me alive this far."

So you begin to see what I mean by death-in-life, though, as suggested by the above monologue, it is more a will-o-the-wisp than an accomplished presence. The winners that I spoke of will admit the legitimacy of nothing but life-in-life, and the mirror image of this, the banner of their sworn opponents, is living death. Perhaps death-in-life has a mirror image, too, which is life-in-death, but I hesitate to reach out to something so fortified with subtleties. The subtle moat has a way of widening, and it is deep. No chasm of the unknown is wider and deeper than death and only in that bottomless unknown is the riddle's answer.

There are plenty who do not even wish you to contemplate the riddle. They will call you very curious names, such as coward, or weakling, if you speak about it.

This belief in a flat life is a contagion that has spread even to would-be friends. Searching on the internet for advice related to suicide, I found a site the text of which showed all the signs of good writing—the absence of confusion and the presence of open-minded sympathy. But even there a discordant note intruded. The relief you are seeking in death, it said, is something that can only exist in the mind of someone living. The good intention, to ward us away from self-destruction and what is presumed merely death-in-death; and so we are back again in a world where there are only winners and losers, advertisers and cynics, impatient entrepreneurs and buttonholing pessimists, exploitative bosses and angry picketers. A world, in short, of bullies.

That there is nothing after death is ultimately no deterrent since nothingness is precisely the riddle. The nothinger the nothingness, the more compelling the riddle.

The action and the reaction of human beings are powered by the poignant tension between life and death, and I have feared being caught and mangled in the for and against of this mechanism. Humans and their implacable, conflicting purposes have terrorised me.

After my phone call to the Samaritans, I reflected that I have relied almost completely on a single trick for survival. When humans have approached—especially in groups—I have evaded entanglement in their disputes and schemes by crawling to the edge of a cliff, lowering myself down, and dangling there. In this way, first, I escape casual detection, second, I am thankfully in no position to be useful to anyone, and third, I can sense the ultimate and lasting escape just below my limbo-treading feet. I feel the motion of the air and am chilled and soothed by an apprehension of the deadly, plunging vacancy whose topmost breath this is. I hang here like a question mark, and as long as there is no answer, this suspension is also safety. I hope no one kicks my fingers away before I am ready.

I seem to have come to another period of my life in which I need to dangle. Realising this, I have decided to write a dangling story, for myself and for all those who are tired of the bullies of success and the bullies of cynicism, neither of whom will allow death to be ours.

Stand with me in the shadow of a tombstone and cool yourself. I intend to muster a tale in which death is beautiful—a tale of the improbable and picturesque. I will be called sentimental; I will be called resentful. I will figuratively submit myself to the clichéd rite of L-O-V-E and H-A-T-E in tattooed capitals on my knuckles, as if romancing some place where I would be strung up as meat in minutes. I have no choice. By this unlikely means I shall survive, until I can survive no longer and I am nothing but a diviner's entrails signifying all I could not endure, and after having laughed so long, then the bullies will see horror.

But now I shall strike up the tale . . .

GRAVES

(A Distressing Novel)

I. Necropolis

AN urn finial, grappled by vines, at the corner of a stone stairway. Here Damien pauses. The stairs lead to a descending avenue of mausolea. He senses the influences here combining to bring forth one of those moments in search of which all that would otherwise be the savings of his solitary life are spent. People never show more than a casual interest, and he can satisfy that by saying that he loves to travel, which is not exactly a lie. If they were to question closely, they might find the details of that travel eccentric, but they never do. And if it were mere ghoulishness, it might even be the kind of thing to boast of in an internet 'about me' statement—it is so hard to know what is taboo and what is tame these days. Instinct tells him that whatever is hard to understand, whatever hard to explain, remains under the shadow of human suspicion, and the moments he devotes his private time to seeking are ineffable. It is as if his life is dedicated to tracking down the perfect summer breeze.

He does not take out his camera yet, knowing from experience that this desire to capture a moment, if hastily indulged, is liable to prevent it. Anyway, there are things photography cannot record.

So he halts here, with his left hand upon the stone of the balustrade next to the finial, and with something languid and faintly grandiose in his stance, as if he looks down now upon the whole world. But that is precisely why his feet have slowed at this spot, he decides.

He is still young, but already he has followed the skittish beam of an attendant's electric torch along the grid of pathways between graves one summer night in Zôshigaya, seen the stone angels and broken columns among the mist-exhaling, ivied trees of Highgate, wandered forgetful of all time the citadel-park of winged hourglasses at Père Lachaise where the narrow houses of the dead stand like streets of dovecotes in which nest only shadow and silence, listened to the homely tones of the volunteer guide, explaining with familiarity the distinguishing traits of the stacked skulls of St. Leonard's ossuary, been witness to the tribute paid by autumn, in fresh reds and yellows, to the spirit of human continuity where the slopes of Kensico are a neat, endless now of monuments and epitaphs, felt warm peace in the scent of pine resin and paraffin as he watched an ant crawl over the marble of a grave in a well-tended site overlooking the Sea of Crete, and already his instincts have been gloriously confirmed by the ten decorated skeletons of the Basilica of Waldsassen, posed and made opulent by Adalbart Eder the goldsmith for whom death was no barrier to speech—the dazzling encrustations of pearls, rubies and other myriad jewels on the bones with which this craftsman communed, impressing Damien as the ultimate efflorescence of decay.

These are only a few of the treasures densely packing the sepulchral reliquary of his remembrance.

In threading the globe as he has, with the dotted line of his travel, he has sewn so many such sights and impressions together that the world has become to him one ever-ramifying city, and that one city a necropolis.

Such is the view the corner of which he has stepped into at this moment.

A visitor to a museum may find the exhibits to be desiccated fragments with not much more interest in them than an average history lesson at school, until, for some reason, a particular bas-relief brings back the living breath of a day two thousand years vanished. For Damien, in his survey of graveyards, crypts and catacombs, things are, to a degree, similar. Not every inscription on every headstone will bring the half-limpid, half-foetid transports with whose nuances he is increasingly intimate. He might view a dozen potter's fields in a row with only the faintest of stirrings. But when the feeling comes, anything from frisson to exaltation, the great difference is this—the museum-goer experiences a dead past revivified, but Damien, among the graves, sees even the living present as the slightest portion—differentiated by the minimum contrast necessary for anything be seen at all—of a sweeping vista of charnel majesty, aeon-tiered, beyond vision, in arches of interlocked bones.

The visitor to a famous city might think of the feet that have trod its thoroughfares through the ages; Damien thinks of how the feet now treading the necropolis of the world are to be added, in vanishing, to the ages of the buried. That what *was* no longer *is*, Damien judges an enigma—apparent yet impossible. That impossibility forms the ground on which the living walk. That they live now who never were before is another enigma—also apparent, also impossible. The two impossibilities mirror each other, so that Damien sometimes sees the dead walking their inverted streets with us their mere reflections.

Damien—hand on balustrade—has been, in his mind, teasing loose some knot of summer breeze, to unsnag and unleash it. Preoccupied with this subtlety, he has not noticed until now that the urn finial has become a massive, hollow-eyed skull, and all the mausolea below seem to drip with sepulchral fluids, as if decay were an army of snails, and even the trunks of the green-leaved trees are excrescences of death. All things above earth, weird toadstools of necrophagy; all things below earth, the very riches of the kingdom of decomposition, offerings for rebirth more potent than any entombed with pharaoh.

At such moments, Damien believes without effort that Adalbart Eder surely did talk with the dead.

II. Retrospection

THOUGH it would never matter to anyone but himself, there was a kind of satisfaction for Damien in looking back over the development of his passion for graves. There had been stages, and he found something like a historical interest in comparing them, but the progression from stage to stage did not seem a simple, linear one.

For instance, having just moved into his studio on Candle Street, two minutes from the Thames, he was unpacking his accumulated effects to arrange them in a larger space than he was used to, and, desultory in this reverie-inducing activity, had grown thoughtful over a paper Kodak pouch of printed photographs from those not so distant days when one needed to take negatives along to a shop to be developed—when technologies were miscellaneous rather than monopolised. Taking these photographs to the Stanley knife-scarred table in the centre of the main space, he sat down, rolled himself a cigarette, and, lighting it, proceeded to examine them one by one. The memories associated with the photographs took him backwards and forwards in what felt more like a spider chart than a normal textbook timeline. Having looked at all the photos, he extracted two in particular, like cards from a deck, laid them side by side on the table, and blew contemplative smoke through the air above them.

On the left he had placed a photograph apparently taken from a crouching position, of an empty set of swings behind which, seeming to form an enclosing wall, without gaps, a number of headstones were visible side by side, like a greyer, more featureless version of the advertisements that line a race track. The location was a small children's playground in a town in Wiltshire.

Damien remembered exactly why he had taken this photograph, and the several similar photographs belonging to this film. The playground, a walled-in, almost-square area of turf, was not obviously attached to any building or institution. It had once, and until very recently at the time the photograph was taken, been a cemetery. Someone, for some reason, had decided that the graves must make room for a swing set and a see-saw, and so all that remained of the cemetery was the headstones, which seemed centrifugally thrown to the walls, the grassy turf area, beneath which the dead were perhaps still decomposing, being now cleared and flattened.

Damien had been sufficiently fascinated that he had hoped to catch something unusual in the photographs he had taken. Looking at the photograph now, he wondered whether the world had changed so much in the intervening time that no one would leave any traces to suggest a playground had once been a cemetery if a similar decision were made today. This seemed, to him, very likely. Everyone was familiar with the paradox that prudishness forbade the mention of sex in front of children even though children were precisely the issue of sex. Damien had come to see that prudishness also blushed at the ribaldry of death, which as much as sex was necessary to the production of children. America had tainted everything.

This photograph did not show it, but others belonging to this film did—next to the playground, separated by a wall, was what remained of the original cemetery. The wall surrounding this area, unlike most of the wall around the new playground, was over head height, as if constructed that way in an act of deliberate concealment. There was one entrance, from the street, a door of flaking paint and weathered planks with nothing to indicate what lay behind it. The very wall it was set in was crumbling and uncared-for, giving the impression that, though no living human might claim the place, to enter was to trespass. Yet the door had been open whenever Damien tried it, and what was contained within the high, crumbling walls was merely graves and an almost fantastical growth of weeds and grasses. The stones, subsiding here and there, as if some section of the yard might collapse at any moment like a mineshaft, were so crammed that Damien had almost been convinced of the absurd idea that these were all the graves that had once taken up twice the area, before the playground was made way for, and that the method of cramming had been to push in the containing wall so that it swept the graves along before it.

It had not been in casual curiosity that he had first explored this burial ground or returned to linger there. But what had it been? No single word was adequate. Fascination? Excitement? Enchantment? 'Intoxication' was close, but even that was a dull approximation.

In memory, Damien was at the scene once more. He moved between the close-packed graves with a quiver of anticipation, as if in nearness to possibilities he could not name. It had recently rained, that first time, and the atmosphere was clammy—cold, and yet, with the algae-green surfaces of the soaking stones on all sides, forcing on his imagination the idea of a jungle humidity. Never before had a cemetery affected him so sensually, so viscerally; and therefore, never before had a cemetery affected him so spiritually. He buzzed with some undifferentiated yearning that was not the domain of hunger or sex or sleep but which it seemed surely he must gratify here if only he knew what the act was that the yearning called for and belonged to.

What made him feel this here when his fascination in other cemeteries had been so attenuated? Here, the slow chaos of decay was palpable. It was hard not to see, in his mind's eye, the buried remains mingling in a soil-choked orgy of putrefaction.

Cemeteries, of course, were gardens of a kind. Gardens of stone, at least to the outer eye. But this garden was losing its orderly stamp, becoming brambled with its return to the wild.

And the peace that was sown here was all the sweeter for nature's encroaching disorder. Reading epitaphs can be an experience of dust and emptiness, as if the words no longer have anything to refer to. But, patched with lichen, and smoothed here and blemished there like the coins of a bygone age, on cracked and on slanting stones, the epitaphs of this cemetery had a more threnodial obscurity and brought to mind the sensitivity of a naked human body in the inhospitable and melancholy climate of a northern country. The forgetfulness of this garden was a greater and wilder and more quivering forgetfulness than most.

On that first occasion, Damien made his personal tour of that crowded, crannied place in complete absorption. Its compression and neglect had a pestilential quality. As some substances are compacted into diamonds or oil, so it seemed decay was compacted here into a thrill that no imagination once touched by the seductions of death could resist. The indecent number of snails in that place, on the paths and the stones, were like the overflowing of his own delight. When he exited back into the street, it was with the secretive smile of one who has just visited another world, and he brushed from his coat the many seeds that had stuck to him from the heads of the rank and rain-wet grasses, more carefree in his actions than a lover adjusting clothes, though with a like consciousness of impropriety.

That cemetery had reminded him on his first discovery of it, as it reminded him in his recollection of it now, of Baudelaire's poem, 'The Joyful Corpse'. For one thing, the poem mentioned snails, as if they were a particular signifier of the liberation of death; as if it is especially through communion with snails that the secret joys of decay at last become familiar and real. More fundamentally, burial was depicted, in the poem, as a fulfilment beyond all words. But this was where things had become problematical. How was one to experience that fulfilment while still alive? Yes, of course there was premature burial, if an accomplice could be found, but that was Poe-esque nightmare, not Baudelairian fulfilment.

With the Baudelaire poem, the chart of Damien's mania for graves began to expand, unfolding from the point marked by the photograph. Although he had read the poem some years before discovering the Wiltshire cemetery, and had recognised something in it on first reading, he felt sure that its significance had swollen retrospectively in relation to the cemetery so that the later event influenced the earlier. In short, the traffic of influence between present and past became two-way. Life had given Damien plentiful occasions to observe this phenomenon. With the present so much influencing the past, it became harder and harder to say exactly how and when his mania had begun. Anyway, as this photograph on the table reminded him, he had come to associate the freedom and the yearning of childhood—that is, the closest thing to the spiritual essence of a reason for life itself—inextricably and very nearly exclusively with graves, with graveyards, with tombs, with death.

But the chart of his obsession unfolded in other directions, too. One of these was represented by the photograph he had set down to the right of the first. There were thirty-two photographs in this film, largely divided between photographs of the playground and cemetery and photographs from a week-long writing course he had attended at a farmhouse in Somerset. There were a few miscellaneous shots from other times and places, too, but these were of little interest to him. The photograph on the right was from the writing course. He had been interested enough in poetry at that age to make some effort at formally developing his skill. In fact, this writing course—specifically for poetry—must have marked the high tide of such efforts.

The photograph had been taken from inside the farmhouse. It showed the frame of the open back door, with the faces of four of the attendees looking in. Damien was among these four. He was bunched together with a young man and woman on the left. They posed playfully in such a way that their heads peered round the jamb at different heights. The fourth figure was somewhat to the right, on her own. She appeared as if about to walk away, looking over her left shoulder in casual disdain before doing so. It was either chance in timing or skill on her part that had caused her to be photographed in this poised and expressive attitude.

That the writing course photographs shared a film with the cemetery photographs perhaps indicated the occasions on which they were taken were close together in time, though it was true sometimes a gap of months or years might separate, for instance, the penultimate and final occasions recorded in such a film. Damien's memory was not reliable on such questions, though if he examined the strips of negative images also kept in the paper pouch, he should at least have been able to determine which came before and which after.

What pleased and intrigued Damien was essentially this: whether or not these otherwise unrelated occasions had arisen in quick chronological succession, they were related by this photographic film. They had since—retroactively—become related in other ways.

Damien had, after the writing course was over, corresponded with all three of the other attendees in the photographs on the right, but in the case of two of them, this correspondence had sunk, within a year, into a more or less respectful apathy from which there was no return. His correspondence with Sadie, by contrast, had returned more than once from deeper abysses than apathy, and, seemingly in defiance of probability, continued its crabbed, unsteady course to the present. She was the one who, in the photograph, stood apart.

He inhaled especially deeply as he rested his gaze on the figure of Sadie, as if he wanted to swallow, once and for all, the elusive satisfaction that nicotine addiction was actuated by but never quite achieved. Inevitably, he exhaled, once more, the smoke of his resigned failure. But if there had been anyone present capable of divination by cigarette smoke, or merely sensitive to the nuances of exhaled breath, they might have detected, in despite of the resignation, or prevailing over it, a sense of perseverance, even defiance.

He recalled to mind now three things about Sadie from those early days.

His earliest distinct memory of her was an occasion close to the beginning of the writing course. At that age there had still been a ticklish excitement to meeting new people left over from the schoolboy instinct for making friends, and he, David—the other male attendee in the photo—and Sadie, as the youngest on the course, had gravitated into a kind of trinity. With any two of the three, it might not have worked, but the chemistry of the short-lived trinity seemed to serve a very specific purpose.

The three of them had lounged together with the unconscious intimacy and vanity of youth in the reading room when, seemingly by chance, no one else was there, and somehow the conversation had, by swift and skilful combinations of the casual and the edgy, made a diagonal move into the territory of greatest preoccupation for their age group.

David was three or four inches taller than Damien, and had a lean, vital presence perhaps honed by the kickboxing that was apparently one of his pastimes. Sadie was reclining on a settee of the outmoded kind whose cushions are edged with a stiff pie-crust of embroidery. She was complacent in the attention she now commanded, her hands behind her head, her left ankle on her right knee, in an attitude that hovered archly between natural ease and self-conscious statement. She was blonde and she was pretty—pretty enough that, at a poetry course, it almost invited incredulity. Elsewhere, her looks would not have been so remarkable. Her skin was pale, her lower jaw wide, and under her freshness lurked an odd tinge of sluggishness. But she was funny, and nonchalantly wielded the scalpel of a surgical charm.

There came a point, quite early on in the conversation, when Damien noticed David *lean in*. This was not only a physical manoeuvre. His focus on Sadie became verbally, and in undefinable ways, more acute, to the elbowing exclusion of Damien, and Damien gave up the race as lost. However, Sadie's unavailability soon became apparent, putting the two young men back on an agreeably equal footing.

"So, are you going out with someone?"

Sadie laughed.

"Going out with someone?" Her intonation expressed with precision that she considered the phrase juvenile, though herself not above using it.

David merely raised his eyebrows and turned up the palms of his hands to indicate that was what he had said and he was waiting for the answer, at her leisure.

"Yeah," she said. "But probably not for long."

"It's not going well?"

"It's going fine."

"What's the problem then?"

"Just the usual. I've got it all worked out now. Do you want to hear my theory of going out with someone?"

"Of course. The floor is yours."

"So, after you've had a bit of experience you know not to, like, think you're going to spend the rest of your life with the next person you meet, so you start to get picky. After a while you meet someone, anyway. You're not sure at first, but you get to know each other a bit and you think you genuinely like each other and you can be honest with each other and avoid all the usual problems. And, you know, actually it's really great. And that's the point that I'm at now.

"But then you remember that you can't spend the rest of your life with just anyone and you start to wonder how long it will last, or how long you should let it last, and the other person says, 'What's wrong?' and you say, 'Nothing's wrong,' and he says, 'There is something wrong,' and basically, from this point you're doomed. If you don't talk about the problem you drift apart in silence, and if you talk about it you end up arguing. At some point you realise you can't be honest with the other person anymore and you've forgotten why you wanted to be, anyway. You get really angry with each other for turning all your trust in each other to nothing, and then one of you ends up saying, 'I don't need you. I can live my own life,' and it's over.

"Then some time passes and you meet someone else and the same thing happens again, except it's either worse, because you've done it before, or it's just boring and over very quickly. And so on until you decide never to go out with anyone again, or die or something. And that's it."

Sadie smiled, apparently in the knowledge of how accomplished her summary had been. It was a smile that seemed to say, "There—didn't I make that look easy!"

David was laughing.

"You really have got it all worked out," he said.

"I told you," said Sadie.

This monologue of Sadie's had a complicated effect on Damien. He was never to forget it. All three of them agreed that Sadie's every word had been not only true but almost transcendently eloquent. Thus they formed a triangle outside of sex. A kind of bitter, mocking, Platonic triangle. On the one hand, the monologue raised the teasing hope that Sadie's current relationship would not last, and that she viewed it lightly. On the other, it revealed a ring of ice around her forming an existential moat in which would-be adventurers might easily become trapped and frozen. Damien strongly suspected that David had a better chance than himself of passing through this ring, existing within sex in the same bitter and mocking way that he currently existed outside it.

In fact, both remained outside.

Damien, being naturally imaginative, and with his imagination boosted by the vigour of youth, although shocked by an almost unfathomable coldness in Sadie's otherwise friendly tone, and emotionally retreating from it, nonetheless was stimulated to daydreaming speculation about what a relationship with this extraordinary person, her brain as spiky as a sea urchin, could be like.

Contact details were exchanged early on, but Sadie clearly found nothing to hold her interest on the course. She left halfway through. This was the second thing that Damien recalled. If his company had not been a sufficiently compelling reason for her to stay, at least he could console himself that she thought enough of him to include him, with David, in the circle—or triangle—of her confidence by expressing to him her general contempt for the other attendees, for the tutors, for the course as a whole.

After Sadie abandoned the course, one of the older women—Damien suspected, in an instinctive bid to neutralise the scorn of the younger woman—penned the following lines, to the amusement of the remaining company:

> Sadie Bean
> Is seldom seen.
> Where did she go?
> We do not know.

And the third thing that Damien remembered as he studied this photograph of a poignantly juvenescent Sadie, was the first attempt he had made to meet her outside the environment of the writing course.

He was making a trip to London for reasons now forgotten, and his connecting train was at the station of the town where Sadie lived. This knowledge proved irresistible, and, deciding to take a chance, he left the station and made a call to her from a public phone booth (this being in the days before mobile phones had become *de rigueur*).

The spontaneity of this decision made him excitable, an excitement that increased when Sadie's voice answered the call.

"Who is it?"

"It's me. Damien. Guess where I am."

"I don't know. Phone me later."

"I can't phone you later. I'm in Swindon. I haven't got long."

"I'm in bed."

"Do you want to meet?"

"Phone me later."

"But—"

"Get *lost*."

She hung up. There had been a distinct finality to the anger of her last two words and Damien was certain that he could not phone back. Somehow the timing had been unfortunate. His excitement had combined with the fact of his having to get to London that day to make him insensitively forward at a time when she was still in bed and wanting to sleep. It was like when two people bending at the same time bang their heads together. Even realising all this, he was hurt. Like a child who believes a stranger has no right to scold him, he was resentful at Sadie's anger. He had no choice, however, but to accept his disappointment and carry his private hurt back to the train station to resume his journey to London.

The hurt was with him, like something he couldn't swallow, throughout that day and the next, but somehow the politics of humility wrested power from the politics of resentment inside him. He saw with quiet sobriety that the situation was his fault and, rather than phoning again, after a few days had passed, he wrote a letter of apology. She responded promptly with a brief but refreshingly breezy letter that managed to sweep from his mind the warning note of her voice on the phone. Its basic import was: For future reference, I have no time for people who have no respect, but I accept your apology, so let's be friends.

In this way was beaten the beginning of a strange path. Shaken from solipsism into gratitude, Damien was surprised to find himself in a pleasing and difficult friendship with a perpetual stranger. It was not that they met often or corresponded with especial frequency, and for long periods Damien would go without giving Sadie a solitary thought, as if she had never been a part of his life (which was natural, after all), but there were occasions, in Sadie's presence or away from her, when it was as if Damien looked down at himself and saw a single silver thread in the fabric of his sleeve, here and there catching the light, and didn't know whether this was some kind of flaw in the garment or whether the essential value of the fabric was concentrated here as in a highlight.

Sadie's existence ran through his own in just such a way: usually forgotten, but when remembered, precious and troubling.

Or that is how things had been until about five years back. Then Sadie herself had precipitated another watershed in Damien's graveyard obsession, without her being aware of it.

But she would be aware of it.

How peculiar and appropriate to come upon these photographs now; it was as if everything had been predetermined.

He put them back on the table, and though alone, did so with understated theatricality as if he were his own solipsistic audience. He stood, then, and surveyed again the space he still had to prepare for the months and perhaps the years ahead of him. The task he had in mind was so immense that it was tempting to linger and dream, especially as this was his nature. But dreams also demanded work.

He put his hand in the box in which he had found the photographs, and took out a round object in bubble wrap. He snipped away the sticky tape with a pair of scissors to reveal the skull of a human child, minus lower jaw. He placed it on the table, between the two photographs.

III. Watershed

IN 2006, Sadie was in her mid-twenties. She was old enough to be aware of a kind of inarticulate compound fracture in her existence, as if the very air of the world had invisibly delivered her a blow the injury from which was only to be discovered, with distressing pain, after a delay of years. She had never encountered anything that truly defined or addressed this pain in a problem-solving way. It was presupposed—but not described—by an ever-evaporating oral tradition in youth culture; though the contents of a blown mind could be inventoried, the process behind the event could not be reflexively examined, and the edges of the event could not be determined in order to place it in context. She was half-aware, however (and only half-aware), that even if the spire of hope had been shattered so that its clock was set in a foil of ruin, the ground from which she viewed it remained firm beneath her. In other words, if she had been provided with a number of lives—as a cat is supposed to be, or in the manner of a video game—her existential shock was that common to youth, of having lost the first of one's allotted lives, and was not the thin, ethereal fatalism of age, when one is on one's final life.

It was the right time for her to start looking into what had previously been overlooked, and to begin the discovery of what had never been signposted. Damien had come to mind, and rather than there being a clear reason to take an interest in him, there had been something more like a 'why not?' combined with a not overwhelming sense that his existence was the mouth of a footpath overshadowed by heavy branches—a road so little travelled it might not even be a through-road.

Both she and he had plateaued in the adult world of tertiary education and work just long enough to be perturbed and paradoxically excited by intimations of some vast, apocalyptic boredom to come. He was in the first stage of his London life, sharing a Nunhead house with three others who had been strangers to him when he moved in. She had a position as lecturer in Norwich, which gave her financial independence and little else. They had always represented, to each other, abstract aspiration and unnamed potential. So, when Damien took stock of the spaces open in his life and invited Sadie to stay the weekend with him, she, taking stock of the spaces in her life, accepted, each mildly surprised by the actions of the other, both of them reassured by the theoretical presence of the third parties in the rented house.

It was the morning of a pleasant Saturday at the beginning of a Bank Holiday weekend joining April to May and the weather, after recent wind and rain, was of such a halcyon complexion that it seemed almost to have erased from the world the consciousness of such a thing as the 21st century. Close by the train station from which Sadie was to start on her short journey was a florist, flowers arranged outside in a dazzle of colours more cheerful than beautiful. Water evaporated on the pavement from where the flowers had been sprinkled and sprayed. Despite the lack of subtlety in the display, Sadie stopped here, in the mood to be receptive to other than habitual influences, and chose a bouquet of chrysanthemums, yellow and white. She bought them, handling them with the confidence that conventions call for and allow, seeming to recall, as she did so, that in the ancient world—Greece, perhaps?—an offering would be made before one set out on a journey. Her present expedition required no such precautions, but this was why the idea pleased her; it seemed gratuitous.

She boarded the train, put her travelling case on the overhead luggage shelf, and wrote something in the card for the bouquet. The train pulled out of the station. She finished what she was writing, sealed the card in the envelope, took a volume of poetry out of her shoulder bag, and started reading.

During the journey, her attention did not remain for long upon any one thing. She would read a poem or half a poem, and then gaze out of the window, at scenery made vaguely luxurious by the fact it was passing. Then she would lean back in her seat and observe with a critical inner eye the intricate spirals of her thought, caught in the day's golden light like the gossamer pattern of an orb web.

The uniqueness of one's own existence, once recognised, seemed to require grand plans. If that uniqueness did not become the centre of the universe's emptiness, it would remain merely an infinitesimal point. One's uniqueness, therefore, required plans on the scale of the universe itself in order to be salvaged, and in order to turn universal emptiness into plenitude. But, then again, the whole idea of grand plans seemed a form of deference to traditional authority and therefore an unwitting abdication of self-sovereignty—to fret about such plans was still to be distracted by the public spectacle and the parade of public ideas, and therefore to keep oneself peripheral. As a gesture towards the exploration of life's possibilities, visiting Damien was even comically small in scale, but this comic smallness was something Sadie could appreciate in a truly solitary manner. Thus, she thought, she might even hope to slip off the deadly path of the expected.

Two stations before her destination, she sent a text message, and received a prompt reply. Damien met her on the platform. Coatless and casual in the mid-spring air, his whole presence gave the feeling that occurs sometimes when the eyes of strangers meet with accidental familiarity. He offered to take her case, but she declined by holding out the bouquet and saying, "Take these."

When he asked who they were for, it was hard to tell whether he was joking. Sadie adopted the particular tone of sarcasm necessary to indicate the answer should be obvious: "Er . . . They're for you."

"Oh." He still seemed uncertain. "Thank you."

And he carried the flowers with a visible mixture of diffidence and pride.

Nunhead Station had an island platform and beyond the tracks on one side, vine-strangled trees and shaggy undergrowth framed a view of the City of London with the skyline markers of the Gherkin, Tower 42 and so on, giving Sadie the impression that she had arrived in the kind of slightly chill, refreshing suburb in which England sometimes seems to specialise. However, once they had descended the steps to the exit and crossed over to Oakdale Road, she saw that there was very little foliage about. As they walked, she noted the terraced houses with their chimney pots like bits of jawbone against the sky, forming, together, one of those seemingly endless streets in Greater London where the homely atmosphere of each building, differing always slightly from its neighbours in its iteration of the type, produces by this variety within repetition the paradoxical impression of a barren cosiness.

They arrived, at last, after passing a Seventh-day Adventist church, at the house where Damien had a room. It was on a corner where there was a turning to the right. On the opposite corner was a pub with a rounded right-angle of frosted-glass frontage, and a little farther up the road that ran between these two corners was what appeared to be a park, enclosed by wall and railings.

During the walk and on their arrival here, as they squeezed through the garden gate and into the narrow hallway of the house, Sadie was aware of a mixture of comfort, awkwardness and freshness, which signalled that even after a long acquaintance they were still in the relatively early stages of getting to know each other.

Damien told her that she could sleep in his room, and he would take the sofa in the living room. This seemed the obvious arrangement, for more than one reason. Still, he appeared unsure whether to show her to his room immediately.

With Sadie's help, he put the flowers in a disused pasta sauce jar, then tore open the seal of the envelope.

Sadie had never previously been present when Damien had opened a card or letter from her. She observed his reaction to her message. The handwriting and composition were as impressive as the message itself, the overall effect being almost like a copperplate inscription on a wall plaque. The letters were tall and narrow, not what is generally called feminine, with abrupt barbs here and there in Sadie's idiosyncratic manner, and occasional loops that pouched slightly too large, like cysts, indicating, in symbiotic contrast to the barbs, a slothful intractability. Towards the end of the inscription, the letters wobbled where the train had pulled out of the station.

This is what she had written:

> Never believe that the small things don't matter.
>
> "I will connive no more
> With that which hopes and plans that
>   I shall not survive . . ."
>
> Chin up, old stick.
>
>   Sadie B.

She could tell from Damien's eyes when he looked up at her that he found it quite unusual.

He nodded, perhaps involuntarily, before speaking.

"Who's the quote from?"

"Edna St. Vincent Millay."

"Thanks." The word seemed forced out in a cough, as if he were admitting something.

He proceeded to make them both mugs of tea with a bustle and unaccustomedness that suggested this was an occasion. They went out into the small back garden to drink them. Sadie burnt her tongue a little. Conversation was bitty, but beneath the nervousness was the usual fatalistic relaxation of such situations, like a metaphysical liver forever processing the toxin of the knowledge of death, as proof that even in an unhealthy age the health of nature is part of our person.

The garden was bordered on one side, where the road was, by a privacy fence of layered, wavy-edged wooden planks, grey with age. Another, similar fence separated this garden from the neighbour's. But opposite the back of the house itself was a wall surmounted by railings, pressed close to which was a seeming wilderness of twiggy, leafy trees and undergrowth unmolested by the bureaucrats to whom such lack of regulation would normally be an affront. There was something curious about the contrast of the seemingly wild character of the area beyond the wall with the wall itself and the domesticity of the street.

"Is that a park?" Sadie asked during a lull in the conversation.

"No. It's a cemetery."

Damien seemed, inexplicably, almost to stutter on this last word. Without knowing why, Sadie felt embarrassed for him and changed the subject.

The drunk tea went down like hourglass sand—another reminder of the fleetingness and unsatisfactoriness of such situations. Still, they had the weekend ahead of them, to settle into like a beanbag. They could watch a couple of DVDs, go to a pub, talk about poetry, take advantage of London—whatever was most conducive to the lowering of barriers in the strange mutual siege of friendship.

After they went back inside, Damien washed up the mugs and said, "I'll show you my room. Your room. Y'know."

He took the chrysanthemums and the larger of Sadie's two bags, and she followed him up the carpeted stairs. Outside the door of the room, he relinquished her travelling case, but there was a curious fumblingness to his manner as if he were not sure what to do next. A smile twitched and stiffened on his face. She thought he would say something, but he only turned wordlessly to open the door, as if time had run out for avoiding such an action.

Immediately he had done so, he disappeared inside. Sadie was delayed by the need to retrieve her travelling case. She heard Damien telling her to come in. By then he had deposited the flowers on a table against the wall and was opening the sash window.

"To let some air in," he said. Then, "The sheets on the bed are new." And he looked at the floor, seemingly perplexed with himself.

She looked around, unsure what to say, and then Damien looked up and caught her eye for a second.

"Just put your stuff anywhere," he said, and half turned away, seeming to act the part of looking at something in particular.

It did not matter to Sadie where in the room her luggage was, but for the sake of moving the situation along without fuss, she deposited her shoulder bag on the bed and positioned her travelling case on the floor next to it. During this operation, she continued to notice what she had first noticed on entering. There were things here that somehow deviated from the very wide band of neutral value in terms of decoration—that neutral band denoting a background against which any guest might be received with reasonable comfort. It was not a *passive* background, though its theme might have been called passive; it felt like something that is obtrusively shown. She was confused as to whether she was expected to notice what, after all, she could not help noticing, or whether, on the contrary, she was expected to act as if there were really nothing to notice at all. She had no precedent from past experience and there were no spoken words in the present moment to guide her. For this reason, it was not difficult to persuade herself, once they left the room, that there hadn't been anything much to notice, really, and whatever odd little trial she had just undergone, she had presumably passed it. But there was a contradiction between having passed a trial and there being nothing to pass, and this contradiction prevented her from entirely forgetting the matter.

Downstairs again, Damien cooked pasta. Sadie helped him a little; little help was needed. Their conversation was sparse, but there was conscious goodwill in their co-operation with all the small preparations for the meal.

Before the meal was ready, one of Damien's housemates came home from work. A girl by the name of Bianca, she had, to Sadie, that look that people have on the first day of something entirely new, such as university. Bianca was obviously well used to her own life by now, but it was quite incidental to Sadie. Still, her presence was reassuring. She breathed that inexplicable normality so taken for granted—by definition, even—among the human inhabitants of a globe of stone and water where both elements transformed ceaselessly within cycles apt to catastrophic aberration, and from which escape could only be into the unknown of death or the slightly lesser unknown of the unbounded darkness in which the globe was suspended. She spoke to Damien only briefly, and even more briefly to Sadie, before going upstairs to her room.

While they were still at the dining table, at the edge of the sitting room, another of Damien's housemates, Gerrard, arrived, heated something in the microwave, and ate it in front of the television, the volume high on *Flog It!* As watching a DVD was, for now, vetoed by Gerrard's monopolisation of the television, once they had finished eating, Damien suggested quietly that they go upstairs; Sadie was more or less relieved to do so.

And so they entered Damien's bedroom again, this time without distractions or immediate excuse for a retreat. It was now that a strange fatalism snared them. They were meant to be deciding their activities for the rest of the evening, but neither was willing to make a definite choice. They wanted to do something, but nothing quite roused them from the lassitude of indecision. The stubbornness of boredom was upon them. But boredom and belonging are curiously linked. It was as if, in truth, they did not want to go anywhere. And perhaps progress cannot be made when there are unacknowledged distractions.

Sadie found herself looking around the room and realised she had given mental priority to a different problem. There was nothing definitively outrageous in the graveyard memorabilia that formed the room's predominant decoration, but the overall effect of it bothered her. Was this a male thing, she wondered. She remembered the way boys at school had never tired of scribbling pictures of penises, usually ejaculating, on their exercise books, desks, and anywhere ink would mark. Girls didn't make doodles of vaginas in the same obsessive way, or in any way at all, that she was aware.

These serried photographs of graves on the walls, and the various objects displayed on the tops of the chest-of-drawers and other items of furniture, gave her a similar feeling. Partly it was the uniformity that was troubling. A young male who had a few soft-porn posters in his bedroom—for instance—might offend the prudish or politically correct, but was unlikely to disturb anyone deeply. If the posters were uniform in their theme, and showed every sign of being organised according to detailed principles, the effect would be more unsettling.

Who would adorn their living space in such a way without embarrassment? But Sadie sensed that Damien was not quite unembarrassed.

Domestication, or its lack, applied to humans as well as other animals. Hence, a human with a touch of the undomesticated weird about them could provoke feelings of danger in the way a poorly trained dog might. There was something like this about Damien, but he seemed half aware of it himself, and even—himself—frightened of it. Sadie had a measure of sympathy for this. Damien was genuinely strange—not merely fashionably so. But she would perhaps have let her repulsion overrule her attraction had it not been for a peculiar calm she also sensed in him, which sat alongside his strangeness and fear.

As if to break the spell of boredom, he had opened a drawer and was showing her his collection of DVDs, in case she was interested in watching any once the television was available. With clumsily assumed casualness, he held up the boxed set of *Six Feet*

Under and said, "Have you seen any of this? It's . . . er . . . quite interesting. Each episode starts with a death."

Sadie suddenly recalled Damien's awkwardness when he had told her, earlier, that the wooded area abutting the house was a cemetery. She felt that she could no longer avoid asking the question on her mind; her remaining choices were only those concerning delivery and tone of voice.

"Damien," she said, "have you got a thing about death?"

He laughed in a brief but slightly giddy fashion, then seemed to see that his response did not quite coincide with her tone.

"Well . . ." he began.

"I mean, with your photographs of graves and everything."

She wanted to ask him about the proximity of the cemetery, too, especially given some of the objects decorating the room, but somehow the question resisted formulation.

"Well . . . the thing is . . . It's a bit difficult to explain, actually, but . . ."

He had stopped talking and was looking at her, as if for help in how to continue his sentence.

"You're not a necrophile, are you?"

"No. No." He shook his head. "I'm . . . I'm a thanatophile."

"What? That's the same thing."

"No. No. It isn't."

"How is it different?"

He exhaled and looked up at the ceiling, seeming to wonder how he had suddenly got into this conversation.

"It's really not a big deal," he said. "I can explain it, but it might take a while, and I don't know if you'd be interested."

"We're not doing anything else, are we? Now might be the right time to explain things. Especially as I'm supposed to sleep in this room with all these graves."

"Sorry . . . You can sleep downstairs if you like. I don't mind."

"You're avoiding the issue. Life's too short to avoid the issue."

Damien nonetheless remained silent and motionless. Without her knowing exactly how it had happened, Sadie's role had become that of prising Damien open like a mussel. She could not tell if she wanted to, or if she had no choice.

"I'm interested, so explain it."

He looked around now, put down the DVDs on the table with the chrysanthemums, and drew up a cushionless wooden chair in front of it.

"There's too much of a build-up," he said. "What I mean is, it's not such a big deal. It's just . . ."

"If it's not a big deal, go ahead and explain it."

"Okay. It's graves I'm interested in, not corpses."

"What about the pictures of corpses on your wall?"

"That's because . . . mainly a grave isn't a grave without some kind of mortal remains. The point is the graveyard. I've visited mortuaries. I'm a nurse, as you know. But that's not what interests me. I mean, I suppose that's interesting in its own way, but that's not what all this is about." He gestured briefly and with the cramp of inhibition to the walls of his room. "It's the graveyard that . . . attracts me. Not the mortuary. And that's because, you see, the graveyard is where you say 'rest in peace'. It's got some kind of spell over it that the mortuary hasn't. With the mortuary, you're still thinking about pathology and . . . it's like an echo chamber for all the violence and fear of the world. Then, in the graveyard, it's all quiet. It's not even a creepy quiet—that's what people don't understand. There's a cemetery right behind this house and it's . . . it's a friendly place."

He had said it. Perhaps he wasn't hiding anything. Why, then, did he squirm like this?

"So, that's it? So you didn't have to make a big deal out of it."

"No. I said. I said it wasn't a big deal."

But he stared at the floor, seemingly disconsolate.

Then he opened his mouth. His confession had begun, and now, even if the process was as painful as the purgation of the body during illness, it seemed he was unable to stop.

"I want . . . to understand death. It's not even that. It's more like . . . I love death. That's it, you see. Thanatos—death. Philia—love. That's why I said 'thanatophile'. Somehow . . . somehow I know that only death can ever fulfil me."

With his final words Damien had exhibited, in tone and demeanour, the relaxed fatalism of someone who had exposed a long-concealed shame. Sadie felt an instinctive revulsion at the apparent disappearance of inner conflict in him, at words uttered as if completely unopposed.

"How can it fulfil you if you don't exist?"

"Somehow, it will."

"You're looking for fulfilment, but because you can't find it in life, you trick yourself into thinking you'll find it in death, but you won't, because you can only ever find anything while you're still alive."

"No." Damien appeared agitated and rose from his chair. He picked up the DVDs from the table behind him, as if about to put them away, but then paused in indecision.

"The problem is, you can't be alive and dead at the same time. That's why you stay alive, taking photographs of graves instead of killing yourself. If you actually killed yourself, you wouldn't be able to fantasize about death anymore. In a weird way, it's a kind of egotism. If you just accepted there is nothing after death, all you'd have left would be life. You wouldn't have to hang around graves and you'd be much happier."

"No!"

Sadie felt herself sprayed with water. The chrysanthemums and DVDs were scattered over the carpet. Water dripped from the table. The empty pasta sauce jar rolled on the floor near her foot.

She must have looked away for an instant, because she hadn't seen what happened. Damien was staring at her with an expression balanced between tearfulness and anger.

"You can be dead and alive at the same time," he said with great deliberateness.

Partly out of shock, she began to laugh.

One of Damien's photograph albums had been open on the table. A couple of chrysanthemums lay crossed over more graveyard pictures. Damien picked the album up in dismay and began to wipe and dab at the water with his sleeve.

IV. Incubation

A spasm, like shame, passed through Damien at the memory.

Ever since he had come across those photographs, the memories had been scuttling out of their old hiding places. On more than one occasion, he found himself going into a trance, only realising he had done so when he came out of it to find himself placing an item on a shelf as if frozen in the act of reconsidering a chess move, or smoothing a throw over the back of a sofa with a gesture that had become a caress.

He could remember exactly how he had felt when Sadie had suggested that happiness consisted in accepting death was the end. Already he had been aware that the conversation was being drawn towards trouble; he had felt himself losing all flexibility. But his sensitivity had increased proportionally to his stiffness. Sadie's words had been like gently groping fingertips at the back of his brain. There was a membranous spine to his cerebral cortex, and those fingers of Sadie's had deftly located it, instinctively understanding this spine was a key, and they had gripped and squeezed. Then had come the dumbfounding sensation. Because Sadie had not been content with a brief squeeze. No. Instead, with her grasp firm, she had scooped and upturned the entire brain and its underside was exposed: it was a helpless horseshoe crab that had curled in on itself for protection, but now, inverted, its hideous appendages struggled helplessly with the empty air.

There was something fundamental about the feeling, as love is said to be fundamental. He was not sure it was even an emotion; it related to a number of emotions. With the memory, he had half-awoken the feeling again, and needed to go through the mental ritual he had developed. First, and simply, he must face the question: might he really be happier believing there was nothing after death? He could, with great calmness, introduce this belief to his habitual thought processes—had done so before—but he knew that this was sleight of hand. The idea of nothingness existed precisely within a living human mind— Sadie's very assertion working against itself—so that it could only be believed as nothingness if one did not pull back to see the picture of nothingness framed by mind. For him to believe in nothingness, then, would be deliberately to banish his self-awareness and play the role of immanence. Very good. First stage of the ritual accomplished. But could he be wrong? He could be wrong that there was consciousness after death, quite indubitably, but he knew, if it were possible to know anything, that he could not *happily believe* that life terminates in nothingness. The idea was so intractable to conceptualisation, it could only be called nonsense. If, for instance, Sadie had succeeded in convincing him to be happy because there is nothing after death, she would have more surely killed him than if she had pulverised his skull with a mallet. That was why he had reacted as he did: spiritual survival. If someone occupying this body was happy believing death the end of everything, it would not be him. It went beyond the question of belief (he could feel the invertebrate legs thrash again). The belief, so-called, was him. If it was madness, then he was, himself, madness, and a cure would be fatal. And, at this point, he had to wonder about other people. Most people he knew—Sadie, for example—did not believe in anything after death. They had chosen to ignore the frames of their own minds. If not, he had no explanation. It was as if they were one-sided pages. Such a thing seems impossible. But that these one-sided pages proliferated around him was peculiar and uncanny. They were people, but how did they embrace their own personhood?

The ritual closed with this mystery.

Life's sacred ambiguity restored, Damien found the image of the scattered chrysanthemums returning to him. Why had Sadie indulged his outburst? It had surprised him at the time. He considered the question in the manner of a tactician nervous at the thought of underestimating an adversary. Perhaps by then she had been sufficiently accustomed or even attached to him that the splash of water and the glimpse of his raw being were not an intolerable affront. Or perhaps this outburst itself cemented an attachment, conveying to her conscious or unconscious mind her accidental discovery of another human being's inner sanctum. He had been very careful after that. It had been unguarded occupancy of the first person that had made him vulnerable and provoked her attack. Thereafter he made sure always to gird himself with repression when he spoke to her. They could even discuss the same subject, but as long as he maintained a certain level of self-accusation—treating himself in the third person—he remained untouchably safe and she betrayed no hostility.

Whatever the incident had meant to her—life's opacity and unpredictability, the occasional viciousness that escaped the black box of its innermost mechanisms, were all particularly acute in the areas of other human beings' judgements and responses—it had been pivotal for him. At the very least, it had precipitated him more quickly down an inevitable path; perhaps it had decided his direction where it had been undecided.

He could not say exactly why it was, but it had been after that incident that his thoughts and imagination had been drawn more and more persistently to the fate of the human body.

Had it been the accusation of necrophilia? Perhaps. It seemed Sadie was correct about one thing: according to all the dictionaries Damien afterwards consulted, 'thanatophile' had the same meaning as 'necrophile'. He felt as if he had been turned into a ghost by this, with ghostly motivations. But this discovery might also have played its part in his growing consideration of the flesh.

The attraction of graves was twofold: there was what might superficially be called the picturesque element, which is what he had espoused to Sadie, but there was also the morbid element. These elements were entwined. Obvious though it was, this truth had long remained unconscious for Damien—half-conscious, at best. After Sadie's visit, he came to appreciate it with growing distinctness.

Somehow, he thought, putrescence held the key to everything. It was where no one wished to look—the last place, so to speak— and that was where the secret was surely hidden. It was precisely through the morbid element that he would at last come to know the supreme peace and fulfilment of the picturesque element. The thought terrified him, but proved impervious to all his attempts at banishment. It was like a magnetic cloud—irresistible in a way he had never encountered before. He knew that he had, at some point, been robbed of the power to say "never" to this thought, so, instead, he repeated "later" and tried not to dwell on the fact he really *meant* "later".

So began a process for which the term '*danse macabre*' might have been coined.

Here he was, again, in a weed-grown cemetery, standing in front of a backward-slanting headstone. Rain fell, at a different slant. It darkened the stone in spots that multiplied and ran, and Damien shivered at the sight as if the stone were his flesh. Cold tingles in his sobriety, like ripples from raindrops on a puddle, were harbingers of the peace and fulfilment he always sought. But, as usual, when he became aware of the proximity of that vast, silent, silver taste for which his soul was meant to be the tongue, he became aware also of its elusiveness . . . or incompleteness . . .

He remembered, suddenly, a poem by Sylvia Plath:

I am vertical
But I would rather be horizontal

Somehow, that expressed the matter. Verticality was the attitude of aspiration, solitude, endeavour—a spine, a single numeral, a broken column. The horizontal attitude was a different dimension. It was the attitude of completion and connection, of effortless dream, of a level at a quantum remove from the upright will.

These thoughts took him down, beneath the soil. Decay was the very root of the beautiful, chill flower to whose scent he had responded as to a caress.

How had the custom of burying the dead begun? There must have been a time when humans or hominids left their dead for carrion. Nature would have been the only undertaker. Nature, in that sense, had been gradually banished. But had the first burials been a question of necessity or of a shift in consciousness? Whichever it had been, funeral rites were now as if an eternal human reality. The discovery of putrefaction was in some sense the discovery of eternity.

And that was the buried secret.

In the clothes they had worn in life, or clothes for some formal occasion that would never formally conclude, dressed either way for personhood, the corpses were put away in the earth. The earth is a great beyond, like the sky, but fingers can delve and divide there, and a deep hole refilled can lock in the unthinkable stench.

A body might be embalmed, but there will be changes—a chaos more certain than order. The changes within a life have continuity, so that someone who knew that life in the child might recognise it still in the woman or man of ninety years. In the earth there is an encroachment of brokenness. What might have been recognised has passed, and its traces are obliterated in patches that spread and merge.

And supposing the remains are not embalmed? Then nature does eternity's hidden work without hindrance.

Damien was familiar, to a degree, with the disfigurements of death. But rather than curtailing his imagination, this familiarity gave it potency. What he was thereby able to see with the mind's eye was of greater, not lesser, breadth.

Some bizarre displacement would affect the eyes of the dead, and the lower jaw would go crooked, as if this erstwhile human being had been pistol-whipped by some cruel and invincible hand into a brutish stupidity from which there was no return. In this corporeal empire, the heart had been a soundless gong, whose beat, second by second, declared that all was well. But now the gong was stilled, and the blood was stagnant that had circulated order, and the stupidity of ruin was the new rule, in all the thoroughfares of blood, and the new rule was no different to anarchy. Blood soured to blackness. The great neuronal library of the brain was flooded and razed, turning into a swamp of pulped memory through which the gases of decomposition bubbled.

The limbs twisted like those of a dehydrated toad. The body was convulsed, mindlessly, as an earthquake convulses the land. The skin, like an overripe apple, browned, blackened, became slimy with liquefaction, broke out in white spores. The corpse continued its slow, slippery thrashing in the detestable slurry of its own decay.

But this was only one among many millions of the dead, secretly partaking in the global citizenship of putrescence with a hive-like wriggle and buzz of activity to parallel the unending purposefulness of the living.

The efficacy of the offerings made in the polis of the rotting corpse was beyond doubt. The mantle of the human shape, vacated by the animating principle, sagged and collapsed into an Indra's web of copulating insects. More than was possible in the experience of love or lust during life, this was a consummation. Without any human lover of the opposite sex, the body was nonetheless consumed by a heaving swarm of procreation, and was likely the ancestor, in decay, of more insects, worms and microbes than the once-living person might have been of human offspring.

And commerce and miscegenation joined the polis of one corpse to that of another. There was a vast economy of decay, necrophagy and reproduction. As a beetle or grub was a speck in the pointillism of a corpse, so each corpse became a speck in the pointillism of the greater cosmopolis of putrefaction.

Most could not even see the cosmopolis, so what hope was there that they would see the great tasselled banners of eternity rising above it? What hope was there that they would smell the incense whose pillars of white smoke rose up from the temples of the cosmopolis and supported vaulted eternity?

Damien knew; there was none. But he must not betray that which, with increasing acuity, increasing certainty, he could see, that which came to his nostrils from the buried beyond, and sometimes more pungently, sometimes more subtle-sweetly than anything in the life as-yet-unburied.

Where before, thanatos had occupied the greater part of his thoughts on his cemetery visits, after the incident with Sadie, Damien found that nekros gained ground, until it was close to being half of what obsessed him on such occasions. And he was afraid its expansion of territory would continue.

To the extent that the corpse cosmopolis was unexplored, the ghostly banners of eternity remained elusive, as belonging to a realm remote in space and in time. There were moments, however, like wakefulness within a dream, when it seemed sure what they signified was real. And so, in imagination, and in second-hand ways, and to some degree in first-hand ways, Damien turned his attention to the physical details of human mortality, its causes and its symptoms, and to every stage of the decomposition of the human form. Each specimen he studied, in imagination or in fact, while seeming to take him towards the goal he kept veiled in his mind, on the other hand, took up just a little more time; the prolonged luxury of avoidance was also the agony of courtship. What he examined in fact, it should be noted, was so far only what he could examine without more than minor risk. However, the barrier of risk that surrounded the dead became palpable to him.

❋

And then, after the houseshare in Nunhead and before the current studio on Candle Street, there had been a very dark period in a one-bedroom flat in New Cross. During this period he worked hard, socialised little, and kept everything hidden. In some ways, this was merely an extension of the Nunhead phase, but in another sense the New Cross period was a twisting outside in of all that had occurred in the preceding period. As a neighbour to Nunhead Cemetery, Damien had served a solitary apprenticeship, rich and raw, in all that the grave had to teach. It was as if a wolf had come of age in the forest. The adventure of it echoed with a wordless thunder that not another soul would ever know. Now, in New Cross, Damien templed his fingers and meditated on theories in whose symbols and mysteries he felt sure no one he spoke to was initiated. His new domestic isolation, and the fact he had been moved to an alternating late shift at work, served to accentuate certain facets of his existence. He kept himself short-haired and closely shaved, and he associated the discipline of such grooming with an inner mixture of tension and exhaustion.

His preferred contemporary author was Houellebecq, for the sting of angst and the consolation his work gave, as if years of anger and bitterness had just been released from a slingshot stretched by the mechanisms of intolerable contradiction as far as it would go. This was the kind of reading that suited the sense prevalent in his life of having to find windows of time—small, tightly shut windows they were. Damien had come to be preoccupied, as with a gatekeeper's riddle, by something Houellebecq had said concerning his first novel, *Whatever*, in an interview: "I hadn't seen any novel make the statement," ran the quote, "that entering the workforce was like entering the grave."

Like entering the grave.

In one sense this characterisation of work was entirely true, but in another sense, entering the grave was precisely what Damien wanted in the hope of it affording what the workplace never could: relief. In either case, there was something in Houellebecq's twinning of work and death.

As a multi-storey car park is built for no other purpose than to accommodate parked cars, and is barren considered architecturally, or as a natural environment, so Damien's life at this time seemed built only to accommodate work. Even in his self-contained flat, feeling his entire life to be owned by those who paid the wages that, in turn, paid the rent, he was no longer as uncompromising in his décor as previously; he lived as if watched, going so far as to discourage in himself muttered soliloquies, or the more outré accompaniments of masturbation that he had allowed himself in the numbered carefree hours of his life. However, pigeons, hobbled by mange, may still scavenge sludgy morsels in a car park, and the homeless may drink there, in the grime, until they are moved on, and there is most likely to exist an entire universe of microbes and crevice-dwellers who do not deign to consult humans on the subject of what is beautiful or useful. And in this way, Damien's real life, his true interests, survived.

There was nothing on the walls now except a couple of commonplace prints—an old poster for James Whale's *Frankenstein* and Salvador Dali's 'Young Virgin Auto-Sodomised by the Horns of Her Own Chastity'—both plainly framed and hanging from pre-existing hooks. The flat had been partly furnished, and Damien had invested in a 'vintage' cabinet with drawers and shelves. The flowers in the vase on the cabinet were changed with some regularity. The books, compact discs and DVDs on the shelves were selected and arranged as if for display in a shop. Paperback volumes of Orwell and Graham Greene gave the impression of sobriety rather than strangeness; even Bataille had been banished from view. Along with much else.

The cemetery photographs, filling innumerable flip-pocket albums with almost forensic monotony, were put away in the drawers. Other images and objects of a similar nature were kept with them, or in boxes in the cupboard. Some of the objects had been stowed in a safe storage unit that Damien had begun to hire. Damien had virtually no visitors in this flat, but was at times aware with what ease a visitor might be able to discover all he had hidden. Imagine, he thought, an acquaintance casually tugging at and then carefully sliding open one of the heavy drawers, taking one or two things from within, examining them, then hastily returning them to the drawer and pushing it closed at the sound of a toilet flush.

Among other things, Damien had also now begun to collect images from police and hospital files. In conjunction with the other items these drawers contained, they might easily suggest to the discoverer alarming areas of mental inquiry and absorption in their possessor. Since the incident with Sadie, Damien had withdrawn, in reaction, into a tingling sensitivity about such discovery.

However, it was also possible—and Damien largely counted on this—that the drawers would remain untouched by any hand but his, and the few visitors that happened to appear, invited or otherwise, would not even guess that the flowers in the vase on the cabinet, by which occasionally he would burn incense, were always flowers taken from graves.

This flat, therefore, afforded Damien the comfort that a burrow affords some nervous rodent, ever twitching with potential reaction to threat. He did not so much relax here as marinate in his own unease. A cigarette in this environment of watched time and furtiveness, where any small, sudden noise—something dropped on the floor of the flat above—felt like an unexpected bruise on one's flank, was a microcosm of the greater interplay of existential torment and solace. The sanctuary of smoke was necessarily fragile. It would last only until the ash drew too near to the filter for Damien to continue smoking. As a lit cigarette must burn out, so, too, must the safety of solitude be invaded. It was this that was threatening—this more than death. The threat— essentially the threat of work—had the bitterness of death about it, but it was, on the other hand, the faint but acrid threat of death in the cigarette that gave its sanctuary the slight authority it had. The smoking of a cigarette, then, became the event and the landscape in which Damien lived.

He would smoke near an open window, even on winter nights, dispose of the ash and extinguished butts immediately in the bin, and often clean the ashtray.

One night towards the end of October, he returned from a late shift and, still in his nurse's uniform, sat down on the sofa and lit a cigarette. He was too exhausted and apathetic even to open the window this time. After a few drags, he retrieved from his back pocket a folded pamphlet he had picked up from some wire rack of similar literature during the course of his duties. It was an unremarkable specimen of printed matter, but he had become intrigued. He had been struck precisely by its quotidian nature. The pamphlet concerned domestic violence. Its background colour was the same light blue as his uniform and on the front and within were a number of photographs of anonymous people who presumably represented some particular demographic vulnerable to physical abuse, or else, in some cases, who were there to indicate that anyone might be the victim of such abuse. The camera focused here on a bruised eye, here on hands gripping the push-handle of a lawn mower, and so on. Overall, the people, or parts of people, pictured, looked 'ordinary'. This, in turn, held the near-subliminal implication that such abuse is ordinary and that, in turn, the ordinary is inseparable from such abuse.

Domestic violence.

Damien pictured a lady with grey curls kneeling to tend to her geraniums. Her husband, smoking a pipe, perhaps, appeared at her side, stamped on her hand, then, scooping her secateurs from the ground, stabbed her shoulder, before turning and walking away, leaving her sobbing pitiably. Damien couldn't quite resist the pipe, though it was outdated now.

There was something so, as they say, terribly English about the phrase 'domestic violence'.

The trick of the pamphlet was this: it was a designed arte-fact, and yet it looked like a piece of reality itself. Reality was as fundamentally seedy as this photograph of an old lady with dishevelled hair and an unfocused gaze, or this one of a slightly obese young man in a wheelchair. Photographs with different lighting, text with a different font, and so on, would give an utterly different impression. But this—domestic violence—was the ultimate reality. That, it seemed to Damien, was the message that England existed to prove and enforce. The worst thing was that the dreariness was never allowed to take wing and exaggerate itself into the liberation of the Gothic. No. The English chose for their literary saints the likes of the execrable Alan Bennett, ob-sessed with tepid dramatisations of old women falling downstairs and breaking their hips. This was the kind of life that England wanted to impose on him. It wanted nothing left of him at all. It would not rest until his soul was deposed and destroyed, the hole where it had been filled in with the caulking of domestic violence and Alan Bennett.

Most of his life was already finished—to use the decorators' term—with precisely this kind of caulking. It was not so much that Damien's imagination led him on to forbidden realms. Again, no; there was something more dreadful than taboo at work here. It was that it was especially his *imagination* that did the leading, and any imagination that germinated and took form in England was incongruous and therefore risible, by contrast with everything else. Against the foil of domestic-violence-and-Alan-Bennett, imagination was automatically that which is to be mocked. He feared that the aesthetic transplant he contemplated to fulfil his existence would not take, because he was rooted in English soil.

Modern life is dull anywhere, thought Damien, but contem-porary England is uniquely dull. He remembered a recent visit to the Pitt Rivers Museum in Oxford. No wonder the English had plundered the world for marvels and stolen the gods of the heathen idolators; there was a lack at home that the English did not have the imagination to supply in any other way than theft. The things in that museum! An array of the bandicoot-striped and the dodo-feathered, the prehistorically natural and the mediaevally artificial, the numinously whimsical and the grinningly sinister, as if the cosmos were a great, twisting, reticulated crocodile, crawling and clanking, every jointed limb and every scale prickly and glittering with terror and manic delight. And on that crocodile had been a single microbe of dullness, and the microbe had slain the crocodile, skinned it, and hung its skin on the walls to admire on a Sunday afternoon.

There was in a case in the upper gallery, Damien remembered, a war helmet made of the poisonous spiny puffer fish. It had once belonged to a warrior of the Micronesian archipelago of Kiribati. Imagine going into battle with your stingray jerkin, your shark tooth-studded mace and your spiny puffer fish helmet, leaping from your boat onto the shore, and straight among the ranks of your enemy! You would know you were born. No doubt the gods had really lived then. Or the Great Spirit—the polytheism of such cultures was sometimes exaggerated, he knew.

Damien sighed out the smoke he had inhaled.

It had been the shrunken heads that had attracted him to the Pitt Rivers Museum. They did not strictly fit in with his thanatophilia (he persisted with the word), because they seemed to imply restless rather than restful spirits, but he was quite prepared to make what was, after all, only a slight detour from his usual interests for these. 'Prepared', of course, suggested the attitude in advance of the event. When he actually found the shrunken heads, he was a little disappointed. There was—it was true—a fascination to them, a kind of repugnantly mellow nausea at being in the presence of something that seemed to suspend the laws of morality; the moral equivalent of the disorientation of a suspension of the laws of physics. The same question arises in both cases: Is this real? Yes, they were, and blinking did not change this. There was also a satisfying, gnome-like appearance of evil. Curious, Damien reflected, as these were supposedly the victims of the monstrous deed rather than the perpetrators. But being the victim of any such extreme act as this tends to confer an aura of evil, or so he theorised. Still, part of the reason he kept looking was because he wanted something more—something unbearable, perhaps. Something that would haunt him.

It was then that something occurred that made him chuckle inwardly. A woman, perhaps in her late thirties, with one of those middle-class accents that make their owner sound very busy and capable, was approaching down the aisle, accompanying her son, who must have been, Damien guessed, about eight—perhaps younger.

"Shrunken heads," she was saying. "Right. Let's see. Down on the right. Ah, look. Here we are."

The young boy, like Damien, had wanted particularly to see the heads. With her hands on his shoulders, the mother positioned him before them. Her left hand still on his left shoulder, she began to point at the jars with her right, explaining with that capable voice, as if she were not reading the details for the first time from the notices next to the jars. Damien could tell, though the boy barely moved, that he was impressed—impressed in what way, he was curious to find out.

The boy could not have been listening to his mother. Without waiting for her to pause, he began, slowly, to shake his head, and in a voice of infantile dismay, said, "I don't like it."

"Don't like it?" his mother repeated, looking him in the face from above. "Spooky?"

The boy nodded.

Efficient in assessing her child's desires and needs, she immediately led him away.

That, thought Damien, is instinct. Instinct and imagination. However much or little he understood about death, the boy knew when something was malevolent. Damien envied him.

As long as children could be unbearably spooked by shrunken heads in glass cabinets, dullness had not entirely prevailed. But was it too late for Damien? Would he be carried off by dullness rather than death? Would he die in some hospital, like the one where he worked (his death a busman's holiday)—a hospital reeking of domestic violence?

Returning to the present from his thoughts, he put the pamphlet to one side and extinguished his cigarette. He needed to unwind before he could sleep. Getting up, with aching exhaustion, from the sofa, he went over to the cabinet and pulled out, to the sound of friction, one of the top drawers. The album he took out was of the A4 kind designed for special occasions such as weddings. He had dedicated this one to the microcosm of decay. Not the dead matter that decomposed, but the decomposers themselves were the subjects here. Lurid reefs of fungus, landscapes of mould with the monotonous beauty of glaciers, magnified microbes, the carrion worm apostrophised by the poets, slugs, beetles, unidentified slime—decomposition was real work, not mere ethereal fading away, and these were the angels who accomplished that work. Only angels could form the hinge between life and death as these did.

As he turned the pages of the album, without hurry, a feeling of calm began to spread through his veins. He had been frightened by aesthetics—by the thought he had chosen an aesthetic that would be obliterated by a rival, which would thereby claim the crown of reality. But these microscopic angels were beyond aesthetics. Suppose a tabloid newspaper were to report some ultimate act of his that he had committed in a more or less Gothic spirit, and were to portray it, under a vulgar headline, as just another sordid specimen of domestic violence; their word would not be the last. The paper would be abandoned somewhere— perhaps the weedy verge of a railway line. It would get stained and soggy in the rain. Snails would crawl over and devour it. The decomposers would so change and redistribute its form that it would vanish as into nothing. No, he reassured himself, he did not have to win that impossible battle of aesthetics.

✳

While his domestic energies were, during this period, conservative, at work he was making some effort to reshape himself, tempering skills from the material of experience. On the NHS Jobs website he saw a notice for a position in the radiology department of a hospital that had some staff-sharing arrangements with his. Previous experience was not essential and training was to be provided. He applied, and was quietly gratified to see that his competency was recognised as more than adequate. Of course, he was asked about his motivation. That was as solid as iron—he merely translated its essence into acceptable language during the interview. In general, throughout this relatively unremarkable career manoeuvre, he was reassured and obscurely thrilled by a sense that purpose is power, and this sense increased his self-sufficiency, which, in turn, increased his capacity for silence. And yet this silence had about it the quality of memorising something for some great moment of recitation in the future.

In particular, it was the existence of an M.R.I. scanner in the radiology department that had attracted him. This fascination had existed in him for some time, so the notice for the job had had the appearance for him that a wide-open door might have to someone who longs to rifle through the drawers of strangers, read their diaries and dress in their clothes. He had hesitated before the opportunity—but not for too long.

He even felt some kind of significance in the joke, never quite resolving itself into a convincing punchline, that it was the machine's magnetism that drew him. The fascination itself was similarly unresolved. Although his new duties took him into the proximity of the machine, and he dealt with those on whom it was used, he did not operate the machine itself; that was an entirely different and, for him, inaccessible career path. Still, he learnt more than was necessary to his job concerning its functioning, and the physical fact of the machine in his life lent these out-of-hours studies a gravity they might not otherwise have possessed. He had been let through to a kind of frontier of human activity, even if his role at that frontier was something like janitor.

The delicacy and sophistication of the machine were as impressive as physical scale can be in the great works of nature and human beings—works such as mountain ranges or cathedrals. He understood the sense of intellectual potency with which some were intoxicated—especially on the research side of things—when they worked with such a machine. There was even something archetypal about it. The magnetic cylinder into which the human was conveyed, as on a slab, resembled partly a tomb and partly some portal of initiation. The cylinder surrounded the patient, swallowed them, made strange, unnerving sounds. It saw into them. They became a transparent object of gnosis, a vessel of data.

At times, Damien wondered whether he had been seduced by precisely the same influences that had seduced those whose nemesis he aspired, someday, to be. The quest for eternal life had been present in more than one pre-modern culture—there were the alchemists, for instance, and the Daoist magicians. In these cases, though, there had always been an esoteric, less literal way of understanding the quest. Modernity repudiated the exoteric and literal form as superstition, because that was the only form it was able to discern. In fact, it was precisely the exoteric—the superstitious—aspect of the quest that modernity, recognising it as it repudiated it, carried on.

As if from the magnetic field of the machine itself, Damien found himself charged up with such portentous thoughts as he went about his daily work, maintaining the outward air of pleasant triviality so important to the professional environment.

The times when he was in attendance for a patient's scan, he was almost always struck by the same paradox. The equipment they were operating cost hundreds of thousands of pounds. As if in a military campaign on the side of knowledge against the forces of the unknown, its purpose was to stick countless coloured pins in a map of the human brain, or other area of anatomy. It was especially in relation to the brain, though, that the images thus generated carried with them—consistently—a cultural implication that was more and more widely accepted, as if it were some new piece of social progress, such as the ban on smoking, sensible and pleasing, of the kind that teachers might incite their pupils to teach, in turn, to their parents, a cultural implication that Francis Crick, that great benefactor of humanity, had even made explicit in 1994 in his book *The Astonishing Hypothesis*: that a human being is a brain, and a brain is a set of impulses that can be accurately charted. This raised the question: if a human being is nothing more than this pixellated diagram, why are we developing such expensive and complex equipment to preserve it?

These feelings, about the relatively worthless human being having medical treatment involving the relatively more valuable M.R.I. scanner (which was the physical locus for all contemporary notions of authority) were not Damien's own feelings. Rather, he felt them imprinted on the soft wax of his being, and he had to erase the impression repeatedly. He was convinced that such feelings were culturally encoded in the situation itself, though for most people they remained at the subliminal level so that cognitive dissonance never occurred and could never therefore become the occasion for a wondered questioning of the assumptions underpinning current societal norms. However, even though the feelings were generally subliminal—that is, not consciously articulate—they were powerful. That was the real reason children and adults alike were afraid of the dreadful, merciless noises the machine made, and why so many were overcome with claustrophobia at the thought of it. The machine was an expensive reality that saw through them; it could negate them like a blowtorch melting snow.

Sooner or later, surely, unless some philosophy that was simple and modern enough to unify people reclaimed the value of human beings via the soul, the paradox represented by the M.R.I. scanner would take its toll and people would simply give up on caring for other people, who they would now view as nothing more than digitally mapped zones of predictable colour.

Of course, to value money (and technological sophistication) was itself a human imposition on reality—Man being, as Protagoras said, the measure of all things—but Damien knew that culture and education had degenerated so lamentably that this simple fact could no longer be grasped on a wide scale. At least money could be measured, that is, counted, and therefore valued—what gave money value could not be measured. Money and technology would thereby be the only remaining residue— the fossil—of the human soul, and people would worship that fossil, automate it, sacrifice themselves to it, just as they had sacrificed their children to Moloch in the ancient days.

There were occasions when Damien's general apprehension of the paradox became particularised in such a way it was as if the three dimensions of consensus reality were rendered flat by the greater reality that reached forth from them. That greater reality—life itself—spoke on such occasions, for moments at a time, with an unmistakable voice, beyond all sophistry, electric in its vibrancy, all-comprehending in its soberness, utterly simple in its familiarity. It told him that humans were doing wrong. It told him that the brazenly degenerate had led to the subtle and insidious and that the subtle and insidious would lead ever back to the brazenly degenerate.

One of these occasions was to remain a vivid event in his soul for years to come, though perhaps no one but he would ever identify it as an event at all. He had been doing work under supervision at the paediatric unit of a different hospital than the one where he usually worked. He had some paediatric experience already from his degree, but was being watched until his competency was established. The patient in question was a ten-year-old girl called Debbie. It did not seem, to Damien, so very long ago that he had been Debbie's age, but the inexplicable thing called time had performed some kind of unrepeatable, unreconstructable stunt, and now his entire state of being was different. He was aware of the oddness of not being able to talk to Debbie, as it were, in her own language, but of having to use the superficially similar language of an adult addressing a child. This, and the fact he was still supervised, made him oddly self-conscious and, in turn, conscious of oddness in the whole situation in which he was contained.

As he applied 'magic cream' to Debbie's hand, where a cannula would later be inserted, took her blood pressure and asked her mother about allergies, he began to wonder about childhood itself—this thing that meant a different-sized body, a different way of talking, a different view of the world. There was something about children—in them the mystery of human existence was closer to the surface. It was not simply that they always represented the future (despite our attempting to relate to them by remembering our own past), though their status as carriers of hope was of an importance hard to exaggerate. There was also something—before they reached the age of rebellion—about their imperfect grasp of convention, which meant their inner sources of life were relatively unmediated in their expression. To watch them was to be aware of the eeriness of the human situation, of the inescapability for humans—however they might try to deny it—of existential nakedness. Children were all as if from the moon, casually yet in bewilderment finding their way on a planet not their own. Their animal grace was at one with their intelligence. Debbie, for instance, when her slim hands were free, picked at her ear so naturally there was no reason it could not be the action of a princess.

What did this girl have to do with the coloured brain map that, in a little while, they would construct of her for her own good? Indeed, it was for her own good—how could he argue against it? Yet, without hope of argument, that is, with the inevitability of the coloured map, he felt chillingly afraid the coloured map itself would replace the good against which no one could argue.

For now, and no doubt for a year or two more, Debbie still moved naturally as a leopard among trees in a world where reality has no need of consulting numbers. That was why he felt the strangeness of it all so keenly this time.

Debbie was put to sleep for the duration of the scan. Damien saw her sliding into the tube of the scanner, a plastic helmet covering her face. At the moment the scanner made a tweeting noise, as if in imitation of a bird, but at some point the grating, carnivorous drone would begin. Not required now, Damien left, but the image of the girl being fed into the machine remained in his mind. He hoped that there was something in the innocence of such sleep, something that the scanner could not see, that would overcome, somehow, the atrocities he foresaw in the century ahead, springing like brambles from the shadow-tracks of all the good things against which there could be no argument.

Damien did this extra work in radiology for almost two years, but since he was only a staff nurse, there was no obvious professional route by which he might work more closely with the machine. He grew tired of being so near the inaccessible, working in the presence of the engine that powered an enemy ideology while being forbidden to reach out his hand to it. Finally, he determined that he needed as much time and energy as possible for projects regarding which no one could help him plan a career path. He withdrew from nursing in radiology as from a bitter dead end.

Of the few visitors he had here, most did not call for social reasons. Only one visitor stayed overnight. This, of course, was Sadie.

As on the occasion of her first visit, to the Nunhead house, he gave up occupancy of his bed in deference to her. But his deference now was deft rather than fumbling. He had, in the last couple of years, made a systematic withdrawal, but with this caution had come also confidence, of the kind that might quietly grow among entrenched soldiers as they stockpile ammunition, receive fresh intelligence and make improvements to their plans.

Once more, the visit was fitted in at the weekend—this time a short rather than a long one. Altogether, it was a success—even, somehow, a surprising success. Sadie arrived on the Saturday afternoon, and in the evening they decided to take advantage of the familiar convenience of Indian cuisine. Before the Kingfisher beers were more than half drunk, Sadie made what could only be called an announcement. Of course, she was the kind to be embarrassed by announcements, and so had delivered it like a tennis player giving a backhand serve. Damien was at once stunned and underwhelmed. It was an odd feeling, already known to him. Life had happened to someone, and he wondered how. His incredulity on such occasions underlined the fact that he was entirely too consistent within himself for life ever to happen to him.

Sadie was engaged. Jason, the fiancé—both Sadie and Damien pronounced this word as if it were an amusing anachronism—was someone Damien had met a couple of times. Tall, slender, with a dark cowlick hanging over his smooth forehead, Jason was the kind of person who managed to combine outward likability with the suggestion of inner sensitivity. Sympathetic towards Sadie's artistic tastes, himself thoughtful and articulate—though more the former than the latter—Jason worked, without signs of deep frustration, in life insurance. In other words, he was one of those reassuring people who show a modest interest in the arts, but no desire to participate. Despite Jason's possession of so many attributes that were, to a detached assessment, in his favour, nonetheless, Damien could only accept the engagement as fact because the truth was in Sadie's voice. Reality stood before him complete, but he could form no idea of what equations and computations might possibly explain it. He gave up hope of understanding almost immediately.

After an initial, mutual pause, when Sadie had let the news trip from her lips with planned off-handedness, both of them had decided this was a very good thing, and that the future looked very pink—even an effervescent pink. The meal became celebratory. The decision, and its declaration now, was something straight, clear and indisputable, and therefore felt like a sudden release, as if a cord that had been stretched taut for too long had been snipped, and some things were now rightly immovable and others newly freed to the movement of harmless enjoyment. In all this, Damien most remembered some rather odd comments from Sadie, which he was sure he had not solicited.

"Anyway," she had said, "you have to marry someone." Then she had paused, and qualified this. "Well, you don't have to. But if you do marry someone, you don't have to think about it anymore. That way you've got the question answered and can concentrate on other things."

From her tone it could have been inferred that her attitude was one of detachment—on the one hand frivolous and on the other merely practical. But by some peculiar gnosis, Damien felt his mind identify a certainty beyond this surface tone: this would be one marriage whose bonds were indestructible.

Damien had smiled, having nothing to say in response, and, indeed, those had been almost the last words spoken on the subject of the future marriage. In the wake of this subject, there came the expanding feeling that they could talk about absolutely anything—all by virtue of the one thing they had just talked about and now must never speak of again.

Indestructible bonds. For Sadie there is only life, Damien remembered, and those bonds are till death.

It seemed natural now to talk about David from the poetry course at which they had first met.

"Did you ever hear from him again?" asked Damien

"Yes. I met him again, but only once. Didn't I tell you?"

And from there the conversation pursued various memories, which had, at some point, taken on the nostalgic quality of the eternal. As if suddenly, Damien and Sadie realised they were good friends and had been so for a while.

At the end of the meal, they ordered coffee. The plan was to go back to Damien's flat, drain a bottle of wine between them, talk into the small hours, and retire to separate beds (Damien's being the inflatable one). Damien felt life spotlighting this moment. It was one of those moments that expands to include a panoramic and non-linear sense of situation, as if time itself is taking you to one side, out of the narrative flow of your own life and into the place where the narrative is devised. He had had something in mind before inviting Sadie this time. But he hadn't anticipated her news. Had it changed anything? He pursed his lips as he considered this.

Something had changed, but he was not sure what, and there was no conclusive reason why he should abandon his plan.

Damien was still not entirely used to the restraint imposed, in city life, by the close proximity of neighbours above, below and to the side. Back at the flat, conscious of that restraint as one might be of a constant chill, he put some music on low, judging the volume finely, uncorked a bottle and poured the wine.

After they had imbibed, with Saturday-night leisure, two glasses each, talking not with animation, but in that easy, pause-loosened way that comes when expectation is dissolved, Damien, who was sitting on the floor, raised a hand as if remembering something, and shuffled over, crablike, to the cabinet. He slid open one of the drawers and looked at Sadie where she sat watching on the sofa. He felt something like a smile approach the surface of his face, but was unsure whether it had manifest as any expression apart from a mixture of knowingness and sadness. Anyway, he was opening the forbidden drawer, as if lifting a skirt to reveal a garter. In fact, this drawer was not one of the most forbidden, merely the one containing those books he wanted close to hand but not on display. He drew out a volume from its familiar place.

"What's the book?" asked Sadie.

Damien raised it to show the title, *The Final Fallacy*.

"Listen to this," he said, and read aloud:

> Let us take the materialist view that the mind is
> exhaustively encoded in the physical brain. In such
> a case, there is nothing in theory to prevent such
> a code being transferred to an artificial brain—a

computer. Suppose, then, that the coding of your brain were transferred at the last possible moment before the death of your brain to such a computer, an advanced one of the kind that many today now anticipate, and suppose that a clone of your body had been prepared in advance with a 'blank' brain from which any previous coding had been erased. After your death, the coding is transferred next from the computer to this. According to Locke, the continuity of memory is the continuity of the person. The clone remembers being you and just is you. To remember being you is, by definition, what it is to be you. Congratulations! You have survived the death of your—first—body.

But what if there were two clones prepared and you were downloaded into both? Which, then, is you? Locke's principle returns an unequivocal answer: both.

But that can't be right.

Your spouse might at first suspect something is wrong with Locke's principle when he or she—let us say he—finds himself suddenly a bigamist without having married again.

But what if we go further? Let us say, for instance, that your spouse chooses one of you by tossing a coin, unable to tell you apart. Let us then say that the rejected you kills the other you in a jealous rage. You are now both alive and dead at the same time. Moreover, you have simultaneously succeeded in committing suicide (killing yourself) and survived.

Damien looked up from the book.
"See?" he said. "Dead and alive at the same time."
Sadie's eyes held Damien's, and his held hers.
He smiled a little on the left side of his mouth.

"He says it's not right," Sadie said at last, taking control of the conversation as if easing the hands of a drunken friend from the steering wheel. "He said, 'But that can't be right.'"

"What do you think?" asked Damien.

"I dunno. Maybe it can't be right. Maybe it's not you."

"Because there is no you? That's what you're thinking, isn't it?"

"I dunno."

Damien slid the book back into the drawer, and, after a little groping, brought out another. On the cover of this was the title, *Never Mind*. Damien found a page that he had apparently marked for reference.

"Listen to this," he said, and began, again, to read:

> We are in the business of explaining and at this point we turn to the conscious Subject as more matter for business as usual. To complete our task we must move from unknowing single cells to the cognisant multiplicity of organised cells without having left anything out or, worse, adding any magic ingredients.

> These criteria for the explanation are viewed by some theorists as bringing us into confrontation with a particularly sticky dilemma.

> On the one hand, if you formulate a theory, as required, with all the working parts in place, and which by virtue of that very fact resembles an automated factory, deserted of what we might call the 'personnel' of any Subject, many will suppose you have practised a vanishing trick or missed something important.

> If, on the other hand, your factory is not fully automated—that is, if the Subject has to press this, pull that and move something else manually, or if the theory has the Subject as an overseer of am-

biguous duty, entirely hands-off in his job, then you
have failed to arrive at your stated goal—a complete
explanation.

"An automated factory." As Damien read this part, knowing
that with this phrase consciousness was resolved into tangles of
neurons and ganglia, he envisaged what he had envisaged before:
half-mechanical, half-biological levers in the membranous factory of the brain, moving spookily backward and forward like
the unseeing feelers of a cockroach.

"So," he said, "in the end there's no difference between living
matter and dead matter, is there?"

Sadie considered.

"Life would be a 'magic ingredient'," Damien added.

"I suppose . . ." said Sadie, "that what he's talking about is the
gap, isn't it? Science is explaining more and more of the workings
of the brain, and will one day explain everything."

"Do you think it will?" Damien's voice had the lightness and
clarity of detachment.

"I don't know. I suppose it must, if everything is physical."

"And there's nothing after death," said Damien, "so nothing
leaves the body. There is only matter. Therefore, if a living body
and a dead body are not made different by any magic ingredients,
they are the same thing, just like a clockwork toy that is moving
is exactly the same as a clockwork toy whose spring has wound
down. And therefore, it is not only possible to be dead and living
at the same time, but that is unavoidably what we all are. The
only thing 'living' can possibly mean is that dead matter moves
in a particular way. So living is only something built on top of
being dead, or is only a subset of being dead. We are all dead and
alive at the same time."

Damien had stood up as he said this and placed the book,
open, face up, in the alcove of the cabinet where the usual flowers
were on display, in their vase.

"But you don't believe that?" asked Sadie.

Damien smiled.

"Do you?"

Again, they held each other's gaze.

Still looking at Sadie, Damien made a strange, slow, deliberate sweep with his left hand and knocked the vase over so that the flowers and water spilt onto the book.

He began to laugh, almost deliberately, it seemed, or as if seeking escape from walls that closed in from both sides: the wall of irony and the wall of sincerity. Sadie looked at him in puzzlement; in puzzlement she joined in his laughter. The laughter of each seemed to understand the laughter of the other, but it was not entirely clear that either of them understood their own laughter.

With a playfully affected sigh, Damien launched himself away from the cabinet and toward the windows behind the sofa. He opened the top window. Then he retrieved the book, wiped the water off it, took it to the window, and posted it into the outside night, as if through a letterbox.

He closed the window. Then opened it again.

"Do you want a cigarette?" he asked.

"I don't smoke."

"Oh. Of course you don't. I think I'll have one."

He had got away with it.

This was only a relief if he did not think of what, at some unspecified point, came next.

For the rest of the weekend, at least, he would not think of it.

V. Resurrection

LIKE creeping ivy, his secret life had to take over.

If anyone found out, Damien thought, they would think it was sudden, unexpected. But it was not sudden. A drift of unspoken experience had, over the years, taken him too far from his fellow human creatures for him to speak now. And . . . perhaps they would not find out.

At this stage of his life, fox-like and secretive in his New Cross flat, he was familiar—the very 'of course' of familiarity—with all of the seven London cemeteries founded in the Victorian era to relieve the pestilent overcrowding of the parish church grave-yards: the 'Magnificent Seven' as they had later been dubbed. He had also visited most of the numerous remainder of burial plots that the capital, squeezing an expanding populace into its limits by all the imperatives of human ambition and survival, seemed to produce despite itself, like ruptures in the fabric of progress. He had spent nights within cemetery walls. He had slept on a creeper-veined slab as if he were a tomb carving. He had watched the stars appear between the branches of grave-sheltering trees as if each new pinprick of radiance were a chime to signal sanctuary. As the stars were thus distilled from the night, he had heard foxes and owls and known that the enclave of death was the enclave also of the wild. He had felt the gossamer stirrings in his heart of aliveness, unsmothered by the smog of human opinion and unchecked by the fences of human convention. He had with patience allowed and observed the emergence of the nocturnal

70

tenderness and fear that awaken with knowing it is from this patch of ground, abode of animal and bramble, corpse and cross, that one may see clearly; and how tremulous the spirit at the clarity of this view, of sagging clay houses and concreted streets, where people sleep in intermission between one interpersonal campaign and the next in the ongoing border disputes of daily life.

In other words, when it came to looking for something specific in the burial plots of London, there was no need for him to make haste in a shallow reconnaissance. He was already versed in that unusual lore. With the steadiness of grounded knowledge, he made his search. And when he had positively identified a grave that appeared to meet all his conditions, he thrilled with uncontrollable shivers, knowing that there were no obstacles for him to remove and that the timing was a matter of his personal decision.

It was a child's grave, not far from the enclosing wall and screened from the view of the nearest footpaths by a comforting group of trees. The burial had taken place in the middle of the twentieth century. The grave was new enough to escape the worst depredations of the body snatchers who had provided useful materials for the medical profession in earlier centuries, but old enough that the parents were likely dead themselves and that a desecration—as it would be called—might go unnoticed, or not be soon detected.

But he had little guidance in this matter. His reading suggested to him that a wooden spade would make less noise than a metal implement; he acquired a wooden spade. The same source served as a reference point for other tools and equipment. Rope, for instance, would make the task considerably easier. There was some amount of reassurance to be gained even from such fragments of information as this. Help, even in this matter, seemed a friendly thing, and surely friendliness was goodness without morals. Though historically he might not have been alone in what he planned, however, he certainly belonged to no company united by an official reference text, or even by the will to be identified with each other. There was no way of knowing, for instance, whether the grave he was now contemplating contained anything, or whether someone had been there before him. How many secrets of time were now beyond recovery? Was this peculiar crisis of his more common than he imagined? There were many questions he would have liked to put directly to someone with prior experience—practical questions and other, more wide-ranging questions. The practical and the personal seemed, in this matter, of equal existential weight. The internet was useless for such questions, for anything—he had discovered—that burned unnameably in the soul. He was not interested in vulgar bragging or cynical sneering, which is what, on the internet, those things closest to personal testimony always were—vulgarity and cynicism both in bad faith. He did not wish to meet any of those who seemed to share his interests. Those who shared his interests only a little perhaps had more in common with him than those who shared them deeply; the former tended to be psychogeographers of a melancholy cast, the latter merely trash. He was between them, could speak to none of them, a necrogeographer. In the end, perhaps, the secret-keeping silence of history, which the internet had begun to interrupt, was not only merciful, but seductive.

So, he set a date, and marked it on his calendar only with a cross. Once the logic of this date had occurred to him, he could not dislodge it from his mind. He would carry out his plan on the winter solstice.

It was late September in the year 2010 when the date was decided. This meant there were unalterably to be three months of waiting. They might be three months of mental preparation, or three months within which doubt would erode the foundations of the plan. As Damien experienced them, they were both things, and other things besides. The temporal distance between the present and the appointed time seemed to shrink with great swiftness. As if it now held too much to pass at such speed down the narrow channel of the predetermined, Damien's mind swelled into a bank-bursting lake of quivering hesitations, unexpected euphoria and uncommon insights in the weeks preceding the solstice and the deed to which he had mentally devoted it. The effect of this was ultimately that when the waters untied the knot of the lake in flowing out the other side, they had the momentum of a renewed spontaneity in addition to the momentum of accumulated purpose.

✻

The bag, a black, forty-four-inch holdall, made him feel like he was departing on a journey, one-way, to somewhere he had never been before. As would be the case on such a journey, the bag was the anchor of his security. A traveller needs a timetable and ticket, though travelling, to many, is synonymous with freedom. Damien, too, had his timetable. He had bought a watch with a luminous face (more discreet than the glow of a phone), and had noted that the sun was to rise at 8.04 a.m. tomorrow. Instead of a ticket, he had, inside the holdall, the body bag he had purloined from the hospital where he worked, and various pieces of equipment for the essential task, or for contingencies.

He entered the burial ground before sunset, which came at 3.52 p.m. that day, and hid between two raised graves by the wall where brambles provided cover, trying to gauge when it was safe to emerge. But there were no clear signals for this; it was a matter of when he felt ready. Even now, the loudest thoughts in his head were telling him that he was doing all this out of bravado, that his play-acting would never have the force to carry him through to the real job that had to be done, that at best he would end up contenting himself with staying the night here, as he had done before, though, given the winter chill, probably not even that. The counter-thoughts saying that he must not back out of his commitment seemed obviously weak and superficial. And yet, after he emerged from his hiding place, he found himself simply following the next step of the plan, and then the next.

Or perhaps not quite simply. The most difficult thing was the first cleaving of the earth with the spade. It was worse than lifting up the skirt of a stranger. In theory, it was easily done, but he could not make himself do it. However, he could not walk away, either. He tried, but returned to the graveside as if fastened to it by a length of elastic.

Is it possible to step outside of oneself? This is the question that lends to every life the fear of death. It is the essential, the most avoided question. The closer the blade of Damien's spade was brought to the soil of the grave, the more intense the question became, like magnetic repulsion.

When, at last, the blade bit into the soil, the magnetic repulsion evaporated, and Damien was left only with a feeling of weakness and disgust. Nothing was preventing him now from doing what he had come to do, but nothing was propelling him, either. Every single spadeful of dirt would have to be moved with conscious deliberateness.

Damien glanced at his watch. Already it was past seven. This gave him time, but people were not yet generally in their beds. He was much more than nervous, but he would not wait. He would continue, and finish.

And so he carried on.

Like a man running a marathon for the first time with little training, he did not know how long it would take, or if he could complete it. He concentrated on the next spadeful, and the next, fearful with each. Two or three times he froze at sounds so slight they might only have been in his ear. He was aware on each of these occasions that, should luck be against him, he was helpless, at least in the question of avoiding discovery, and he had no confidence in his ability to take counter-measures should discovery occur. Still, he had mapped out an escape route in his mind, and his holdall also contained a small battery of non-lethal weapons such as pepper spray.

On each occasion that something alarmed him, however, nothing happened. Perhaps there had only been a hedgehog in the grass or the slither of a falling leaf. Eventually he would let out a breath, still not certain that there were no human eyes upon him, and resume his task.

His shoes and the bottoms of his trouser legs were filthy now with mud. His gloved hands, too, were streaked with it. Somehow the turned soil had made the night wildly luxurious. His mind was famished, and all that met his senses was a feast of fascination. His eyes had adjusted to the dark. In fact, when he realised how much they had adjusted, he blinked. He seemed to be seeing colours, even at night. Was it an illusion? But how could an illusion make him see better? He was blinking as if something was in his eyes, but it was the lucidity of his vision that made him blink. Glancing about to test this vision, he saw even what was still—the nearby wall—quickening like kindled fire with the elemental energies of its solidity. Everything seemed to draw vampiric sustenance, with great inhalations and exhalations, from this opened wound in the soil.

And still there was nothing to do but continue with his indefinite task, advancing with steadiness to an unknown conclusion.

After a long time, the hole was large enough that he could stand inside it. Indeed, he had to, in order to keep digging. But his head and shoulders still protruded above ground level.

He was aware of wanting to cry, but being unable to. He was himself. Who else could he ever be? And yet things had got too deep and it was too late for him to be himself. He had stepped outside himself, and this was how it felt. But only how he *felt*—he told himself; it was only feelings, and he was surely still there behind them. Surely? To step outside oneself is to step into the inhospitable freedom of 'this is all there is', but no sooner did he step into 'this is all there is' than he began to suffer with existential double vision. The pressure of it all was terrible.

But there—there was the coffin. Now he wanted only to finish it all quickly and get away.

The wood was still firm, but he had anticipated this. He hauled himself from the hole and took a mattock and a rag from the holdall. Then he slid back into the grave.

He worked for some time with the intensity of a burrowing

animal. The unbearable contradiction of being himself and not himself had disappeared as if sleep had brought forgetfulness while his body was active.

After a while, he scrabbled up again for the rope and the body bag, and again returned to the pit. He had changed his gloves for surgical gloves, and now he wore a white mask over nose and mouth.

His satisfaction rising in bloated ambiguity, like a gorge, Damien secured the rope in a noose beneath the armpits of the object he had successfully unburied. His task required the utmost haste on the one hand and patience with details on the other, and so his mental condition was one of frantic concentration, the feeling that at any point in the process, something vital might slip from his nervous fingers and precipitate a calamity such as his being caught, and therefore frozen, forever, in the state of not being himself—frozen there in the eyes of a world not susceptible to the euphoria and the nausea of double vision.

This must have been the reason he did not hear anything until a voice came from directly above him.

"Man, what you doing here?"

The words sank through his back in chill vibrations, percolating to his bowels. He knew that to freeze now would mean a steep escalation of trouble, but he could think of no words and no actions by which he could find purchase on the situation.

"Hey. You hear me?"

"I . . ." He cleared his throat, to find his voice and to grasp the handle of the moment. "I lost something."

"Man, I can't hear what you're saying."

Damien considered, and then realised he was considering. Whoever this interloper was, he had allowed Damien to consider, and Damien was grateful for that. To consider was human.

He turned to face the source of the voice, and spoke before he took in the figure that stood above him, but he knew that the white mask still covered his nose and mouth and that this might muffle his words.

"I lost something," he repeated.

And then the specific reality of the person at the graveside began to imprint itself on his consciousness in such a way that he could feel the subtleties of the figure and the voice permeate the mind-body totality of his own existence.

The figure stood in an attitude of unbudgeable idleness. His curiosity was unapologetic; it was plain he was not going to drift away until he was satisfied. In the night-gloom, Damien thought he saw a kind of tasselled shawl around the shoulders of the one addressing him, and wondered half-consciously whether he had come from a festival of some kind. Sound and shadow disclosed the existence of a large glass bottle in the possession of this stranger. It was larger than a wine bottle, suggesting almost the kind of vessel that might be seen in the display window of an old-fashioned chemist. For a moment, Damien expected a jester's cap and bells, but the man was bare-headed.

"Have I seen you before?" the man asked now.

Damien shook his head. "No," he said.

"What's your name?"

"Jason."

"Jason? Jason? I'm Steve. Have we met before?"

"I don't think so."

"Hey, Jason, I've got to ask you something. Are you sure we haven't met before? I feel like I know you from somewhere. Man, I wonder where my friend is. He said he was going to pick me up an hour ago. I've got—" he seemed to delve into his pocket with one hand, "—seventy-two pee. I need to get to my friend's house in Harington. Can you lend me ten pound?"

"I don't have any money."

"Five pound?"

"I've got no cash at all."

"Have you got a cash card?"

"There's no cash machine."

"Have you got a card?"

Damien didn't respond. There were no immediate escape routes from the situation, but he did not feel like playing along in the hope of getting to the end of the ordeal sooner.

A leak had sprung inside him, and he could feel himself filling up with misery. Out of spite and helplessness he did nothing but stand and let the waters of misery rise, flooding and ruining the furniture of his inner self. He wished he knew whether Steve understood the situation. He wanted to refer to the corpse, to what he was doing, but each time this intention extended itself inside him, it stopped short of realisation, deflected by the same uncertainty. And this was why he was miserable and spiteful. If he left the situation long enough, he knew, a buckling might occur and the ceiling of the unthinkable might fall in on him. Still he did nothing.

Had Steve seen, before Damien had kicked the torch and redirected its beam, the child made venerable by decay, that sight as uncommon as a living angel?

"Hey, Jason, are you okay? You look like you've got worries on your mind."

Damien said nothing.

"What're you doing in that hole? Something smells bad down there."

Damien reached up to pull the mask away from his mouth and nose. There was the relief that always comes in removing a mask, even when that removal increases vulnerability. His breath was no longer stifled. Whatever microbes it contained, the night air was sweet, chill, without friction. This freedom of air mediated between Damien and what was at his feet. Somehow, the corpse was the very opposite of his vulnerability. He was intimately connected with it—that was why he was vulnerable—but the corpse was an enigma, repelling all mentation, though it might provoke. For an instant it was absolutely clear. The corpse was simultaneously Damien's ultimate Achilles' heel and his ultimate invulnerability. What he needed was not just to be linked with this corpse, as he already was, but somehow to change places with it.

"I'm a sanitary technician," he said.

"That's your job?"

"Yes. It's actually 'mortality services sanitary technician'."

"Why're you working at night?"

Damien sighed.

"It's like roadworks. You know how they do that at night sometimes? This is like that. Some jobs . . . people don't normally see."

"Do you want some rum?"

"What?"

Steve shook the glass vessel he was holding, and it made a swilling sound.

"Real Jamaica rum. The good stuff. Try some."

"No. Thanks. It's okay."

"Try it. It's good. It's not a trick. Look."

Steve uncapped the vessel, and tossed it back with what, considering the size of the bottle, must have been a practised steadiness. He took three gulping swigs and wiped his mouth with the back of his left hand. Then he crouched down at the graveside and extended the bottle towards Damien. At first, Damien repeated his refusal, but the truth was he wanted something to drink. He discarded the rope he had been holding, took the bottle in both surgical-gloved hands and swigged once, twice, three times, to match Steve. Then he passed it back. Steve nodded and took it.

"Steve," said Damien, "do you know where a cashpoint is?"

"Yes, I know one. It's not far."

"If you help me finish my job, I'll pay you a tenner. Don't worry about paying me back."

"What do you want me to do?"

"Not much. Just stand there and pull this rope when I say."

Steve stood near the headstone, as directed, and Damien passed him the rope. Damien calculated as he manoeuvred, the situation presenting him with a series of chicanes he had to steer past. He did not want to do anything with the torch still in the grave, so he picked it up and placed it by Steve's feet. Its beam was directed away from the grave and onto the headstone. Damien would have to feel what he was doing in a newly intense darkness, but he was ready for this. The first task was to get the body bag into the right position. As he was engaged in this, he heard Steve speak, seemingly to himself.

"Philip James Draper. Died nineteen fifty-two. Eight years old. Very sad. Very sad."

"Okay," said Damien. "Pull. Slowly. About two or three feet. A bit more. A bit more. Stop. That's it. Now, same speed. Lower it. Lower. Lower. That's it."

He untied and removed the rope, sealed the body bag, then tied the rope again around the bag. What now? He put the tools that had been in the grave with him on the graveside turf.

"I'm coming up," he said.

Scrambling unsteadily out, his limbs aching with cramp and tingling with pins-and-needles, he took the rope from Steve.

"Can you open that bag over there?" he asked, pointing to the holdall.

This was the part he had most feared, but Steve showed no signs of abrogating his complicity with Damien's pretence. The fumblingness of trying to fit the body inside the holdall was almost unbearable, like undressing in front of someone and tripping over your own underwear. But each hitch went unchallenged so that the event, however abashed, grew to its majority in a world that seemed much wider for its indifference. Some of what had been in the holdall had to be removed to accommodate the very common but somehow nameless thing that had been newly introduced. Most of these could be transferred to a smaller bag that Damien had also brought along, but some, it seemed, would have to be left behind. This was troubling.

"That's a nice bag," said Steve, indicating the holdall. "Where'd you get it?"

"Er . . . the internet."

"That's a nice bag." He clicked his tongue in admiration.

"Right, let's go," said Damien, and kicked into the grave the few items he could no longer carry.

"You not taking them?"

"I'll pick them up next time."

Steve seemed to know the terrain very well. A sense of collusion moved within Damien, slicing the water of his inner feelings like the blade of a rudder, as he followed Steve to one of the lich gates. There was certainly a sense in which Steve's appearance was lucky—he only hoped it wasn't too lucky. From the other side of the lich gate, Steve helped Damien lift the holdall and the rum over, and then Damien climbed over after him, feeling like some unknown Houdini.

They headed off along the pavement. Damien carried the holdall in his left hand. The rum passed back and forth between them. For a while Damien gave no thought to where they were going, but soon remembered Steve had claimed to know the whereabouts of a cash machine. The road was dipping down to a junction of some sort, with a park and housing estate beyond. It looked like the wrong kind of area for a cash machine. Slowly, apprehension began to grow back in Damien's stomach. Nonetheless, the rum continued to pass back and forth. Past the junction they turned right through the estate. So far, they had encountered no other people, except one or two, on the other side of the road or in the periphery of Damien's vision. The estate seemed in the grip of an iron silence, like a prison in suspended animation. Damien was surprised there was a way through, its silence felt so very much like a dead end, but the way through appeared soon enough, and then they were at another junction.

Steve appeared to be considering which way to go. Then he pointed and shouted in triumph.

"Taxi!"

The taxi was letting out passengers a little way down the road. Steve ran towards it, clearly jubilant at this serendipity. Damien followed, hampered by the holdall. After only a couple of strides, it occurred to him to question why he was doing so. He could take this opportunity to run away. But a feeling of quavering fatalism washed over him as he contemplated escape. He should do it, but he wasn't doing it, and the longer he hesitated, the harder it was to make that break for it. Run away with the holdall? That would make him all too memorable to Steve. God knows what Steve was really thinking. He seemed to have a genius for projecting an ambiguous attitude. It was obviously an act, but there was something in its very obviousness that charmed. It was as if he was letting you in on the joke that he was dodgy, and in doing so he rendered it nothing more than a joke, and so disarmed you.

Damien smiled to himself, troubled though he was. He decided he liked Steve.

Maybe the taxi would be useful to him, anyway.

Steve was talking to the taxi driver by the time Damien got there.

"We've got a bag, too. Can we put it in the boot?"

The taxi driver nodded from his seat, opened the driver's door, and went to the back of the car.

"Going on holiday?" he asked Damien.

Damien laughed, then realised that, oddly, the man seemed to be expecting an answer.

"No. No. This is my work bag."

He was afraid the next question would be what his work was. He didn't want to give a different answer to the one he'd given Steve, but he surely could not give that answer this time.

However, the question didn't come. The man shut the boot with a hefty crunch. Now Damien would not be able to retrieve the holdall until . . . when? Until they got to wherever they were going. There was nothing he could do but be a passenger for an indefinite, presumably brief, period.

Damien got in on the right side. Steve was already sitting on the left, leaning forward to talk to the driver.

"Harington. The address is 27 Laidlaw Grove. Also, can we stop at a cashpoint machine on the way?"

"Yeah. No problem."

The car pulled away from the kerb, with that sensation for Damien that a car pulling away sometimes gives a passenger, of giving oneself up to an irresponsible escapade of the kind that calls for a snatch of theme tune. However, the city remained impassively silent. The driver's hands pawed the wheel as he turned a corner, and the light of the sleeping streets slid coldly across Damien's face. He closed his eyes. Distance. Distance. He wanted to be far away from everything.

"Hey, don't sleep, man." It was Steve.

"We'll be there soon," he continued. "I'll introduce you to my friend, Simon. He is a genius with computers. He's building a program to predict things. Anyone who invests in that, they're gonna be rich in the future."

The taxi pulled over.

"Cash machine here," the driver said over his shoulder.

Steve got out readily on the left side, then came back. He leaned in at the door.

"The cash machine," he said.

"Oh yes," said Damien, and got out on his side.

He took out his wallet and slipped a card from inside. When he inserted it into the machine, Steve stood close on his right. Damien looked pointedly at Steve, waiting for him to look away, which he eventually did, then he entered his pin number. Then Damien noticed Steve was looking at the screen again.

"Ten pounds, right?"

"We'll need more than that for the taxi."

"I thought you said ten pounds."

"I was going to get some more from somewhere else. This taxi will cost twenty pound, at least, to Harington. Maybe thirty pound. But you need to get more out for the party. I can get us some MDMA. Say eighty pound, altogether."

"Eighty pounds?"

"Ninety."

Damien sighed. The bag was in the boot, of course. He looked around, thinking. Not far away, he noticed, was a police station. The lights were still on inside, visible through the glass doors. A young woman, perhaps Spanish, perhaps in her late twenties, who had apparently been wheeling a travel bag along, was karate-kicking at the doors and screaming, "Are you gonna arrest me then? Are you gonna arrest me then?" She was surrounded by five youths on bicycles, sitting on their saddles with their feet on the pavement.

"Eighty pounds. Okay," he said, and punched in the figure. He took the money and slipped it in his wallet with his card before Steve could say anything.

When they were back in the taxi and it had pulled away from the kerb to continue their journey, Steve began talking about his friend Simon again.

"Algorithms—that's the word. That's what he does. He makes algorithms to predict things, and he is working on the ultimate algorithm for chaos."

"Chaos?"

"Yes. He will predict chaos. Anyone who invests in that will be rich."

"You can't predict chaos," said Damien. "That's the point of chaos—you can't predict it."

"This is the ultimate algorithm," said Steve. "It will predict even chaos."

"Really?"

Damien thought about predicting chaos. The thought seemed to turn into a feedback loop in his head.

"You should invest in it. It's a good investment. I will introduce you to him."

"I'll think about it."

Damien was impatient to get out of the taxi now, and responded to Steve's conversation only in order to keep him satisfied that he was listening.

After some time, Steve looked around at the streets passing outside the taxi windows and was animated with apparent recognition.

"Almost there," he said.

He began to direct the taxi driver, unnecessarily, as it seemed. Damien was mildly surprised that they were going to a real place, which the interaction between Steve and the driver confirmed.

Eventually, they were standing on the pavement outside 27 Laidlaw Grove. Damien had been anxious about retrieving the holdall, but now it was in his grasp again. He paid the taxi driver, and the taxi drove away, leaving them in a part of the city quite unfamiliar to him. It was, anyway, one of those numerous areas of Greater London where closely ranked houses formed an angular maze, as if a cutting had been taken from the residential area of some unnamed smaller town elsewhere in Britain and grown to fill the needs of a denser population, stretching, therefore, into streets of more dizzying sameness, with fewer hints that their desert of cement and clay will contain, or give place to, an oasis of some different mode of existence than mere containment and habitation. There was a bareness to such places that made Damien's feet hurt as he walked them—he thought, out of psychic rather than physical reaction. However, he had grown used to them, and knew that these stony-seeming houses were also, in many ways, warm with life. He remembered such warmth now, its usually untidy traces in the environment marking, like skid marks on a road, where human life had been, but since he had not been here before, the coldness of the stony exteriors, reminding all to be strangers to each other, predominated. The house in front of which they had stopped, too, was entirely dark and silent. Damien was perplexed—there was no party here.

"Come on," said Steve, and began to walk off down the pavement.

"Wait. This is twenty-seven, here."

"That's not the house. I always give the wrong address. It's not far from here."

It was at this point that Damien was especially tempted to walk, or possibly run, away. Yet, once more, he followed after Steve. All his emotions were in a state of suspension. Something inside him was raising an alarm, telling him he was doing something dangerously stupid. And yet he could not quite convince himself that this was true. This weird condition of being in intense fear but doubting the fear, persisted long enough for it to be torturous. "I have to do something. I can't just keep following like this," he told himself. But he continued to follow.

After one or two turnings, Damien began to hear the kind of dance music that had been ubiquitous since the nineties, and which, he now realised, evoked associations of time, place and person as distinctly and colourfully as a moving hologram. Even that dull, yet high-energy thud, which made him think of drink going dead in the small hours—as in Larkin's poem about masturbation—was warm and human. His mind was wonderfully eased by it.

Soon an ambience of many voices could be heard under the beat. Would the emotional tone of such chatter, Damien wondered, be familiar to someone from the fifth century if you could go back in time and play them a recording of it? Was it as timeless as it sounded?

They turned into the street where the party was being held. It was immediately apparent which house was their destination. No doubt this party was being received by neighbours with the same mixture of tolerance and seething uptightness as uncounted similar parties across London. Police might be called, but more commonly, if there were complaints they would take the form of repeated bangings on the wall, or else someone would knock on the door and remind the first person who answered it that some of us have work in the morning (this would be unavailing, however, as the person answering the door would be too drunk or otherwise spaced out to pass on the message in any effective way). All of this passed through Damien's mind, along with the rest of the knowledge of parties he had accumulated in his life, and he judged that for all its agitation, discomfort and seeming insecurity, a party was a safe place to be—a ship whose decks might get washed by the spray of a storm, but which would not sink. And, as they approached the house, the light and the voices—even though the latter belonged entirely to strangers—half-reassured him with a sense of sanctuary. If he could stash the bag somewhere for a while, he could use the situation to plan his next move in his own time. It was easy to get separated from someone at a party. He would not have to say goodbye to Steve.

Steve approached the front door, raised his hand to ring the bell, then stopped.

"Man, what happened to the rum?"

"Oh, I still have it—in my backpack."

"Okay. Good. Best get it out for the party."

Steve rang the bell while Damien took the backpack from his back and retrieved the still more-than-half-full bottle of rum. Steve had to ply the bell twice more, but just as Damien was becoming nervous about their prospects of gaining entry, the door was flung open, inwards, and three or four party-goers stood in attitudes of dramatic welcome in the hall space at the foot of the stairs, as if they expected to share a kind of knowingness with those on the doorstep. By this time, Damien was brandishing the rum, and Steve did not even have to complete a sentence before they were beckoned inside.

The door closed behind them and Damien was aware of having to work fast.

"I need to put my bags somewhere," he said to Steve.

"Chucky," said Steve to one of the three people still in the hallway, "where can we put our bags?"

Chucky, a young man with corn-coloured dreadlocks piled on his head, answered with the casual authority of someone intimate with the house: "Tessa's bedroom. Just up the stairs, past the toilet, first on the left. Should be a pile of coats and bags already there."

"Okay," said Damien, and passed the rum to Steve. "I'll be right back down."

He did not wait for further permission, but ascended the stairs with the momentum of sudden release. There was a small queue for the toilet, along the landing to the next flight of stairs, and the next stairs, too, were occupied by people smoking and drinking. Ducking into the bedroom, however, Damien was surprised and glad to find it unoccupied. He stopped for a moment to survey the unexpected stillness. A shiver ran down him and rebounded in ripples. It was odd how quiet could occupy a room even in a house full of music and dancing, and how ticklish that quiet could be. Anyway, he had not been misinformed. There was the pile of bags and coats, to the right of the bed. Degraded as it was, Damien recognised this as a middle-class habit. He wondered whether he should try to bury the holdall underneath these bags and coats, but then, perhaps, this would do more to excite suspicion than if he placed his bags carefully by the side of the others. He walked over, set down the holdall and slipped his backpack once more from his shoulders in order to place it on top. For a while he stood, contemplating whether there might be a more advantageous ordering of things, or whether he could now easily walk away. At least, he had no desire to hurry downstairs to where the congregation of people was densest.

There was something intimate and touching about this congeries of personal property—this makeshift cloakroom. Everything here had a just-dropped softness, seemed fresh with the scent of absent owners.

Tessa—that was the name that had been given for the owner of this bedroom. There was something touching, too, in the equality—the lack of chivalry—that meant she had been made vulnerable in having her room designated the cloakroom. There was a dynamic at work either of trust or of carelessness, or perhaps of a compound of the two.

A wardrobe stood near the left-hand corner against the wall in which the door was set. Damien walked over to it, idly, and opened the door. These tops and dresses, on coat hangers, surely belonged to Tessa. Damien knew very little about dress design, but he noticed one that even had something of the Laura Ashley style about it. He took the fabric, near the hem, between his thumb and fingers, and savoured the tactile impression. Sensation and sentiment, he reflected, were closely related. He felt he understood, from the information of his fingertips on this garment, the feelings, simultaneously, of a parent and a lover. The lover knew the poignancy of gain and loss, from and to absolute strangeness; the parent knew the poignancy of constancy and restraint in the midst of endless change.

He let the hem of the dress drop back into place, and closed the door. Then he moved over to the window, which overlooked the back garden. The kitchen door opened onto the garden, which was L-shaped, with Damien viewing from the top of the L to the bottom, which swung left. From the kitchen, a few of the party guests had straggled outside, smoking and drinking. They were looking for something other than mere noise, but they found only chill and fragments of conversation.

In the horizontal bar of the garden's inverted L, there was a hedge, and behind the hedge, a fence. This double barrier, however, was not entirely effective in excluding the uninvited. A fox, with movements light as whisks of snow, was investigating that quarter, habituated, it seemed, to treating the rare empty moments of an urban environment as appearing and disappearing pathways and patchworks of the wild. Its coat was silvered by the electric light from the kitchen. The humans in the garden only occupied the vertical bar of the L. They had not seen the fox. Damien, himself unobserved, saw both. As more humans entered the garden and moved towards its bottom end, the fox flitted away into the hedge. Damien was aware of the lingering resonance from his shiver when he had first entered the room; the resonance grew inside him, nourished by quiet and distance.

What did the people here want, really? Did they know? There was sex, of course, but even that relied on things unspoken and indefinite postponements.

He began to think about a doctor at the hospital where he worked. She had insisted, in his presence, more than once, that it was simply impossible for a human being to come to terms with death. And yet, she had three children whose unfaceable deaths would have to be faced because of her. Had she thought differently at the time they were conceived? What did she think of her task as a doctor? Was it to keep people alive in the fear of death for as long as possible? Could you, in fact, commit yourself to fighting death without thinking about it? In any case, her attitude was typical of people he knew; she was merely unusual in that, as a professional working in the presence of death, she was at the very front line of the attitude, one of its exemplars. But how was this seemingly intolerable contradiction maintained in her and in the society she typified?

There was a kind of answer, which might also explain why the world was so wild and dizzy, with merely tantalising glimpses of something else. In making death unthinkable, these people had trapped themselves in the unthinkable forever. Only by not thinking about unthinkable death were they able to procreate, and so ensure that there would always be humans contained in the fatal bubble of the unthinkable. There they were, at the centre of the bubble, in the tragic throes of sex, perpetuating the spell by whose power the bubble kept its binding force. If they only understood, for once, that death was not unthinkable, the bubble might burst. The consequences of that, Damien did not know, but how could they be worse than being trapped in the unthinkable?

He began to roll himself a cigarette. He was not sure that he needed it, and yet, in some peculiarly detached way he told himself this was exactly the kind of situation in which he really needed a cigarette. Having lit it, he could not find an ashtray, so opened the sash window a crack in order to flick ash outside. He supposed he should go downstairs after this cigarette, but then an urge coalesced within him to open up the holdall and take another look at what he had brought here. Only moments after he became aware of this urge, there came an opposite reaction in him of extraordinary revulsion, and he did not want to look at all. And then again, he needed to look, to overcome this revulsion, but it was too risky, and so on.

Smoking, and contemplating the bag, he felt his mind settle on a mournful image, full of that kind of grief that must have been known to various heroes of myth who looked back when they had been told not to. The image was this: a river of insecurity and a child set adrift on it in a box. The river was time. The child in the box had gone into a tunnel for over fifty years before emerging from the darkness once more into the tilting, many-voiced, prismatic insecurity of the world. What peace was there, with the destination of all unknown, except to let oneself be carried through the world on that flow? Here we all are, still flowing, thought Damien, and none of us can do a thing about any of it. This child, he thought, has the answers to all our secret questions, or at least can reply to them with the same depth of longing and unknowingness with which they are asked, if only, that is, his language can be translated.

He had not quite finished his cigarette, and was still pursuing his train of thought into regions of dim apocalypse where shadows of consolation danced with *ignes fatui* of soul-menace, when the door was catapulted open with unnecessary violence.

A young man and woman virtually fell through into the room, and looked about, laughing.

"Oh, sorry," said the young woman.

"Sorry," the young man echoed.

"I'm just having a cigarette," said Damien, raising his right hand in evidence. "Don't mind me."

But apparently they did mind, as the acknowledgement that had first extended to Damien in apologies withdrew and the interaction between the couple became exclusive—a consultation in lowered voices preliminary to their leaving the room.

About to slump into solitude after the exit of the couple, Damien stiffened again into alertness when the door swung open once more and a familiar figure appeared.

"Man, you still here?"

"Just having a cigarette," said Damien.

"Have you got fifty pound for the MDMA?"

Damien nodded and took the money from his pocket.

"Okay, wait here," said Steve.

"I'll come down," said Damien.

"No. I'll come back up. We need a room, so best you wait here."

Steve left with the money. Damien went back to the window and flicked the shrivelled butt of the cigarette out into the garden. Then he closed the window, walked away and sat down on the carpeted floor with his back against the foot of the bed. Having been told to wait, he felt powerless and miserable. He bowed his head and sank into himself. Now, while Steve was in search of drugs, might be a good time to make his escape. The conviction suddenly flared up in him that this was true—that this was an opportunity he must seize. But then he wondered what would happen if, carrying the bulky holdall, he met Steve on the stairs. His spirit, which had been roused, sank back again into weariness. He took the injunction to wait as both punishment and protection, as if he were safe in prison.

A strange new desire began to grow in him. He became aware of the double bed whose foot he leaned against. It was empty, and he had the impression it was clean. Perhaps it wasn't entirely clean. Perhaps it had a faint, natural smell, like a pile of dry, dead leaves in a wood where some small mammal curls up. In any case, it seemed to him that there was nothing he wanted more than to slip beneath the duvet covering that bed, to stretch himself out upon his back and let his limbs explore that intimate emptiness, and then to curl up on his side. He wanted to dissolve in this strange bed, to become no one, and to pupate from no one to someone else, someone entirely new and other than his current self.

But looking down at himself, he saw his clothes were patched with drying mud, and he knew that to spoil the bed was against the spirit of what he desired. He had to be clean, himself, to enter the bed. Once more he was stuck in his indefinite purgatory.

The force field that imprisoned him in defeat worked only one way and did nothing to hinder the passage of time. Soon enough the door of the bedroom opened again, as if Damien's leaden concerns were utterly without substance. This confused him, but also revived him somewhat. In human life, the inconsequential is like oxygen, sustaining without judgement.

It was Steve, with two others, one male, one female. There seemed to be no accounting for their appearance here. The man was young and bearded, his presence frothy, as if he were physically made of a lighter than average substance, his figure like that of some mustelid animal that had learned to walk on its hind legs, elongated towards the top and as if balancing through constant weavings of motion. The woman, in a colourful, one-piece dress that made an elegant stencil of the contours of her body, was as if sculpted for a pop video, and gave off an appropriate scent, almost citric in its commitment to uniformly high notes.

Damien swiftly formed a conviction that Steve had asked all three of the other people in the room (that is, Damien and the two new arrivals) for money to buy drugs, with the prior intention of pocketing the surplus cash. He didn't mind. If anything, the notion revived him further and increased his sympathy for Steve. We all need our little tricks to get by, he thought.

There was a delightful question, which in its suggestion of complicity seemed also to absolve all present of existing sins. The question was: on what surface would they cut the drugs for snorting? The young man and woman searched the room, demonstrating their virtue in a flutter of usefulness. Since there was an obvious absence of vinyl and compact discs, for a while it seemed as if they might be thwarted in their design. Damien, belatedly, joined the search, but before he could muster more than a perfunctory motivation, the woman found something. There were some shelves to the right of the bed on which were carelessly arranged two dozen or so tattered paperback novels. The woman selected one of these, according to criteria she did not disclose. It was Murakami Haruki's *Kafka on the Shore*. Steve took this with semi-professional approval, sat down on the bed, and produced a transparent plastic bag from a pocket somewhere in the layers of clothing that swathed him like a puzzle in fabric.

"Does anyone have a card?" he asked.

The young man took one out of his wallet. It looked like a club membership card. Using this, Steve began to chop and arrange the MDMA on the surface of the book.

With everyone else's attention on the white lines being prepared, Damien felt a shuddering loneliness open up around him. For some reason, it was Sadie he thought of. She seemed now impossibly distant, as if he would never meet her again, until, perhaps, time faltered into ruin and the universe was obliterated, and even though, in the meantime, her image might always be close to him. He told himself that she didn't matter, but this only intensified the poignant glow of her image in his mind.

The young man had left the room in search of a chair. Not feeling so intrepid, Damien decided that he must sit on the bed, and so he did, as if to include himself in a campfire circle. The flames of this fire were chill.

The young woman had drawn up a chair from somewhere in the room, obviously pre-empting the young man, and now looked across the expanse of the bed at Damien. To Damien's surprise, she was smoking—a straight cigarette—and was tapping the ash into a drink can, presumably empty.

"What's your name?" she asked.

"Jamie, er, Jason."

"Jamie?"

"Jason."

"Estelle."

"Estelle?"

"That's right. How do you know Steve?"

"Well . . . work."

"What do you do?"

"He's an investor," said Steve.

"An investor?"

"A speculator," Damien corrected. "I speculate."

"What do you speculate on?"

"On?"

"In."

"I speculate on many things."

"Is that work?"

Damien smiled sadly.

"In a way, yes. You have to assess things. And then, you invest. It's very uncertain. Like gambling."

"He's investing in Simon's project," said Steve.

"I'm assessing it," said Damien.

Just then, the young man returned with a four-legged backless stool and sat down between Estelle and Steve.

"Okay," said Steve, his tone indicating that the subject was about to change, "who's first? Estelle, ladies first."

Estelle did not demur. Wordlessly, she put aside cigarette and can, and knelt by the bed where Steve had placed the book, now striped with four white lines.

"Does anyone have money?" Steve asked. "Ten pound."

Everyone appeared slightly confused and wary, but Steve soon made it clear he meant to snort the lines with, and then everyone relaxed with the realisation of how unnecessary their suspicion had been. David, the young man, produced a five-pound note, and this was pronounced adequate.

Damien knew that one of the white lines was his—the second, third or fourth—and as Estelle vacuumed hers up into her nostril with the siphon of the rolled-up fiver, he was stricken suddenly with the feeling that this was definitively a bad idea. But it was nightmarishly irresistible, as if Damien's mind had been caught up in a vortex circling a drain, the centre of which was the MDMA.

Damien was last. He tried not to think of the three noses that had preceded him, inserted the five-pound note, and snorted with sustained determination until only a trace of the line was left. He could feel a burning thread at the back of his nose, trickling down into his throat, so sharp in taste that it made his sinuses numb. There was the suspicion of damage to delicate tissue, along with a recklessness growing on the warmth of the spreading numbness, a feeling of simultaneous indifference and excitement.

He put the five-pound note on the book, not wanting to pass back to its owner something that had just been in his nose. Looking, as he did so, at the book's cover, he felt suddenly very sorry for himself, as if the MDMA constituted the only crumbs that Murakami Haruki had left to Damien from his enormous international success. Bitter crumbs. Still, he thought, there might be some solace in the bitterness if one had the will and the discipline to find it.

He stood, and then sat down on the bed, next to the book. There was general sniffing in the room and a little laughter.

Estelle now picked up the bottle of rum she had brought in with her—Steve's rum. It was close to empty, but there was still enough to share. She took a swig and passed it to Damien. He noticed an absurd swell of warm pride within himself at this sign of favour, and was quietly triumphant to be swigging from the same bottle immediately after her. The fiery trail of the rum in his stomach seemed to blend with the more even, disembodied radiation of the MDMA. Estelle nodded as if she knew this was precisely what was happening to Damien.

Damien passed the bottle to Steve, who swigged and passed to David. Almost immediately, Steve began to prepare four more lines of MDMA on the cover of *Kafka on the Shore*. The bottle came back to Damien from Estelle, and still had rum in it. A rhythm, of sorts, was gathering.

This time, when the lines were ready, Steve invited Damien to be the first to snort. When he had finished, he noticed David was skinning up a joint. There was some conversation but he was only following it imperfectly. He was returning too much to his own thoughts, and this was a worry. Nonetheless, he had to congratulate himself on behaving so normally. Yes, to congratulate himself was the best thing.

"... and my friend woke up with Hugh Fearnley-Whittingstall ejaculating in her hair. And she was like, 'What the fuck are you doing?', and he was like, 'That's just what I do. I come in people's hair. I'm Hugh Fearnley-Whittingstall. That's just what I do.' So, anyway, she didn't go back there again, and she never told—"

David was relating some anecdote a friend had told him, but it didn't seem important, and Damien, suddenly impatient, interrupted.

"Could I scrounge a fag?" he asked Estelle, in the spirit of congratulating himself, but realised he was beaming at her much more expressively than he had intended, as if his simple request were somehow magnificently charming.

She took her bag from beneath her chair and fished out the cigarettes, passing one to Damien with the manner of someone already used to supplying him with tobacco. She proceeded to light the cigarette when it was between his lips. For some reason this was extraordinary, as if she had calmed a wild horse with a gesture. Then it was her turn to snort a line. Damien thought he would watch this, but quickly changed his mind, stood up, and walked over to the window, not really knowing why except that he wanted to get up and move, and he was used to smoking by windows.

He opened the window a crack and blew smoke towards the aperture. The garden, he saw, had emptied of people. Perhaps the cold had been too much for them. The fox was there again, though, unless it was a different fox. Could the foxes help him, he wondered, in disposing of very old meat? What did foxes eat? He took another drag on his cigarette.

When he turned back to the room, he had an odd sensation. His thinking seemed to have been heightened in some way, but he was no longer sure he could keep up with his own thoughts. How had he traversed the carpet from bed to window? There was no path or designated route. Stranded, for the moment, in the corner, he surveyed the room and tried to take in his situation. There was activity here. Three strangers. The activity seemed distant. It was redundant activity in that everything was already over. Life after death, as maggots are life after death. Or rather, life in death, wriggling in the grooves of decay. But it had all the authority inherent in the fact of existing.

From where he stood, Damien's view took in these ungovernable apparitions of human life and the holdall at the same time.

He was stranded here, as if there were no past. These people came from nowhere, and yet they seemed to have things to say to each other.

Damien tried to retrace how he had come to be here, so that he might retread the steps he had taken from bed to window and work out various contingency plans by which he might escape this peculiar situational island. The whole of existence, he realised, had to be traversed on a tightrope of thought, and it was incredible that he had not yet fallen. One had to be confident, but not overconfident. Balance, balance, balance. People spoke always as if there were something else, but balance was the thing. There were two realities and . . . but the tightrope of thought seemed to be dissolving, leaving him high . . . suspended . . .

He tuned into the conversation, and thought he could make sense of it. Steve was snorting his line now, and David was talking to Estelle.

"Google Earth?" he asked.

"Yeah."

"I don't know if Google can do it, but I don't see why not. They probably can. The military can, and they're all in it together now."

"So you reckon Google can hear what we're saying now?"

"I don't know about now, this minute, but . . . maybe."

Steve finished his line.

"It doesn't bother me," he said. "I always thought they know everythink anyway."

"If they know everything, right," said Estelle, "if they know everything, how come they're so useless at their job?"

Damien could feel a realisation gathering in his brain, like lightning flickering in neural clouds.

It could not have been an accident that Steve had brought him here. He had taken drugs, of course, but that was not the essential cause of what was happening to his brain and to the world. How could it be when the drugs were contained within the world and the world within his mind? No, the real cause of all this could not be doubted. It was because he had descended and risen again. He had uncovered secrets, and this was his reward. There were two realities, one in which nothing was possible and one in which anything was possible, and it had been his job to get from the former to the latter, with a spade. That was the meaning of his whole life, if not the entire universe, and it was unfolding tonight. The only question was, would it unfold without his doing anything further, or were there still tasks to perform and secrets to uncover?

"Jason?"

Estelle was offering him what appeared to be the very last of the rum. Unsure what to do with his cigarette, he flicked it out of the window and walked with ginger steps to take the bottle from her grasp. He was disturbed to discover the floor solid beneath his feet, despite the lack of any coherent tightrope-thought in his head. Nonetheless, he took the bottle and sat down again on the bed, where Steve was preparing more lines.

"What do you think, Jason?" asked Estelle.

"What do I think?" He looked around and considered.

"Can Google hear everything we say?" Estelle clarified.

"And should we be worried?" David added. He passed the joint he'd been smoking to Estelle as he said this.

"Can they hear everything?... No. Maybe they want to, or they're trying. Maybe they even want us to think they can hear everything, but maybe what they really want is for us to believe that nothing exists unless Google knows about it."

"What do you mean?" David got out the question before Estelle, who started but didn't complete it.

"They want to make us all extroverts. Without . . . without anything inside. Without the ability to look inside. If everything is external, they can know it all, and keep watch on it and control it. That's what they want. They can't exactly destroy the internal, but they can make everyone believe it doesn't exist, so the internal world becomes depopulated and loses all its power. But in a sense that just means it's not being watched. I'm sure they'll think they're watching the internal world, with brain-scans and so on, but really this will just be another way for them to try and deny that internal things exist. And in the meantime, there'll be something in the pipeline. Something really desperate and impossible, like a huge, undead rat floating through the sewers of the internal."

The next four lines were prepared and it was Steve's turn to go first. Estelle passed the joint to Damien. He took it and inhaled sharply, surprised at the queasy immediacy of the rush. His brain felt like a hot air balloon whose remaining tethers to the earth were now untied. His heart seemed to be beating too high in his chest, with an icy heat, as if all the information that usually gave a sensation of heat had been flattened into digital coding.

Steve had finished and it was his turn for a line. He didn't know what to do with the joint, but Steve, tactfully, correctly or opportunistically, took it from him.

Less than ten minutes later, he found himself sitting on the bed, talking again.

"If Google can hear everything we say," he said, with the peculiar sensation he was listening to himself talk without making it happen, "then Simon is in trouble. He would already be in trouble whatever we say now. Just think, Google runs on algorithms, and Simon might have the algorithm that unifies all algorithms. It would have to. That's the only way to predict chaos. That's what Google want. If he doesn't want to work for them, the first thing he needs to think about is protection. Normal protection is not going to work. He needs to use reverse psychology. He needs to announce to the world that he has the algorithm, which will create a force field around him from the world powers competing for his secret. Any investors would have to do the same. Everything except the algorithm itself needs to be super transparent. Maybe even the algorithm. No, that wouldn't work. Too many terrorists.

"We have to tell Simon all this soon."

"I don't understand what you're saying, man," said Steve.

"It's all right. Simon will understand. I don't have my phone. Could I phone him with yours?"

"He'll be at the party later. That's why I'm here, man. He's coming."

"Good. Predicting chaos, you see. That's what they want. But we have to fight fire with fire. The first question is, how do you predict chaos, since that's exactly what's unpredictable? That's the noise outside the signal. The Greeks had a word for it. Begins with 'a'. Anyway, so imagine you clear up those crumbs. Bitter crumbs. But they turn sweet. It all makes sense, you see. They clear up the crumbs. So everyone knows exactly everything that is ever going to happen. They think there's no free will. That's the only way this can be predicted. So why do they want to predict it? Without free will they can't control it, anyway. Imagine, you know exactly what's going to happen in advance, which decisions are wrong, et cetera, but you can't change those decisions. Your actions and words are just stuff you watch happen, knowing it all already. Imagine that. What would happen in a world like that? A feedback loop, that's what, breaking into turbulence. There are two outlines; always have been until now. One of them is what actually happens, and one of them is our mind where we think we have free will. They look different, because they're not aligned. But, by predicting chaos, we will align these two outlines, and it will be discovered that they are one and the same. So, you've only got one outline. What happens then? Spontaneity for the first time. The outline can change itself now, because it's in focus. It can warp into an explosion of infinite possibility. This is what the patterns mean in sacred architecture, where they copy the ripples of water. Two spreading ripples on a pond. The circles meet and overlap and they kind of plait, like hair. But you can't tell now whether the ripples are going backward or forward. That is, whether they are bouncing back from the other circle or whether the ripples that look like they're bouncing back are actually the other circle itself, spreading through this one."

"What are these outlines?" asked Estelle.

Damien thought, and bit his forefinger. He noticed he'd been chewing his bottom lip whenever he wasn't talking.

He took his hand from his mouth and held it out horizontally, palm downward.

"So this is what happens, see?" he said. "This is one outline." Then he held his left hand in a similar position, but lower. "This is what we think. This is the second outline. Now, if we know exactly what's going to happen, that means there's no free will, so it's like the first outline becomes full." And he raised his left hand until it was level with his right. "And so you get one outline. But because it's full now, it overflows. Like this." And here he made snaking gestures upward with his hands like some variation of an Egyptian dance. "Fwoof. Fwoof. Fwoof."

"Fwoof fwoof fwoof?" Estelle echoed his words, mocking, questioning, or both.

"Yes. It overflows and overlaps. Or . . . the other way round."

And he attempted further hand gestures in illustration of his words.

"I can't quite get the right gestures now, but kind of like this."

After a few moments, he stopped mid-gesture, dissatisfied, and looked around as if coming to.

Estelle passed him the joint.

"More lines on the way," said Steve, who had been busy again with the Murakami.

"Steve," said Damien, "there's something strange about this MDMA." He took a drag of the joint.

"That's because this ain't MDMA, man."

Damien choked.

"What?... What is it?"

"Ketamine. This is ketamine."

"You said it was MDMA."

"No. It's ketamine."

"But . . . It was MDMA. I took MDMA, but I've taken ketamine."

"This is ketamine."

"Have I had any MDMA?"

"Yes."

"Have I had any ketamine?"

"Yes."

"What happened?"

"Nothing happened. We got money for drugs. We bought drugs. We're taking drugs."

Damien offered the joint to Steve, who shook his head. He offered instead to David, who took it.

"I think I've got to dance," said Damien, and stood up.

"You off somewhere?" asked David.

"I think it's important that I dance. I have to work out those gestures."

"Have your line first," said Steve.

"I'll come back for it."

"Then don't blame us if it's gone before you come back."

"Okay, I'll have it now."

"Okay. Ready."

He knelt at the book, and snorted once more, the white line prepared for him, this time with the speed of practice and impatience. He sniffed, stood, and walked unsteadily to the door.

Before exiting, he turned round again.

"I'll be back. You have to trust me. It's important that you trust me."

He raised his finger as if to say more, but nothing came, and he left.

Clearly they were oblivious to the urgency of the situation. Everything had to turn completely inside out and only he could make sure it happened. But could he do it without co-operation?

It was a relief not to be constrained by the rituals and expectations of the room he had just been in. There were still people on the stairs to the next floor, but they ignored him, and he felt himself alone again, as if shivering from a sudden draft. Partly, he felt exposed in being separated from the holdall, having left it in a room with three people in whom, if he was honest, he did not have unwavering faith. He had left the claustrophobic safety of the space capsule and was independently exploring the environment of space. Exploring his environment in this way was, of course, vital, but because the outcome of the exploration was uncertain, he felt as if insects made of ice were burrowing a labyrinth just under his skin.

He descended the stairs in this space-walk, getting used to the gravity, which seemed to be all in his feet. Or possibly, his shoes.

The ground floor was undoubtedly the metropolis of this house, populated by people strange to Damien, and probably, in many cases, to each other. The front room was the source of the music. It was particularly this environment that Damien had to understand, acclimatise to, and master. Some lines of an old Bowie song came back to him, seemingly out of nowhere—the chorus about the man who looked like a jerk. Damien smiled. Anyone who made such a judgement about the chorused man would be sadly mistaken. This was a man of intoxicating and occult power. The song warned we should watch him. He *took care of the room.*

That's it! That's what he had to do. He had to take care of the room.

A silhouetted D.J. was ensconced just in front of a bay window that, had the curtains been open, would have shown the meagre yard of cracked paving stones and almost leafless hydrangea. The ceiling light was off, but there was illumination from other sources—a bedside lamp with an upended shade, and roving coloured lights from among the entrenched equipment of the D.J. The party looked to be past its prime, but not yet close to its termination. There really needed to be a greater density of dancers, but this would have to serve. Still in his coat and mud-patched jeans, Damien slid into the unseen element, warm and gelatinous, whose currents swayed and spun the dancers as wind shakes trees. He felt the currents against his body. He let them move him. As someone learning to swim is surprised when the water supports their body, so Damien was surprised at how the music supported his. For a while he closed his eyes, harmonising with the wave patterns of beat and melody, then he opened them again. He needed to use the synchronicity he had internalised to spread his influence in the room.

Not far from him, at ten o'clock, was a girl in a sleeveless top, with her hair at the right length, and in the perfect shape, for supporting a crown of flowers. Her face had a youthful sweetness to it, rendered slightly threatening by a hastiness of curve around the eyes and mouth, occasional flashes of her smile revealing a snaggletooth, so that Damien immediately assigned to her the totem of a sabre-toothed tiger. She held her arms out before her, as if for balance, while twisting her lower body from side to side. Dancing almost opposite her was a thin-limbed black man, half a head taller than Damien and, like most people here, probably in his early twenties, who she seemed sometimes to be dancing with. Like her, he wore a sleeveless top, his apparently in a stencil-style zebra pattern. He need not concentrate on them as individuals, Damien decided, only on the fact that they all now inhabited the same element. He worked at this for a while, dissolving his body into the music so that the music itself could become an extendable appendage for him. He had to find the right movements—a task somewhere between learning to crack a whip and deciphering a particularly tricky code. But he was almost convinced he was making progress. He could feel an accumulation of energy around his forearms and in his stomach and throat.

Someone bumped into him from behind. He turned around to see a young man—a picaresque quality placing him somewhere between lad and dude—with tousled hair and clad in skinny jeans. This new arrival to Damien's sensory experience was, himself, so slim, that he had sharp dimples when he grinned, which he did, winningly, to Damien, the grin communicating that their accidental contact was a serendipity, an occasion for them to appraise and approve each other's moves. Damien felt himself receiving intense hot power from the feedback of attention. Somehow the two of them were twirling with their arms crooked around each other's necks, in danger of losing their balance and crashing to the floor. Before such a collapse took place, however, the younger guy patted Damien on the back a couple of times and slid back into the musically defined, spontaneous collective of the dance.

Something should happen, thought Damien. That incident had been close, but there needed to be a complete undoing of some kind—a multilateral undoing.

His friendly skirmish with the young man had been to his advantage, however. The exchange of energy had left him with a semi-ecstatic surplus, and this had increased his attractiveness to the other dancers, as was apparent from their approaches and signals. The sabre-toothed empress and her zebra-striped prelate, at one point, manoeuvred so as to allow him precarious docking in their dynamic energy field. He hovered there like a dragonfly, but was unable to sustain that highly volatile position. When the formation finally broke up, he suffered injury to his self-esteem, which meant a considerable loss of the pressurised energy he had been accumulating, but fortunately, he had been in dock to the two of them long enough to have made an overall gain, if only slightly.

After this he felt himself unable to make any significant progress. Even when his invisible appendages soared like sudden beanstalks as he twisted, shrank and exploded on artfully trembling legs, he was frustrated by the sense of an upper limit to all his efforts. It was at this point that a sweat of unease began to seep out of the pores of his forehead. He knew what he had to do. The question was, could he do it?

Everything depended upon mind. If he could think it, in the right way, he could do it. And if it was necessary, did that not also imply it was possible? But then again, was it not precisely the possibility that was frightening—the white light, the complete exposure, of ultimate fulfilment? That was the trouble with the human race since the beginning—fear of the light. How painful, how cramped and distorted the lives they had always lived, in the shells they had made to protect themselves. But now he could change all that forever, if only he did that apparently easy but near-impossible thing, and became the first human being to break the shell.

This was why Steve had brought him to the party—there could be no doubt. Not so he could leave the corpse-child upstairs in the holdall. How could he think that? No. The corpse-child must dance. Everything depended upon this. He must dance, and Damien must make him dance.

Yes.

He could see it, powerfully and clearly in his mind's eye. His efforts had plateaued because he had left the corpse-child upstairs. But he would bring him down and dance him into the front room. At first the other dancers would not understand what they saw, or they wouldn't believe it. But, as he swung the corpse-child through the air, he would weave realisation through the room. They would understand. They would believe. Understand that this was real—that the unreal was real. But would they understand the implications? This was the tightrope, after all. He not only had to walk across it—he had to dance across it. But he would do it this way: just as the stench and the appalling grotesqueness of the corpse-child persuaded them that this was real and they began to grope about for the appropriate way to respond to such a reality—grope about with the danger of closing their fingers around the tried, conventional certainties of horror, disgust and so on—he would put the corpse-child's feet on the toes of his shoes, and he would dance him back and forth with such wit, such playfulness, that everyone assembled there would cast aside all preconceived ideas, and they would see beyond madness, to freedom, to the aching abundance of love, and they would laugh and embrace each other, at the centre of a psychic earthquake of peace that would shift the entire axis of the Earth, signalling the beginning of a new age.

All this would take place, if only in his tap dancing on a tight-rope he made no mistakes. If he made a single one, everything would collapse once more into what had been called 'reality' for the duration of human history—fear, suspicion, materialism, partial-mindedness. And the trap of reality would close upon him with some of its worst consequences. Still, he knew that the very nature of the trap was that it was nightmare—didn't he?—and all he had to do through the worst of it was remain a lucid dreamer, which is to say, what the world calls a madman.

He would dance a little more—just to the end of this current track—and then he would go upstairs. He must not leave it too late.

He opened eyes that he had closed for a while in his imaginings. Glancing about, he caught sight of David, also dancing. Perhaps the room upstairs was now vacated. There was no immediate sign of Steve or Estelle. In his determination, Damien cut himself off from David, as if not recognising him. In modern life, there was an anxiety of doubt surrounding how to value and prioritise, but it was certain that his retrieval of the corpse-child from the holdall was more important than his social acknowledgement of David.

The track ended without any skilful segue into another track from the D.J. The silence was brief but jolting enough to remind Damien of his necessary resolve. He bowed his head, in determination, or perhaps fatalism, and turned to the door by which he had entered. No one detained him, and he climbed the stairs conscious of his aloneness. Now he was at the door of the bedroom. He turned his ear to the door and concentrated, but could hear nothing. Why did it matter if the room was empty if his intention was to brandish the corpse-child to everyone? Was he lacking resolve? Maybe. But not necessarily. He wanted to make an entrance to the front room. The front room was the stage—everything else was the wings. He didn't want to be spotted in the wings preparing for his entrance. But maybe this way of thinking indicated what he was attempting was too contrived, anyway. Even so, he would prefer it if no one was in the bedroom. He exhaled heavily and opened the door. Almost uncannily, the room was still and empty, the light left on, as if the emptiness had been prepared for him.

He closed the door, making sure he heard and felt it click shut. It was odd that Steve and Estelle had gone. He could not think of a reason why they should have stayed, yet he continued to feel it was odd they had gone. The chair on which Estelle had sat had now been returned to its former position next to the wardrobe and David's had gone. Damien went over to the far side of the bed. There was some impression left from where they had been sitting, but the Murakami was no longer there. All of this was distraction and procrastination, of course. This was the difficult task of humanity. Distraction and procrastination. But never being able to escape. Digging graves. All of the work, all of it, digging graves.

Another cigarette.

He rolled it by the window, lit it, and once more opened the window a crack. The smoke was sour in his mouth. It felt like it was abrading his throat, but there was some satisfaction in this. Yet, when he had only smoked a little over half of the cigarette, it became somehow intolerable to him, and he tossed it out into the night, closed the window, and strode swiftly over to the holdall. He unzipped first the holdall and then the rumpled body bag it contained.

There it was. It was in this object that the meeting of possibility and impossibility was made tangible. What is the enigma that is to be sensed in the phrase 'the remains'? That this is all we can believe, and yet we can't believe it; this—this shape of the past tense in the present. This sacred corruption. This substance of disappointment. This betrayal without the satisfaction of a sting. This mere thing whose stillness was violence. This inevitable but never-arriving future, always breaking against consciousness. This friend of worms. This dusty gag in the mouth of heartbreak. This irredeemable token. This shame.

On the one hand it was the ultimate waste product. On the other hand, it was something he had stolen from eternity, as Prometheus had stolen fire.

He could hear the regular impact of the beat from the front room and the almost-individual voices of the other party-goers. This sonic background made him shiver. The corpse-child seemed to recline on it like one of the skeletons of the Basilica of Waldsassen reclining in bejewelled finery on musty embroidered cushions. He had to lift out the corpse-child, as if he were a doctor, delivering it to the world for a second birth.

Just then there were footsteps and the door rattled as if someone had failed to turn the knob properly while trying to open it. Damien was electrified by a spasm of pure panic. He was convinced that he could do nothing swiftly and skilfully enough to prevent discovery—discovery of himself kneeling over a decades-old corpse in a bag. There was no time to fumble with zips. But whoever was at the door was having trouble unsticking the bolt, and this gave Damien a chance to collect himself. He threw someone's coat over the open mouth of the holdall and put his backpack on top of this, pretending to search inside it for something. Deliberately, perhaps unnaturally, he did not react when the door was opened.

"Oh . . . Have you seen Carl?"

Damien looked around at the voice. A young man with copper-brown hair and a pink, pitted face was leaning in, hanging on the door jamb.

Damien shook his head.

"I don't know Carl. No one's come in here . . . There are some people upstairs, I think."

"Okay. Er. Thanks."

The door shut again, with careless force, which made Damien wince.

Letting out a deep breath, he removed his backpack and the coat once more. He sat back on his heels and stared.

Then he moved forward, reaching in with both hands to open the zip further and pull out the child.

But he was aware each moment now of the unlocked door, for which he had no key, and moved gingerly, as if trying to lift something that might burn him. Nerves forced him to hesitate, to freeze, even to undo the little extrication he had done, a number of times, and finally, defeated, he let the child fall back in.

Could he let himself be defeated?

He crouched on his haunches in misery, unable happily to give up, unable to continue. He felt like screaming in frustration, but only managed a couple of grunts, like the noises made by a dreaming dog.

At last, he crouched forward so that his face was close to that of the corpse-child, and he flared his nostrils and breathed in deeply. Almost as if he could not help himself, he put out his tongue and licked the left cheek of the foetid homunculus from bottom to top. And then he licked it again.

The taste was minimal, and yet laced with suggestions of something repellent, as if he had licked a slug. He could not do it a third time. He was unsure if this was entirely psychological, or a physically caused phenomenon, but his tongue was burning and itching, and a prickling sensation was swiftly spreading to his throat. He spat on the carpet and licked his shirt cuff, to little effect. Suddenly, water was an urgent necessity. He zipped up the body bag and holdall and placed the backpack once more on top. In his mind there spontaneously formed the image of some unspecified but virulent disease, kin of all the great plagues of history, spreading through his body from his tongue, replacing all that was clean with all that was unclean, until he was a walking mummy, preserved in the curse of his own fatal pestilence. That he might die seemed a real possibility, but, although the death and the foulness were one thing, it was the aspect of foulness that did most to loosen the moorings of his soul with dread.

The bathroom was only next door. He could feel himself being transformed, and had to do something now. To his unspeakable relief, the bathroom was unoccupied. He locked the door behind him, hurried to the basin, and turned on both taps, letting first the cold and then the hot water run over his tongue. The maddening sensation of prickly heat was not significantly lessened, and Damien proceeded to try all manner of things, licking soap, swilling and gargling and spreading toothpaste in his mouth with his fingers.

Eventually a throb of fatalism sank through him, calming into resignation tinged with empowerment and disquiet. He had done what he could. Time would decide the outcome. Out of habit, as if to complete a ceremony, he washed his hands. He was aware of a change that had been brought about, by its own natural process or by his actions. The disease that occupied him had now stabilised in its aspect of foulness. The death aspect was a concentrated point of the unknown. The foulness could still be felt in fever flushes, but its core was seemingly burnt out, so that Damien had become perhaps merely a carrier for it.

He left the bathroom and descended the stairs to the ground floor. The front room no longer held attraction for him. He wanted to talk to someone. It was not even that he had something to say. Rather, he knew in advance that he was seeking someone to tell him that he had not failed even though he knew he had failed. "But we've all failed," this someone would say. And therein would be the meaning of death, and in sharing this meaning there would be a hopeless hope.

The kitchen, he decided, was the place to go. There were enough people here that their separate conversations could not be easily distinguished until he moved into the orbit of one or the other. What he felt as he passed among them, he thought, was amoral agency rather than diffident restraint, but if this was so, the frictionlessness of the condition left him almost as helpless to instigate conversation. Instead, spotting two unopened cans of Żywiec by the sink, he walked over, cracked one open and took a slurp. After the alcohol he would drink some water, he decided.

Having made the beer his own with a few swigs, he turned to face the room. A tall girl with mousy-blonde hair in a Twiggy-esque bob-cut was standing close by. Catching her eye by chance, he nodded. She returned the nod, so he extended his hand, which she accepted. The handshake seemed an odd formality in this situation, but Damien tried not to worry too much that he was acting in an unnatural manner. He noted that her eyes were an unusually pale shade of green.

"Damien," he said.

She leaned in to hear him better.

"Sorry?"

"Da . . . er . . . Jason. My name's Jason."

"Oh. I'm Emma," she said, and gave a brief, single nod and smile as if happy to confirm and have understood this simple, personal fact.

Most of the significant movement in Damien's being was currently in his eyes and his mind as he assessed and reassessed the figure before him. They spoke, over the music, about indifferent things, so that signs of intelligence and special meaning had to be looked for not so much in words as in inflexion, facial expression, even in pauses. Sure enough, she was human, a fact always—or almost always—at least novel and enigmatic enough to elicit from Damien, when, as now, he was paying attention, a few flickers of admiration, but there was something very odd, which was to say, very ordinary, about this girl.

"I want to experience new things," she was saying. "This year, I climbed a gasometer."

"Climbed . . . a gas meter?"

Damien, for a moment, formed a puzzling picture of Emma standing on a chair in the hallway of a house and pulling herself up by means of the meter affixed to the wall. Sure enough, that would be an unusual experience, technically speaking, but he was not sure it would be an interesting one.

"A gasometer. You know. Where they store gas."

"Oh. Yes. I know. You climbed one?"

"Yes. Good, isn't it?"

Damien nodded.

"Yes. Yes."

Emma gave the same short nod of happy confirmation she had given earlier when she had told him her name. She seemed to do this to punctuate the attainment of each small point of understanding that appealed to her.

"Yes," she continued, "and next year I want to ride an alpaca."

Damien nodded as if in unfolding appreciation of this idea, but could not quite nod his way to a convincing conclusion.

"Do you know what my resolution was this year?" Emma asked.

"Er . . . no."

"To learn one new brilliant song each day."

"Learn? To sing, or to play?"

"No, just to listen to. Do you know any?"

"Er . . . do you know Portishead?"

"No. I haven't heard of them."

"I recommend . . . 'Wandering Star'."

It was the only Portishead song title he could remember at the moment.

"'Wandering Star'. Portishead. I'll remember that. Thank you."

"That's okay. It's a good song."

"What about you? Did you make any New Year's resolutions?"

"No, I . . . I just . . . The only thing I did do was, I made a resolution never to tell the truth, for the entire year."

"Really?"

"Yes. It's a very difficult resolution to keep. It makes you realise how lazy it is to tell the truth all the time."

"Wait. Do you mean you're lying now?"

"Well, as I said, it's a difficult resolution to keep."

"So you've broken it?"

"I suppose I have."

Emma gave another of her short, single nods, but this one lacked the happiness of its predecessors. She looked uncertain, even a little injured. A wave of enormous remorse and pity engulfed Damien and he was unable to speak.

"Excuse me," said Emma, "I'm just going to talk to my friends."

"Of course."

She gave a smile afflicted with the same injured uncertainty as her nod had been, and walked away.

Damien took another swig of lager and decided he needed to go outside for a cigarette. Closing the door behind him, he found himself alone in the garden. He placed his beer on the window-sill, took out his tobacco and Rizlas and began to roll himself a smoke. A strange afterimage of Emma haunted his mind as his fingers worked. How could he have communicated with her? She would live an entire life sealed off from him. Was anything beyond the brief conversation they had engaged in possible between them? That injury—that had hinted at possibilities. But the hurt that suggested a life beyond the immediately visible was precisely what foreclosed any entry to that sweet world. Even these thoughts were preposterous. But how did a girl without transcendence walk and talk and get hurt like that? She surely wasn't a bubble, was she?

Her afterimage, in his mind, tiny, determined, climbed the tall, narrow ladder up the side of the gasometer. She did it for no one but herself. Slowly her svelte, humourless figure ascended to an independent triumph in which no one would share—not even God.

Damien felt like crying. He tried to, but was unable.

He finished rolling his cigarette, lit it, and took a drag.

The words of the song were repeating in his head in a hypnotic, insistent loop:

> Wandering star, your tomb the universe,
> The blackness, the darkness, forever.

She would listen to the song, perhaps. Perhaps there was that. And she would know not everything he had said was a lie.

The blackness, the darkness, forever.

There were no foxes in the garden now, but he forced himself to finish his cigarette, despite the cold and despite finding no more enjoyment in the burning tobacco.

The feeling of understanding his situation seemed to deepen endlessly, and, after each ebb of poignancy came a renewed swell.

Should he leave? Steve didn't seem to be around anymore. No one would stop him. But it was hard to leave the warmth of this house and the potential implicit in the gathering of people and an occasion temporally unique. The dissatisfaction would stick in his throat if he left now. But was the madness of success truly possible? Was he not obscurely—and yet inexorably—doomed to the sanity of failure?

The cigarette had become unsmokeable. He trod it underfoot and went back inside.

There was, to the left, as he entered the house, facing away from the kitchen, an open door leading to another room. This was the room, he realised, directly below the bedroom in which the holdall was stored. It appeared to be a chill-out area of some kind, at least for the duration of the party. Red gauze had been draped over a standing lamp in the corner, and this provided the room's main source of illumination.

Stepping through the doorway, and entering into the new environment, which swelled to surround him like a small red jungle of angles, upholstery and people, Damien realised he was once more in the immediate proximity of Steve.

"Hey, Jason. Where you been?"

"Just . . . Dancing."

"I didn't see you in there."

"I went outside. For a smoke."

Steve was in an armchair with its back to the window that faced out on the L-shaped garden. The room seemed improbably crammed with sofas, armchairs and general seating. This was convenient, of course, for large numbers of people, but Damien found it unsettling. He kept thinking the room must be of enormous size—bigger than it looked.

To Steve's left, on a simple wood-backed chair, sat the young man with whom Damien had danced earlier. They exchanged nods of recognition. Their dancefloor clinch, however, appeared to have done little to promote ease of conversation off the dancefloor. Damien guessed that the young man, whose name turned out to be Russell, did not know Steve very well. Russell was smoking a spliff, and something in the way the two were sitting together made Damien think that Russell had just bought some weed from Steve and was smoking this spliff with him as a matter of etiquette. Naturally, Steve's need for money had been exaggerated all along, but . . . Damien gave up on completing the thought.

There was an empty armchair facing Steve's at an angle of about forty-five degrees. Steve motioned for Damien to sit down. Aware of something peremptory in the gesture, Damien was nonetheless unable, on the spot, to think of a natural means of resisting. He sat down as Steve took the spliff from Russell.

"You need to give me your phone number before you go," Steve said after toking deeply and exhaling.

"I'm not going anywhere," said Damien.

"But you will forget, so better give it me now."

Something occurred to Damien with piercing clarity. In the ordinary course of events it would not matter, ultimately, if Steve had his number. To receive unwanted calls and messages would be a nuisance, but not an insoluble or a serious one. However, it was possible—and Steve's demeanour even supported this thesis—that Steve was playing a shrewd game to which Damien's telephone number was central. As his mind probed this possibility, Damien found that he did not wish to believe it, but if it were true it would explain aspects of Steve's behaviour that were otherwise mysterious.

"Ah . . . Yeah, like I said, I don't have my phone on me," said Damien, secretly triumphant that he had remembered his lie from earlier. "I don't usually take it to work, see?"

"You must have your phone."

Damien patted himself in an independently conducted body search.

"No. It'll be at home."

"But you must remember the number."

Damien moved his lips as if in attempted recollection.

"No . . . No. I can't remember. I think it's all muscle memory. My finger might remember if you give me a keypad."

"What you want a keypad for?"

"To tap my number in. On your phone."

Steve reached with his left hand into an inside pocket and drew out a Samsung Galaxy S4. Still holding the joint, he brought up the contacts list with his right hand, then passed the phone to Damien, who took it with keen interest. He did not know whether to be surprised or not that Steve had a smartphone. He supposed not. He began to scroll down the list. There was one Simon on it: Simon Hammett. Was this the name of the genius? It could be. Damien began to tap in a message.

> Come to the party soon. Steve knows the address. It is imperative we talk. I think I understand some of the big things, but I have questions. E.G. About chaos. Parmenides: "To be and not to be are regarded as the same and not the same." Maybe the key to everything? The universe depends on this. Come soon. Jas

"Hey, Man, what you typing?"

It had taken Steve a while to notice Damien was tapping in something longer than a phone number. Damien did not want to be thwarted, so pressed 'send' before finishing his false name.

Steve snatched the phone back and looked through the different screens for what Damien had done. Damien stared, then, suddenly, he leant forward so that his face was centimetres from Steve's, put out his tongue, and licked from the left side of Steve's lower jaw to the top of his cheek.

"What are you doing?"

Steve recoiled in his seat and shoved Damien back with his forearm. Just then his phone rang. He looked at the screen, stood up and, putting the phone to his ear, left the room.

Steve had taken the joint with him. Russell stood up as if to follow him, clearly wishing to retrieve it, but looked uncertain. Damien also stood up. The blow that Steve had struck him with his forearm had actually had some impact. It was surely nothing serious, but he could feel it high on his breastbone.

Although whiskers had not been especially visible on Steve's cheek, the sensation left on Damien's tongue was of the subtle Velcro friction of incipient stubble. The impression was of such lasting savour that it felt to Damien as if he had stolen something from Steve. But on this count, at least, he did not feel guilty; he felt justified. In this feeling of justification he also realised he was not interested in Russell's uncertainty. He turned away without eye contact and scanned the rest of the room.

In the corner opposite to that where Steve had lately been installed, there sat a young man and woman who he judged to be on terms of casual friendship. It would be easy to take the vacant lounge seat adjacent to them, gently insinuate himself into their conversation, and be in a position of advantage if Steve came back now with any of his tricks.

Smoothly as letting a needle fall into the groove of a record, he carried through what he had just formulated in mentation.

The girl was called Kara. It might have been with a C or a K, but Damien imagined a K and stuck with it. She had hair somewhat reminiscent of Louise Brooks, but with the forward lick of the side-serifs more looped and pointed. Damien almost felt that she had usurped Louise Brooks's haircut, as one might usurp a crown, so that the authority of a historical dynasty was there but with a new, individual face whose idiosyncrasies of character one struggles, at first, to assimilate because of the comparative power of the foil within which they are set.

Her friend—there was something exclusive in the way he was introduced as "a friend" that was at once faintly offensive but also touching, girding the two of them, as it did, with invisible angels of wrath—was called Elliot. His shoulders were high in his stitch-embroidered shirt as if he were forever drawing circumspectly back from something questionable that he did not want to touch.

Damien realised he was no longer entirely capable of following a conversation, even when paying close attention. He guessed a reduction of functioning short-term memory was involved, but there was also the fact that words were shedding their signifying quality like monstrous butterflies breaking loose from their containing chrysalides. He wondered how long this state of affairs had persisted. It seemed possible he had earlier believed himself more lucid than he actually was.

Kara was passing him a joint now, and he took it from her two fingers with his two fingers, with a repressed excitement as if this, indeed, were precisely the shortcut to a secret and thrilling fulfilment to which all else had been a faintly tiresome prelude. It was, true or false, really quite beyond his control now, anyway. As he inhaled on the joint, he could feel his mind solidify and shoot up through his skull in a rapid growth of quartz crystals that trapped all his thoughts in stasis.

". . . research," Elliot was saying. "People who share your politics actually smell better to you. And you're attracted to people by smell. So you actually find people more attractive if they share your politics. A virtuous circle."

"What were the politics of the people doing the study?" asked Damien.

Elliot shrugged as he took the joint from Damien.

"It doesn't matter," he said. "It's science."

"So . . . what if they tried to build a virtuous circle by making everyone smell like a certain kind of politics, so that, say, only liberal-democrats would be sexually attractive?"

"Doesn't work that way. It's not the politics that makes someone smell better, it's if you agree with their politics."

Damien was silent for a moment. His mouth moved without thought.

"What if you're not interested in politics? Does that mean no one can smell you? You're like a ghost in the world of noses."

"Everything's politics," said Elliot as if repeating an inarguable conclusion.

After a while, Damien said, "Everything's mind."

Elliot shook his head and blew out smoke. "No it's not," he said.

"Does politics exist inside the mind or outside it?" Damien asked.

"Outside."

This was not the answer he was expecting. It seemed obviously absurd, and yet dangled before him in spiteful irrefutability.

"Very gnostic," Damien muttered at last.

Elliot glanced at him sharply and passed the joint to Kara.

"What d'you mean?"

Damien felt a quickening in his chest. Elliot seemed roused, as if wakened to a scent he was keen to follow. It was a kind of negative recognition, but it held greater promise of contact than anything he had so far encountered at this party. There was an irresistible slide to what happened next.

Damien could hardly remember what he said even as he was saying it. He asked Elliot what the politics of the Big Bang were. Elliot responded by talking at great length about the scientific method and social justice, though Damien was unable to follow the connection that he made between the two. Kara joined in, supplementing Elliot's argument by talking about evolution and civil rights.

Damien watched her face as she spoke. She passed him the joint without pausing in what she said, and Damien took it without saying anything. He was trying to fix her face in a recognisable character. It seemed forever on the brink of crystallising into the face of someone he had always known, and yet forever melting away into the strangeness of deception. Did she mean what she said? If so, in what way did she mean it?

". . . how we'll put an end to social inequality, an end to male privilege and an end to oppressive cruelty like female genital mutilation," she said in summary.

"Jesus Christ." Damien let out a breath. "That's a bit negative, isn't it? Why do you want to end everything?"

"Don't you? Don't you want to end male privilege and female genital mutilation?"

Damien laughed and shook his head.

"Well, let's not pretend it's a single issue," he said. "Let's take this one thing at a time. No, I don't want to end female genital mutilation. I want the genitals to go on being mutilated. I fully support the mutilation of genitals forever!"

Both Elliot and Kara were looking at Damien in silence. He took a drag.

"It's fucking culture, innit?"

He realised he had said "innit" deliberately and winced slightly at the self-satire. He let out a smoky breath of exasperation.

"Well, bad luck for you," said Kara, "because it will end. You're on the losing side."

"You think I care about genital mutilation? I'm not even going to get into the fact that your so-called winning side is trying to wipe out genital mutilation abroad but is helping its spread here in Britain. You know what's wrong with this winning side of yours? You want it all, but you can't take it all. You don't have a fucking clue that you can't have sex without death.

"Do you know why genitals are mutilated? Because pleasure must be prevented. I'll show you what sexual pleasure is." He stopped, laughed. "That came out wrong." Then, looking at Kara, tapping his head with the two fingers between which the joint was still held, "You don't know what I've got upstairs. The orgasm is a rotting corpse. That's why we're all here, and why none of us can bear it. That's what sexual pleasure means."

He took a final drag on the joint and then held it out to Elliot. Elliot, however, didn't take it. When Damien inclined his head in encouragement, Elliot shook his head slightly, but as if he had done so by mistake and did not want to engage even in non-verbal communication with Damien. It was the invisible and insurmountable barrier again—the one that always ruined everything. It forced one to act in a swamp of fatal self-consciousness.

"Fine," said Damien. "So you're happy to support organised crime by buying drugs, but you won't—"

"He didn't—" Kara cut in with some vehemence, but Damien did not hear her next words since his attention, and that of most people in the room, was shaken from its current focus and redirected to the screams that were coming from upstairs, apparently from the room directly above.

Damien looked around. Others in the room were also looking around, but there was no sign that any of them thought of doing anything.

"Excuse me," said Damien, and put the joint in the ashtray on the arm of Kara's chair. He stood and walked from the room. Once through the doorway, he began to run. He was at the head of the stairway before anyone else had moved towards the bedroom. How slow people were, how unresponsive.

Standing outside the bedroom door, Damien was aware of the freedom and three-dimensionality of everything; everything on automatic until a decision is made to switch to manual control. He opened the door and walked through. There was a girl in the room, with her back partially turned towards him, so that he could just see her right cheek from behind. She was about to turn around. He had seen her downstairs at some point, but had not spoken to or danced with her. She turned completely to face him and gestured with her left hand towards the pile of bags and coats.

"What is it?" he asked.

He saw that she did not have the words to explain. She did not know what it was.

Damien moved forward. The holdall and body bag had been unzipped. He knelt and zipped them up again.

He realised that, although he and the girl saw the same thing, they saw it from very different angles.

Why had she even looked in the holdall? The motive of theft seemed somehow unlikely. All Damien could think was that reality had wanted to reveal itself, and concomitantly to reveal everything else as unreal. The means at its disposal for doing this would be endless. Was the girl's muteness, her feebleness of motion, the result of knowing that she had fallen on the side of the unreal?

Damien picked up his backpack and carefully looped the straps over his shoulders. Then he took the holdall in his right hand. Laws are like force fields, generated by culture and time. Would a visitor from five thousand years ago be subject to the same force fields as a contemporary human? And what if one were to dig up one of the lodestones that generated a field? Would the field collapse?

From the girl's eyes, Damien could tell she needed an explanation. He knew it all, of course, because he had trod the path step by step. But nothing he could say would make sense to her, for whom the path was unknown. And yet, something needed to be spoken.

"This is mine," he said.

She stood aside as he walked from the room. His temptation to quicken his pace was not unmanageable. From the ground floor, a few people watched him descend the stairs. Their eyes were questioning, but not acute. When he reached for the front door, he almost believed that something might still detain him; he opened it with the feeling of grasping something that breaks an otherwise deadly fall. He was glad of safety while yet feeling the lurch and tang of the danger he had escaped. Then he was closing the door behind him and walking with long, determined strides. There was little darkness left, and he wanted to be home before daylight.

VI. Time Lapse

HE had hardly dared to trust in the night buses, but had decided, finally, that it was more realistic to suppose he could find the right buses than to commit to walking all the way to his flat. The journey home was surprisingly normal—cold, depressing, but with the sense, beneath all the indifference and ugliness of the city in the final hours of night, that London was the kind of place one sings drunken songs to. Once he got on the N136 service, he knew that he would be delivered to within a few minutes' walk of his door. Then it was merely the safe tedium of the seeming crawl of the bus.

He arrived home just after seven in the morning, with dawn still some time away, but the peculiar sad freshness of the pre-dawn air on his cheeks.

He collapsed into bed.

Unfortunately, oblivion, when it came, was splintered. He began to be conscious of the energy with which the various substances he had taken still worked within him. What had gone in his mouth had generally served to promote sleep, but what had gone up his nose tended strongly in the opposite direction.

Sleep, even in the intermittent patches in which it came, was not as soothing as he would have wished. His throat and head felt terrible. He was aware—when he had awareness—of passively and helplessly undergoing a number of bodily processes that were coping mechanisms of one kind or another.

At one point—it was now daylight, but he did not look at the time—he suddenly realised, in the middle of an extremely unpleasant spinning sensation, that he had to get to the toilet. Somehow, he managed to stagger his way there, half-undressed, and knelt over the toilet bowl just as he was wracked by painful spasms of vomiting. Poisonous-tasting swill was projected from his mouth, and, though it was good to be rid of this burden, the spasms continued in excruciating dry retching even when it seemed there was nothing left to purge.

The cold porcelain against his temple was a worshipfully merciful thing, a thing of solemnity and sadness, and tears leaked from the corner of his left eye. It was then he remembered there was a corpse in the bath next to him. There was nothing he could do about it and, when he thought all heaving had passed, he staggered back to bed again and lay in a nest of wretched dizziness.

Damien dreamt that he had been involved in a horrific car crash on the motorway. The wreckage was extensive, involving a preposterous number of vehicles. Entire families had died screaming, imprisoned in the blazing shells of overturned cars. A man whose eyes had been lacerated by the debris of a shattered windscreen wandered with arms outstretched, like a zombie, weeping blood. Elsewhere in the newly-formed shanty town of devastation, a little girl nursed her severed arm like a doll and wailed endlessly, piteously. In the confusion, Damien was not sure what had happened to him. His wits had been scattered, giving him a half-labyrinthine, half-panoramic view of the situation; eventually he realised this was because he had also been scattered as a physical entity. The crash that was at the epicentre of the ever-expanding pile-up had done something extraordinary to him, so that his head, his arms, his torso, his legs and various bits and pieces had been violently sundered and deposited at great distances from each other in inexplicable places. As his understanding became more focused, so his consciousness identified with and concentrated itself in one of these scattered pieces—the right arm.

The arm was crawling, without clear purpose, through broken glass, twisted metal, patches of fire. It felt a sadness as strong as its will to survive. All the work it had done for the sake of the person—always the first to reach out, to get dirty, to be bitten or stung, but never given any credit, never even named. It was loyal. It knew the everyday and the intimate. And here it was now, abandoned under circumstances of vast shame that it did not understand, no longer of the person. But even abandoned like this, it would survive. It would do all the crawling and the clutching that was necessary.

And then, unexpectedly, it remembered the left arm, and the hand that had sometimes held its own. The left had known even less recognition, and yet were not the both of them unique in their fingerprints, witty in their mime-like flexibility? Who knew the left like this right did? No one. It could not even say what the specific use of the left was (not that the lefty was lazy or lame), but it knew it would miss the other like nothing else on Earth. It wanted to cry with the loss, but it had no eyes to cry with. There was nothing to do but keep crawling.

When he awoke, to the sound of rain and to darkness, apart from a disorientation concerning time like that of a jet-lagged arrival in a strange land, Damien was aware of the reassuring feeling of having escaped a nightmare. Like most people (he assumed), he had had this experience a number of times. An odd sort of experience when one considered it. In the dream, for some reason, one is facing doom—death or, more often, something worse. And then one awakes, and there comes the recognition of reality. Of normality. But why should this be so reassuring, especially considering what most people seem to believe about reality—that it is something you escape from, not to? But then, if reality is so terrible, that should make reality and normality antonyms.

In a vaguer form, these thoughts flitted and fumbled through Damien's head as he rose from his bed and put on his trousers. The cold in his flat made him feel stranger still, so that he shivered a weird, double shiver, the physical tremor giving way to a frisson almost of the uncanny. He should have been at work, and the timer for the central heating was set for when he would usually come home, not for now. He was aware that his reassurance at having woken was curiously modified; it was not the reassurance of previous experience.

And then things clicked into focus again, or as much into focus as was possible under the circumstances. He had not woken to normality this time, whether it could be called reality or not.

Images and words from the previous night swirled in a collage inside his head, stirring strange feelings, and spiking here and there with unexpected excitements.

> Wandering star, whose funeral is rehearsed,
> In blackness, in darkness, forever.

There was a corpse in his bathtub, and it was not going to disappear. It was work to be done.

He had failed, last night, at the party. Then again, there had been moments, a couple of moments, when he had owned his failure. It had been just enough, he realised, that even with the corpse in his bath, he would not quite go mad. He would not quite collapse under the burden of despair and horror. There was even an element—a strong element—of mere drudgery in all this. Rather tiresomely, but also rather gloriously, he would get through this, more alone in his accomplishment than Emma scaling her gasometer.

But he would need to purloin a scalpel from work, for starters. He would need to formulate an exact plan. And in the meantime, he would hold on to his job, through the winter and for as long as necessary.

128

✻

As he continued to arrange things in his Candle Street flat, calculating all the while for strategic usefulness and for aesthetic effect, the procession of memories not only persisted, but waxed. In the circumstances, this was natural. But then, perhaps the circumstances, considered in the widest view, were not natural, and this was why the expected was nonetheless unexpected. When dislodged from her usual rhythms by catastrophe, dearth or glut, nature can achieve an uncanny fullness and steadiness in her new, unmoored state: rivers of lava that carry all things before them, the animals evacuating the area in unseasonal migrations. So the memories moved in to the flat with Damien, like animals with an instinct for an Ark, but whether the purpose of this Ark was to weather the floods till they subsided or to find the deepest abyss to sink into seemed uncertain. Still, there was satisfaction in the way the memories came.

Days passed in the flat. Then weeks.

If someone for whom a human life is small and ephemeral had watched, they would have seen Damien's effects, his decorations and designs, spread and take shape like the weaving of an orb web. And, each night, as a spider retires to its hiding place behind a leaf, Damien climbed a wooden ladder to a platform beneath a skylight where his bedding was.

And if there had been a soundtrack to the time-lapse activity of Damien transforming his environment, perhaps it would have been the rising chords of a pipe-organ reverberating beneath a vaulted ceiling. Shelves began to line the walls, and were filled. There were specimens of unusual taxidermy, multifarious books and ornaments, and even a variety of strange tools and instruments. A low table was replaced with a chest of reinforced black leather, studded with iron, and covered by a scrap of antique lace. Furniture was procured from auctions and junk shops according to what could best serve the functions and multiply the effects now building in the space through its bewildering correspondences and juxtapositions. Things hung from strings and wires suspended from wall to wall. A partition was put up, and a work desk was installed. Peacock feathers were inserted in an urn that had once contained human ashes.

There came a time when, although it was clear the space would continue to develop, Damien nonetheless felt he had completed it, put some last piece in place: the Victorian death mask at the centre of the mandala mural he had paid another tenant to paint. Then, the inaudible organ chords rose to their crescendo.

He had escaped the English aesthetic, or anti-aesthetic, of 'domestic violence'.

Room 303, the Factory, Candle Street.

Though he was still unsure of arriving at his destination in life—or rather, in life-and-death—Damien at least now felt the satisfaction of hearing and feeling the continuous vibration of the engine in the vehicle he hoped would take him there. The satisfaction was so much the greater for the fact he had built the engine himself. It was an ambitious, and therefore a temperamental, piece of machinery, and he tinkered with it each day, to maintain and to improve.

The Candle Street flat had been a fortuitous find. Without this, his plans would have been hampered almost to the point of hopelessness. It was almost as if the future success of the plans had retroactively arranged its own past, making what was really indispensable to Damien both known and available to him. This flat itself had seemed to conspire with him.

In fact, it was not exactly a flat—at least, not officially. It was rented out as a studio, that is, as a business premises. For that reason, the rent was much lower than it would have been for a smaller living space in this—or any other—part of London. The building in which the studio was situated had once been a toy factory, but now it was an artists' colony with its own bar and live music venue. All the artists who rented studio space here also used their studios as living space, though this was, in fact, illegal. The owner was not only aware of the situation, he knew this was the attraction of the Factory, and had covertly used the cheap-lodgings aspect of the premises as a lure for tenants from the beginning, so that the hundreds of artists living there knew they were expected to collude with him if they wanted to preserve the considerable benefits of the arrangement.

Damien had heard of it from Sadie, who had a friend who had lived in the Factory for a while and had spoken of it enthusiastically as a novel and stimulating environment. Ever since that night when he had been waylaid by and had eventually escaped from the legendary Steve (as Damien liked to think of him), he had been particularly alert to fluxes in his environment and the possibilities they suggested. Therefore he had been sharp about asking Sadie to put him in touch with her friend, and, once in contact, ascertaining almost immediately the benefits that the Factory could offer him, he made a most business-like and tar-geted application to the landlord, Roger Leak, for tenancy.

Roger had the watchful, intolerant air of someone aware of liv-ing a precarious double-life in public (even his shadow-life being well known). He made a farcical show of being strict about ap-plications, but this was only to screen obvious legal investigators. Prepared for this, Damien had presented him with specimens of his artistic work—strange composite skeletons made from the bones of different animals: birds, rodents, snakes, cats and so on.

Soon, the keys to a top-floor studio were in Damien's possession.

Damien felt the advantages here almost beyond number.

To begin with, the economy of the situation would have been an obvious advantage to anyone, but Damien particularly ap-preciated this because he wished to divert his financial resources into more speculative channels to accelerate the achievement of his ends. The spaciousness of the studio was perhaps what he had most urgently desired. After stripping flesh meticulously from a corpse in the tiny, windowless bathroom of his previous flat, and furtively disposing of that flesh at night, Damien had begun to think of enclosed living quarters as a kind of deliberate cruelty on the part of the architects and landlords of Britain. Of course, the greater space was also practically necessary. He needed a workshop—a laboratory, even.

For some time, Damien had wondered whether Steve or anyone else at the party might report him for something, but perhaps Steve had been the only one to know enough to go to the police, and Damien judged it exceedingly likely that Steve would wish to avoid the company of the police whenever possible if there were no extraordinary enticements to the contrary. At any rate, day had followed day, and week had followed week, without any inquiries from the authorities, and Damien felt himself, as it seemed, being let in on the great secret that many live outside the law without ever being detected. The dread of immediate discovery lifted, but he remained uneasy. Although, therefore, it was not a practical consideration, he also felt freer having moved away from the address he had lived at when he had encountered Steve. This feeling bordered on superstition, but its validity for him was undeniable.

Then there were other, miscellaneous advantages to his Candle Street quarters. Strange smells and noises would not be out of place here, and a little eccentricity of behaviour would be easily overlooked. The other tenants, aware first and foremost of their own precarious legal position, would be extremely unlikely to in-form the authorities about any suspicions or even discoveries that they might make. By doing so, they would be jeopardising not only their own tenancy, but the situation of their entire artistic community. In addition to all this, although Damien was aware of a desire on his part, whose origins were obscure, to look down on his fellow tenants as poseurs and fakes, he had to concede that there was something in the environment and milieu that was conducive to creative inspiration. Even outside his own studio, whatever else one might say about the Factory, it could not be called 'domestic violence'. For that alone he was grateful, even before other factors were considered.

Only a few days after he had first moved in, his sleeping patterns disturbed, as it seemed, by the new sense of liberation—a buoyancy that one must get used to, like the buoyancy of the Dead Sea—he had climbed onto the roof of the Factory by a ladder from his studio that ascended through a peculiar maintenance turret smelling of dust and grease, and he had watched as the rising sun worked its changes over the prospect of rooftops and streets. Viewing the city from this vantage point, he had felt himself unseen in a position of privilege and power, as if the lives contained in the buildings that mapped perspective to the horizon were exposed to his understanding and possible manipulation.

The main structure of the Factory was built around a courtyard, creating, even more, the sense of a self-protecting enclave of freedom. The inhabitants of this colony—especially if they didn't have day jobs—kept their own hours. It was not surprising to Damien, therefore, to notice movement across the courtyard from him on the rooftop area opposite. Looking more closely, however, he found surprise expanding within him, to a considerable degree—a surprise he could not measure by comparison because he was alone. The movement was that of a single figure edging slowly along the very brink of the roof, where the access to the guttering was provided by a walkway just wide enough for a couple of cats to pass without touching. The figure was a girl, dressed as if she had spent the night dancing in the club below, with shorts and leggings and a plum-coloured blouse that was now sliding down to expose her midriff—sliding *down*, because she was walking on her hands.

Damien was not sure what he was meant to do in such a situation. Obviously to shout at her would be stupid. If she lost her balance she could easily fall and die, or perhaps be crippled for life. It came to him that the question of what he was meant to do was in itself stupid. Both he and the girl were alone, living their own lives. He relaxed, and watched, and a great sense of peace settled into him. This girl was not a fake. She had no safety net and was perhaps even unaware of an audience.

Eventually, the girl flipped back onto her feet and climbed inside the building, but during the five or ten minutes that he watched her, a change took place inside Damien, almost as if he had been given permission for something—for life itself. He was ever after grateful to that nameless girl, whom he had recognised, when she had flipped back onto her feet, as someone he'd passed once or twice in the corridors of the Factory; so grateful that he hoped never to have to speak to her.

It was perhaps this incident that had done most to convince him that his move here had been the right thing to do. He remembered, a number of times, the poetry course on which he had met Sadie. In those now-remote days he had been searching for some means to open life out like a fan, and he had had a vague idea that poetry might provide such means. Poetry had come to represent to him everything that was ineffable and ultimately desirable, so that, when he had let it slip from his grasp over the years, he had felt himself become lost and, eventually, as one not truly alive. But now he realised that he had not abandoned poetry, or not abandoned that essential thing that had led him to poetry. It had seemed to die in the unwitnessed silence of his life, but now he felt himself about to possess it a thousand times more than he had ever possessed it before.

There were disadvantages to living in the Factory, too. Fellow tenants were sometimes exceptionally noisy, and, since Damien still worked as a nurse, his shifts changing at intervals, sleep was important to him. He was encouraged, in the end, not to use any time unmindfully—to sleep when he could, to work when he could, and whenever he was awake, whatever he was doing, always to engage as fully as he could.

Heating the studio was also not easy, and though it was—by accident rather than design—well ventilated, in the summer, the heat could become uncomfortable, as if Damien were living under a magnifying glass directing the sun's rays on him.

The plumbing was not what Damien was used to, either, and the studio was for some reason vulnerable to infestations of vermin.

However, even these disadvantages often turned out to be advantages in one way or another. For instance, the unusual situation regarding heating and plumbing meant that Damien was not entirely able to lapse into comfortable habit, but was forced to extemporise and to define autonomously his relationship to his environment. This was another reminder to Damien not to let himself fall into the default channels of survival that were promoted by the champions of normality who ruled the age—the advertisers and technologists who were by now conjoined twins.

Then there had been the matter of the cockroaches, which came in the spring a year after he moved in. About the mice he had had mixed feelings, but the cockroaches he had initially detested with a cold, instinctive detestation that almost frightened him. There was a physical repugnance he felt towards the creatures, and he knew he was not unique in this, but he did not, himself, understand why. They were merely beetles, after all, and he did not have such feelings towards other beetles. Many creatures invaded human living spaces—spiders, slugs, flies and so on—and Damien was not always happy to see them, but nothing gave Damien such a feeling of itchy uncleanness as cockroaches, so that the mere knowledge of their presence was like a disease in the mind. It was almost as if they were not natural. They must have been, of course, but just as mushrooms are neither plant nor animal but inhabit their own particular grey area within the realm of organic life, so, Damien mused, perhaps cockroaches, too, were 'their own thing', a scuttling, antennae-twitching, exoskeletal fungus.

Damien's thoughts lingered so much on the cockroaches that he began to perceive what he believed were the metaphysical reasons for his repugnance, behind the otherwise enigmatic physical response. It seemed to him that it was a moral repugnance. Morality was ultimately predicated on compassion and, although all nature preys on itself—one form on another—that compassion was capable of recognising a unity in all living things. Damien would hesitate to crush even a spider. If he did so, he would feel natural remorse. Hideous a spider might have been, but its delicate arrangement of segmented legs, compact thorax and swelling abdomen spoke eloquently of a spirit. In cockroaches Damien sensed an utter void, as if conscience was no longer even relevant in relation to them. He did not like this feeling. In the presence of a cockroach he was rendered, spiritually, a psychopath, since compassion here ultimately failed to find the unity of all living things, and the chain of sacred interdependence was broken.

Nonetheless, at first he had tried to exercise tolerance. The cockroaches had not been consulted regarding the contract he had signed with Roger Leak, and there was no reason they should suffer on account of it. If one of them crawled across a wall occasionally, or even out of the wall cupboard where he kept crockery, bread, tinned food and so on, anyway, there was no real injury in the situation for him. And why should he consider himself above them? Complexity? That was the materialists' vapid answer to all conundrums. Complexity. As if by sequencing ones and zeroes for long enough in the right order you might suddenly produce life, consciousness and God knows what else. Except that, in order to explain life and consciousness this way, they ultimately turned back on themselves, like the philosophical equivalent of an ingrowing toenail, and ended up having to deny that the life and consciousness they set out to explain even existed. So, presumably, there would never be a God-knows-what-else; there was no road ahead for the progressive materialists. But it was precisely this he was struggling with, wasn't it? He was travelling their dead-end road, though he was perhaps not in step with them.

After a while his scruples regarding the cockroaches began to yield ground to his revulsion. Their presence was an affront to him, and he was aware that his determination to be tolerant of them was entirely artificial. This was especially true when more than one of them appeared on a surface at any given time. He could not help imagining their seething procreation in hidden places. The idea of harmonious co-existence, which was in one sense irreproachable, even imperative, buckled and gave way, and all he wanted was to be rid of the damned things. Still, he hesitated to crush them. This was not necessarily a moral consideration. He had heard that if you crush a pregnant cockroach indoors, you will simply spread the eggs and risk putting the seal on any existing infestation. He was not sure how tiny the eggs must be—like bacteria—that they could spread invisibly in this way, or how impervious they must be to the forces that destroyed the host body of the mother, that there could be no hope of eliminating them; he had considered the subject many times. He had received this advice from more than one source, however, and it at least seemed something people repeated with conviction. Still, he found it hard to imagine these invisible, indestructible eggs as anything other than supernatural, and he was not sure that the advice was based on any real understanding of the facts. He therefore had a reason other than moral for not crushing the cockroaches, but, since he harboured doubts about it, he was not sure this was his actual reason; it might have been only an excuse. He could always call in pest control professionals, of course, but that seemed a little too close to calling in health and safety officials, who, at the Factory, were anathema.

A course of action naturally suggested itself, though it seemed unlikely to provide an efficient solution. Unable to tolerate the flagrant, uninvited crawling of the cockroaches over his surfaces, and unwilling to smash them in their flittery tracks with rolled-up newspaper or disused shoe, he found himself forced to deal with the pests as some dealt with spiders. He placed a small jar over them, slid a piece of card between the surface on which the cockroach had been crawling and the rim of the jar, and transported the captive insect in this glass holding cell to a larger cell of the same kind. In this larger jar he put a little water, for drinking, and crumbs of bread, cheese and so on for food. At a convenient time, when he had a replacement jar, he would take the one containing a number of captive cockroaches and dispose of it in a skip near the Factory, hoping that cockroaches didn't have the homing instincts that mice apparently did.

Quite soon after he had started dealing with the cockroaches in this manner, Damien made a discovery. Unexpectedly, he found that the cockroaches were dying in the jar. It looked at first as if they were drowning in the water he provided. He thought this was very careless of them, considering their reputation as hardy survivors. But some of the cockroaches died in other parts of the jar, away from the water. Damien then wondered if they were suffocating. He wondered—something between a smile and a grimace played on his lips at the thought—he wondered whether in his attempts to be humane even within the moral void of his relationship with the cockroaches, he had not visited upon them a greater cruelty than if he had merely pulverised them in indiscriminate rage. More than once, he pictured them as prisoners of war in a Japanese detention camp, himself the camp commander, instituting a system of discipline that amounted to torture and gradual execution. How did they experience the featureless and closed glass environment into which he deposited them?

When he punctured the lid of the jar with a knife to provide air holes, the cockroaches died with the same apparent inevitability as before.

Damien's discovery, however, was not that cockroaches died in glass jars.

It was the smell.

The word 'evil' collocated well with the word 'smell'. 'Evil smell', the collocation, had a mediaeval ring to it. He had not before smelt anything quite like the odour that assailed his nostrils when he unscrewed the lid of the jar after a number of the inmates had died, and by now he was familiar with a variety of stenches that were far removed in their sensual and emotional impact from those known to the everyday olfactory palette of the modern city dweller. Assailed—perhaps the word was inadequate. Molested, might be better; or violated. 'Evil smell' was certainly an appropriate description in its own way, cryptically suggesting the threat of complete moral otherness.

This stink, pungent as the worst cases of halitosis, but with something more penetrating in its signature, was a revelation to Damien. It meant something—something profound and full of implication—but because it was a raw sensory experience, he could not say what.

In any case, it was this stink that led him to consider that these cockroaches, like the studio itself, could not be accidental. They, too, conspired with his goals. They were the key to something, like enigmatic data thrown up by an experiment, and he must respect them as such. The scientist cannot discount data, and the dreamer, if he wishes to understand a nightmare, or remain lucid within it, cannot run from the demon whose influence holds sway there. Respect, enquiry and a mind so open as to be empty—these were necessary.

The stink was not something he could endure to inhale deeply, but a small dose of it became oddly satisfying to him. If only slightly, it enlarged the circumference of his experience.

He deposited the cockroach-containing jars in the skip less often for a while, until they began to take up too much space and he had to dispose of the excess.

Two years passed, slowly or quickly, through the basic enigma of each moment yielding to the next though there is no each or next moment. One morning, Damien was working on the shrox skeleton that he had suspended from the ceiling. In general conception, the shrox was a hybrid of shrimp and ox. The skull was that of a Texan steer. The ribcage, however, had been adapted to make it more like an exoskeletal carapace, beneath which Damien had pieced together multiple pairs of segmented legs, splaying outward at their tips, which by a series of cogs, pistons and so on, could be pumped in a wave-like motion, like the struggling of the legs of an upturned horseshoe crab. The shrox was still missing some of its limbs on the front right side. On the workbench below were assorted bones from which Damien could select the next piece in his task of construction. Before selecting the next bone, however, he paused, and in pausing he seemed to slump, inwardly. In mentally stepping back from the task, as often happens, he had allowed uncertainty to enter his thoughts. He had to take a break at some point, anyway, and there was the question of when he would ever finish his work, and, if he did finish it, whether it would have any value. It was not as if he were pursuing a straight line to a definite goal. Each area of related study and endeavour he had entered upon had been like a new detour. Where was he going, in fact?

He felt he had been working a long, long time, alone, in darkness and desperation, and he was tired.

There was no one to tell him whether or not he was going the right way.

He sat down at the workbench and began to roll a cigarette with the tobacco and papers he had left there.

The utter loneliness of the self-imposed task.

He began to smoke the cigarette, not sure if he could ever get up from his seat again. But when he was only halfway through it, a new urge kindled in him, and he stubbed it out in a cheap tin ashtray, got up, and went over to one of his bookshelves. He had been keeping a journal of his work in the hope of maintaining his mental and spiritual orientation. He also had an idea that it might be of value to be able to leave the world some record of his thoughts. On the one hand, this might mislead people, but on the other, they were perhaps more likely to be misled, and in a more egregious way, if his deeds were interpreted only through the lens of vulgar prejudice.

He unlocked the clasp of the journal with a key from his pocket and turned to the first blank page. There he wrote the date, the 24ᵗʰ of May, 2014, and, beneath that, the following lines:

I can see that I have been working under the pressure of a contradiction. Of course, that's the point. I want to resolve the contradiction. But when one enters into such work, one can become blind. Otherwise the contradiction, though not solved perhaps, grows slack, like a bow that is relaxed, and the arrow is never loosed.

What is the contradiction? That's the vital question. Surely everyone faces it to some extent, and in their various ways.

For me it has been like this: Desperation had impelled me to attempt what might even be called a superhuman enterprise. I must be careful here—the word 'superhuman' might invite laughter. My own laughter, I mean. Why is the task superhuman? I can answer that clearly and firmly—because it goes beyond death.

Let me go back a little.

It is desperation that has been my motive force. Why desperation? Because of the all-nullifying power of death. I labour like some Greek hero rebelling against the gods—labour—because of nothingness. I am not the only one who has done this absurd thing. We feel as if we really are entering the realm of death, going beyond that invisible wall that hems in most human lives with false safety, because we believe in the nothingness. We are galvanised by nothingness.

The contradiction is there.

If I really believed there was nothing—that is,

believed it without contradiction—of course I could not work. If I really believed there was something (put aside the contradiction), what need would I have for work? For now I need the contradiction. Doesn't reality itself need it? Doesn't God need the Devil? It is in relation to the contradiction that death-in-life, life-in-death and mere living-death are all defined.

Nonetheless, I must be careful. Careful of the laughter that leads to inaction, yes, but also careful of the blindness that turns all action to evil.

Think of all the Promethean idiots who have come before. They either gave it all up and became the drunken might-have-beens of absurdity, or, even worse, they succeeded, and were maniacs who did not understand what a child understands.

For instance—the featherweight concept that one does not exist. How does this concept weigh so heavily on one? The way we treat it, it's as if Atlas could not shoulder this non-existent burden. Any child can see the idiocy of this. Any child.

Then again, transcendence, our great hope, without which there is no Gothic arch and no Gothic spire—this also is founded upon featherweight things.

Arriving at a Tube station yesterday, I got on the escalator to the exit and glanced at the electronic posters on the wall as I usually do, and for some reason I was struck by the face of an actress in some stage show. The face conveyed something. Actors are meant to convey things with their faces, of course, but they do this by imitating life, which also conveys things, and, on top of this, actors are cast in certain roles because of the things they naturally tend to convey. They can be well cast or badly cast.

There is at least enough universality in the response to what is conveyed that such things are possible, otherwise the very concepts of good and bad acting would not exist. I didn't think of all this at the time. This is retrospective explanation. What I saw, or perhaps more accurately, felt, in looking at that face, was a tang of eternity. It was transcendence, I have no doubt. But how does one pin such things down so as to convince and therefore to cure the world of the destructive tantrums of doubt? I need something that can be grasped, so that it might be passed on.

What do we have without it? The usual uncertainty, which growing numbers in the present world try to make into a negative certainty, as if there could be such a thing. I do it, too. Of course, that's why I have taken this path and why I am writing this.

I remember the last time I was in a restaurant. I couldn't concentrate on the conversation of those next to me, and kept looking, instead, at the two women sitting opposite each other at a nearby table. I was in a hopeless mood. The women both wore smart clothes, as if they had just come from office jobs. I suppose they were in their forties. They spoke, apparently without reticence. I heard much of what they said and it did not seem it would have made any difference if they had never said it. They were just opening their mouths and making sounds. And they didn't stop. They kept on and on doing it. Then I thought all humans should die, and the race become extinct, to put an end to this maddening redundancy. But something in my mind changed before the end of the meal.

It is easy to despise someone as a yakking ego

squandering the resources of flesh and bone, but this is not the only possible view. We know from experience that we can also see each human as an irreplaceable expression of life. If we can see the same person as a corpse-ego and as a living soul, why do we not simply choose to see them as the latter? If there are no values in the universe, there is nothing to prevent us from doing this, and if there are values, then we are positively compelled. The choice reflects on us, not on the object of our perception.

Well, thought Damien, why *don't* we choose the latter?

He put down his pen.

The truth is (he thought), we do, much or most of the time, and this is true even of those of us who deny it. But we cease to do so when it does not suit us. And perhaps out of hatred of this hypocrisy, or perhaps for maddening, incomprehensible reasons that are both blameless and blameworthy, there are those who claim to hold the opposite view and spend their lives in the service of an inverted hypocrisy.

Anyway, he could not write any more about it now. The real source and meaning of this confusion in humans was elusive, and to try again and again to lunge and strike, only to plunge one's blade into mist, was tiring.

He looked at the time on the screen of his phone. It was almost twelve. He would go down to the corner shop and buy a few things he needed, maybe take a walk along the river to clear his head.

Rather than have to carry shopping farther than the distance from shop to studio, Damien decided to go to the riverbank first. There was a walk here where the ground was something like that of a pier. One had the sense sometimes not just of being next to the water, but actually over it. The walk led to a small park, if one felt the need for 'green space', or one could simply lean on the waterside railings and gaze at the wide and ever-flowing Thames.

That is what Damien did today. Recently, Damien had been so besieged by symptoms of stress and depression that it had not been difficult to persuade the doctor to recommend that he take time off work. Certain assertions, usually purporting to have the weight of science behind them, had buried themselves in his brain like a corkscrew of intellectual evil. They threatened to turn everything that was primary to human life into sinister mockery—this, in fact, was what they were designed to do. But gazing at the waters of the Thames flowing in placid power before his eyes, Damien could think of no reason he should give the corkscrews precedence in his experience above the immediate fact of this vast movement of water and this wide, undemanding air. The world, after all, was the usual antidote to the corkscrews of intellectual evil. This century, however, the corkscrews returned and returned, with special virulence, and to the increasing detriment of the world, their old enemy, which they wished to abolish.

He sat on the ground by the railings and began to roll a cigarette.

What had happened was simple, but infinitely nuanced. The *Is* had decayed. It had been proclaimed explicitly by Parmenides—one could not even think of nothing. Everything simply was. At some point, though, the West had been infected by the scepticism of the East. The difference was, western scepticism had the power of obnoxious certainty behind it, because all the decay was in the body of the mighty, affirmative IS. In the East, the sceptics doubted even their own scepticism and so steered by subtle paradox towards the truth. In the West, scepticism was the one thing not doubted, so that instead of paradox there was mere contradiction: rebellion certain of its own virtue and incapable of acknowledging the sources of its certainty, since they were its publicly avowed enemy. And so the Is decayed. Ontological insecurity and all that other pseudo-philosophical crap, in which fashion mattered more than truth. The black T-shirt of Western thought.

If there was any such thing as evil, there was no more certain source for it than this. And if there was any goal worth achieving it was to rid the world of those evil corkscrews. Even to slow them down a little would be something.

Damien got to his feet again, lit his cigarette and puffed on it at intervals as he leant on the railings. The smoke looked insignificant on the largeness of the air; it was not like smoking indoors.

He did not want to get too distracted by going to the park. After all, there was the tormenting hopelessness and urgency of his task, as always.

He threw his cigarette with a backhand flick into the Thames, two thirds smoked. Shopping, and then back to the studio—that was all there was for it.

On his way back from the corner shop, dangling a plastic bag of groceries, Damien stopped at the gloomy post-room just inside the Factory courtyard where a number of cardboard boxes on the floor represented the rudimentary system of pigeonholes in which all post was deposited, often without any very scrupulous attempt at sorting. After some rummaging, Damien managed to find a bank statement, something he'd ordered from Amazon, and a letter addressed to him in Sadie's distinctive handwriting. He slipped them into the bag with the groceries, returned to the courtyard, went through another, interior gate, and then ascended the grimy, graffitied stairs to the top floor where his studio was.

He opened Sadie's letter first, rolling and lighting another cigarette as he read it at his workbench.

It was the usual kind of letter he received from Sadie. He admired, as he always did, the way she never said a word about her marriage, almost as if she were still single—single with the unavailability of marriage. This gave to Sadie, in his mind, a pleasing and graceful opacity, a quality that was of gem-like rarity in a world where so many imposed and demanded vociferous explanations for everything. He felt sure she was being immaculately careful not to have children. This also was admirable. In the letter, she complained a little about work, mentioned the possibility of a visit to Ireland, expressed a lack of surprise that another young and handsome New York poet, famous for his "naked sincerity", had been exposed as a rapist and serial sex abuser, predicted he would now adopt a poetical persona of tearful apology and quasi-religious guilt, and so on.

The impression he had in reading it was that he usually had—though perhaps more than usually clear—of someone too large for her own life, bitter at the intolerable restraint this imposed on her, and yet tolerating what was intolerable without self-pity, by ceaselessly affirming her own existence.

This note of unemphasised and undefeated bitterness was, however, varied at one point in the letter by something new. Sadie, it seemed, had been writing. In fact, she had been writing for some years without mentioning it to anyone, as she had been entirely unsure whether the results had any value outside of a subjective record of some of her thoughts and feelings. It was poetry, of course. Anyway, she had finally taken the step, about a year and a half ago, of sending some of the poems to a magazine. Two of them had been accepted, and the editor had asked to see more. He had put her in touch with someone at Boudica Books and the upshot was that in a couple of months her first collection of poetry was due to be published. She was her usual restrained self in that she did not reproduce any of her poems in the letter. She did, however, give the book's title, as if she were confiding something, and Damien could sense quiet pride and triumph in the way she ended a paragraph with the five words, "My Chewing Gum, Your Shoe".

There was a reason, of course, why this news struck a different note to the rest of the letter. Work could not, of itself, illuminate life with meaning. Nor, of themselves, could those unmentioned things, marriage and procreation. Procreation for what? The different note in the news of the poetry collection seemed like independent evidence that it was only from something outside such necessary things (so humans viewed them) as work and procreation that the necessary things could themselves be in any way validated. He could not help wondering what Sadie would say to this if he pointed it out. Anyway, good for her.

The letter continued after this news, but for some reason Damien suddenly felt empty, as if some spoon of sadness had just coolly sliced open his belly and scooped everything out.

He looked up at the still incomplete shrox. He should stop procrastinating in these detours. His background researches were never-ending, and would bring no certainty. Probably he had done enough. Now he had to test what he thought he had learned.

He would write to Sadie and invite her to the studio. She hadn't been yet.

VII. The Sorting that Evens Things Out

SHE had received an invitation from him last year, too. It had been early autumn, before the clocks went back, and late enough in the year that people were beginning to sense the acceleration towards Christmas. There had been something odd about the letter—at first, she could not tell what it was. Anyway, she had been left with the impression that, despite his invitation, he did not really want her to come. But then, early in the new year, there had come another letter in which the invitation was renewed.

She had gone as far as to compare these letters with others she had received from him previously. She found something unexpected. The handwriting had changed. In the two most recent letters it was different—smaller and somehow less flowing, as if it was not the result of a living progression of thought, but merely of someone trying to copy the shapes of one word after another without understanding how they were linked.

It was true this made her uneasy, but it seemed trivial, after all. Perhaps what troubled her more, as far as she could isolate definite reasons for her feelings, was the evasiveness of tone in both letters. It was as if he had nothing to say, or at least nothing he really wanted to say, but nonetheless felt the need to fill a few sheets of paper with words to give the semblance of writing a letter. Usually he did not hesitate to write about quotidian things in the sharp focus of detail, making engaging what could hardly be called news simply by giving it his attention in the medium of the written word. In these two most recent letters, however, he seemed to hint at having news whilst declining to say anything specific about it, as if backing off each time in weariness. For instance, he mentioned, in both letters, some kind of work he was doing in the studio to which he had moved, which he also made clear was not connected with his day job, but did not give a single clear indication of what that work might be. The studio was in the Factory, of course, of which she knew a little, so she could deduce that the work was artistic, but Damien didn't say so himself. He only said it was hard to explain, appending vague and baffling equivocations even to this statement. "I suppose I could explain, but I would rather you came and saw for yourself." And so on.

The truth was, she almost decided against accepting the invitation. Then she remembered the times they had met before. Her memories were at variance with her present anxieties, and she decided that her imagination had been triggered in some accidental way so that she was projecting something gloomy and sinister—something she could not even specify—onto circumstances that were actually quite ordinary. Besides, she wanted to show him her first published collection of poetry. When she imagined handing him a copy—as a gift—the shadows seemed to melt away from the vision of the future event. They had first met on that poetry course all those years ago, when Sadie was almost exactly half the age she was now; he was one of the few people in her life she expected to have more than a superficial appreciation of what she had written, and even the mere fact she had written it and had it published.

A coincidence finally settled the matter. Sadie's friend, Justina, who also lived in London, called her and suggested they catch up. Although Sadie had not been especially eager to renew her friendship with Justina, for some reason, during the phone conversation her feelings changed and the idea took spontaneous shape that spending time with Justina would be a welcome respite from a routine that had become airlessly predictable. Once the decision had been made in Sadie's mind to stay with Justina, the further decision, to call on Damien while she was there, seemed to make itself.

This arrangement was freely consented to first by Justina and then by Damien. Sadie even regretted that her nebulous suspicions meant she had forestalled the possibility of spending more time with Damien on this occasion. The idea of presenting him with her poetry debut and parting company with him two or three hours later seemed suddenly bitter-sweet. But there was no need to exaggerate such things, especially now the decision had been made.

Now it was the 30th of May, 2015, her university had just broken up for the summer holidays, Sadie had stayed overnight at Justina's flat in Hackney Wick and breakfasted with her this morning, and after having a long, lazy conversation that recalled student days of irresponsibility, they had gone out to lunch at a place Justina knew. Sadie had then parted with Justina to find her way to the Factory. It was taken for granted that this was not an occasion for Sadie to introduce her two friends. She would spend the afternoon with Damien with the expectation of getting back to Justina's for dinner, but would phone if there was a change of plan. Her travelling bag had been left in Justina's flat.

The Factory was not signposted and the passers-by whom Sadie stopped and asked had never heard of it. Eventually, however, with Damien providing guidance by phone and text message, she arrived at the building, which, with its arched gateway, beneath a cupola, forming the very corner of the street, reminded her a little of the outer defences of a fortress. On the ground floor were arched windows with clouded panes, some of them protected by brown-painted wire mesh. In the upper storeys, the windows had no arches, and though not frosted like the lower windows, tended to be sooty, or else there were broken panes covered with paper or board. Or blinds were drawn. Or detritus blocked the view. The very bricks of the place were a sooty brown and, overall, the building gave the impression of an impenetrable den the activities of whose inhabitants were unknown.

Drawing closer, and avoiding the safety-helmeted cyclists who shouted something incoherent at her that sounded, nonetheless, vicious, Sadie saw, beyond the arch of the entranceway, a stone-paved courtyard. Perhaps there had once been wooden gates here, but now there was an ill-fitting cage of metal bars, with a smaller barred door—to admit foot traffic—set within it. To the right of this was a security guard's office. She gave Damien's name and room number here, but the guard told her that access was for residents only. Before she could frame her next question she received a text message from Damien saying he would be down in a minute and asking her to wait.

After some time had passed, she heard footsteps in the courtyard. Then she saw him. He raised a hand in greeting as he walked, but said nothing. When he reached the archway, he pulled a ring of keys from his pocket, unlocked the smaller barred door, and let her through. His attention on the keys and the lock gave her time to observe him. A strange sadness rippled through her. It was only a passing feeling, but she knew it was one of those passing feelings that reveal, for a moment, something that will remain resistant to solution and consolation throughout a lifetime. She had, during this moment, the absurd impression that this was visiting time at a prison, and that it simply did not occur to Damien, letting her in with his own key, that he might also let himself out.

Having walked through the door, Sadie looked back at the security guard. She wanted to see exactly what his attitude was in knowing that he had needlessly kept her waiting outside, but he looked away, pretending not to notice her. If only people would look you in the eye when you were the victim of their duties.

"Sorry about that," said Damien, closing the door behind her. "This way."

He led her across the courtyard, walking a little ahead rather than beside her. She glanced about, aware that the environment was unusual, and ready to make mental observations. The paving of the yard sagged into pits here and there, as if it had been around since Dickens was writing his novels of urban deprivation. However, there were also signs that the Factory was occupied and modified by the people of subsequent ages, including the present one. There was a tunnel at the far end of the yard, leading to another section of the building, it seemed, and just before this, on the left, were a number of motorbikes. On the right, skirting the inner wall of the yard, was a kind of raised pavement. Some distressed wooden chairs, without arms, had been placed here, of the kind that might have surprising price tags in a second-hand shop in the right part of London—their white paint scratched, their cushioned seats worn. Around these were numbers of empty beer bottles and cans, as well as cigarette ends that had been stamped flat. Farther along, a door with glass panes stood open, but nothing could be seen beyond it except a dusty curtain, hanging from above, a desk with a candle on it, and general gloom. A flyer pasted in one of the window panes advertised live music. Still farther, in the right-hand corner of the courtyard, was a tall, barred door beyond which a drab, concrete stairway ascended into shadow.

Damien flourished his keys again at this second door and Sadie caught up with him.

It had been over a year since Sadie had been in Damien's presence and she was adjusting to it again as one might adjust after arriving in a foreign country that one had returned to a number of times in one's life. On such occasions, one is always reminded that place is also time, as one registers what is familiar and what has changed in one's absence. In one sense it seemed to Sadie that Damien was an example of the perfect continuity of personality through time. His slightest mannerisms struck her as almost uncannily well preserved. But in another sense he seemed disconcertingly different. It was as if all the familiar elements had been subtly rearranged so that one could not remember exactly what the arrangement had been before. His way of glancing up at her when his head was lowered, for instance, was the same, and yet it seemed to mean something different now. If she had to put it into words, it would be something like this: Before, there had been, somewhere in the conflict between Damien's attentiveness and his diffidence, a quality of elusiveness, a suggestion—in what way signalled it was impossible to say—that he was elusive because he had no choice; now the same elusiveness could still be detected, but it existed because he had a choice.

This formulation of the matter did not seem quite correct, and yet, once it had crystallised among Sadie's thoughts, it remained, quivering with recognition like a compass needle ever maintaining its position in indicating north.

The stairs ended in a door, graffiti-covered, which had a hefty, immovable look to it, as if its use were prohibited except in emergencies. But this swung open readily enough, and a corridor was revealed beyond, lined with canvases stretched on wood, bearing paintings all in a style that seemed to be some undisciplined derivative of Expressionism. They came to another door, like the last one, on the left, and passed through this one, too. Continuing along the corridor they had just entered, they arrived, finally, at the door to Damien's studio. There was nothing to distinguish it from the other doors they had passed except a lack of distinguishing features. That is, some of the other doors had notices, stickers and so on decorating them and advertising the individuality of the occupiers, but the door to Damien's studio was plain, unvarnished wood without anything added to draw attention. As well as the usual kind of lock below the door handle, there was also a padlock at just below shoulder height.

Damien paused and looked up at Sadie again, sideways, from beneath the brows of a slightly lowered head. The moment resembled so closely a moment from years ago when Sadie had stood outside a different door with Damien at a different address that time seemed to become transparent between the two moments, so that they were visible side by side. Sadie was almost convinced that Damien was aware of this, too. He said nothing, but his look was the very opposite of vague. His eyes all but spoke, and Sadie all but understood what they meant to say.

He looked away and turned a key in the first lock and then in the second. Then he swung open the door. Black curtains hung in a cubicle shape inside from a square canopy, forming a blind antechamber to the studio. As it swung inward, the door had momentarily opened a gap between the curtains, but this had disclosed no definite objects. Damien stepped into the antechamber, then through the curtains. Then, from the other side, he said, "Come through."

Whatever reason Damien had had for putting up the curtains around the doorway, the effect they had on Sadie was distinct and peculiar. She closed the door behind her and then the curtains flapped at her head as she passed between them. It was as if she had been blindfolded and had the blindfold removed within the space of a second or two, and had emerged into a different world, with the blindfold removed, to that she had been conscious of before the blindfold had been applied. The transformation was so swift and so complete that the most obvious question to present itself was, where did this new world come from? Sadie was not so dumbfounded by what seemed sudden that her mind had been slowed in response. An answer came to her as she looked about herself. This new world had not come from anywhere; it had been here all along, and was now revealed, as surgery reveals the internal anatomy of the human form. This was the internal anatomy of the world. Or at least of a certain part of it that had been known to her for many years. She took her surroundings in as if it were necessary to assimilate and interpret it all rapidly in case a quick response were needed.

There was, indeed, much in common between this and the room that had been recalled to Sadie's mind outside the door. That is, although to a superficial examination the two spaces would look entirely different, only linked by an apparent preoccupation with death, in fact they both arose from the same substratum of systematising spirit. Nothing here, outré as it might seem, had been arranged for effect alone. Instead, a vortex of very real and in some sense rational concerns had drawn all this together. It could

even be said that this was the same room given time and freedom
to develop. What Sadie had vaguely suspected lay beneath the
surface in that remembered room was not only on the surface
here, but brimmed over. Apart from the intrinsic strangeness of
the room, judged by conventional standards, there was an added
strangeness for Sadie because the development from the earlier
room to this one had been interrupted by another room—the flat
Damien had rented before this studio—that had shown no signs
of what had come before and what was to come after. That flat,
like the curtained antechamber she had just passed through, had
been a kind of blindfold, and now she was caught off-guard.

Of course, this chamber had once served some purpose in a
working factory, though it was hard to say what. The dark, skeletal
presence of the factory remained beneath everything. The space
was also intended as an artist's studio, and what it contained was
not inappropriate from that point of view, depending on how
narrow was one's definition of art. Upon the two layers of factory
and studio, however, Sadie could see imposed at least two more
layers—of miniature cathedral and black museum.

The walls were rigged with shelves which, rather than forming simple parallel lines, were like a vertical maze of scaffolding,
recesses inset here and there for objects that would find no place
in a more regular scheme. In this way, the walls were as closely
packed with books and other objects as a printer's tray is packed
with movable type. The 'other objects' were various, and not always readily identifiable. Clearly, however, Damien had become
deeply interested in all manner of biological forms. Here, in a
jar, a centipede was curled up like an ammunition belt; there,
a dissected lizard was stretched in a preserved diagram of itself
between sheets of Perspex. A scrawl in black marker in the bottom corner of the outside of the container looked like Damien's
signature. Other jars contained a starfish like a ripped cushion,
with guts spilling out, a cockerel's head onto which human teeth
had been transplanted, replacing the coxcomb, and so on. An
array of bizarre surgical instruments hung on hooks or in open

boxes reinforced the impression that this was a workshop as well as a museum. Sadie noticed one with spiky curves that was labelled a "trepanning brace". There were also images—prints, paintings, figurines. Sadie's attention was snagged on the barbs of a very unusual mask that looked like it belonged in a public— rather than a private—museum. She felt that the mask was 'at large in the world', as a carnivorous animal would be if liberated from a zoo. Was it Mesoamerican, perhaps? Presumably it was a replica, although its aura of authenticity was remarkable. Bats were represented among the images in various ways, most notably by a dangling skeleton next to what appeared to be a bat automaton of bone and brass, the skeleton and the automaton forming chiropteran twins frozen with their segmented wings in the same swooping attitude. Sadie could tell that all these things had been selected with great curatorial care, and with a guiding purpose that, whether or not it could ultimately be called artistic, showed far more penetrating artistic sensibility than the paintings she had noticed in the corridor they had passed through a minute or two before. The Belgian artist Ensor seemed to be particularly favoured. Prominently on display were prints of his three paintings *Skeletons Fighting for the Body of a Hanged Man*, *Skeletons Warming Themselves*, and *Skeletons Fighting Over a Smoked Herring*. Elsewhere was a reproduction of *The Old Man and Death*, by Joseph Wright.

The studio had a high ceiling. No doubt this made the space difficult to heat, but Damien had made use of this feature. There were pulleys and rigging above head height of the kind that might be seen under the ceiling of a theatre, and Damien had employed these to suspend various items, or otherwise facilitate their occupation of space. Largest among these was a very peculiar skeleton that hung above the central workbench. The horned skull appeared to be that of an ox, but the body had a structure that was not mammalian, the bones that chandeliered from a distinct spine nonetheless seeming to blueprint a basic species patent from among the possibilities of invertebrate life. Above this, two delicate model aeroplanes, propellers blurred with rotation, looped through the air on fixed tracks, perhaps guided by invisible wires. Crawling up and down the ropes and rods they flew between was another hybrid skeleton, this one limbless. Presumably it was intended to resemble some type of giant caterpillar, since it moved in that manner, stretching and contracting, common to caterpillars. However, there was ambiguity in the very fact that this creature was made of linked bones, and this ambiguity expanded into greater strangeness at the creature's head, which appeared to be the skull of a fish, its lower jaw jutting out further than its upper, and its whole mouth crammed with primitive teeth. This aquatapillar clicked and rattled as it moved, and the aeroplanes whirred, giving the impression that they—Damien and Sadie—had not entered a space dormant until their arrival, but an environment of continuous activity.

The studio was well lit, though all the windows were above head height—the slanting skylight over the bed and the vertical arched windows in the right-hand wall, just below the ceiling. In these latter windows, however, each pane of glass had been modified by the application of a colour filter—orange, yellow, blue, green and red. It was partly this that gave the studio its layer of cathedral aesthetic, though the coloured panes were a simple device and the light that shone through them fell on metal girders.

In synthesis, the various components of the studio, both those intrinsic to it and those apparently added to it by Damien, combined to create a different element to that in which life moved and pursued its purposes outside the door. Damien, Sadie now saw, was like an amphibious creature, operating in two separate elements and negotiating each element differently, as a frog will hop on land and swim in water. Here, Damien's movements, even the expressions that played across his face, were different. There was laughter on his lips now, waiting to be released—the kind of laughter that rises to the surface like bubbles in that ambiguous area between the domains ruled by two different value systems, where the laws regarding what one must take seriously are uncertain in their jurisdiction and enforcement. Sadie felt herself adjusting to this new element, too, uncertainly.

"So, this is my studio," said Damien at last. He looked Sadie in the eye for a moment, gave a half-smile, and turned away. He seemed to want to make a dramatic gesture, but abandoned it (as he had done before, many years ago, at a different address). Then his eye appeared to catch something to which he could redirect the thwarted gesture and he pulled a cord that was hanging from the rigging above.

"The shrox!" he said, and along with a new whir and flutter, the large skeleton above the workbench began to move, slowly at first, and then with a piston-like regularity that had about it an emphatic vitality. If it had had legs, as such, it would have been galloping, but its limbs were more in the nature of flippers and it moved in segmented undulations like an undersea millipede.

It was clear, anyway, that Damien had worked exceptionally hard since Sadie had last met him and in these days when the only things that people could agree to respect were firstly what had made unusual amounts of money, and secondly what had required a great amount of work, even though this did not look like it would excite an entrepreneur, it commanded involuntary respect on the second count. It was clear to anyone born in the last century that what was on display here had certainly required more than a steady effort. With the human attention span now generally in a state of ruin caused by addiction to social media, and the electronic democracy of ignorance short-circuiting cultural growth, what Damien appeared to have achieved in isolation—though, in fact, what he had achieved was ambiguous—was so astonishing that Sadie had the sensation of assumptions about the world whose inception she could not remember, now being set to zero.

Damien pulled the cord again and the convulsive movements of the shrox succumbed to inertia.

"Are they real bones?" Sadie asked.

Damien nodded slowly, apparently more in appreciation of the question than to indicate the affirmative.

"Yes," he said. "Mostly. And other organic materials from animal cadavers. But sometimes I've had to make use of artificial materials to fill gaps. I suppose the fact that I've been making hybrids means there's no point in being a purist, anyway." He paused, then continued: "You can see why I couldn't explain by letter."

"I thought I'd be the one impressing you," said Sadie. "With my poetry collection, I mean. Obviously there's no hope of that now."

"There is," said Damien. "There is hope. Have you got it with you?"

Sadie turned her head to the bag hanging from her shoulder and drew a slender paperback volume from within. She passed it, briskly, to Damien.

"This is for you."

"Oh. Thank you. Can you inscribe it?"

"I have."

Damien opened the book to the title page.

"Thank you," he said, flicking to later pages and appearing to read.

Sadie was interested in his reaction, but did not want to fix her gaze too intently upon him, so, after some moments, looked away.

To the left of where they stood, which seemed to be the work area, was what might be called a living area. Here a black leather chest, with a circle of antique lace draped across it, and a vase of flowers in the centre of this, served as something like a coffee table. On one side of this chest sat two armchairs and on the other a settee, all with the look of serendipitous junk-shop finds. Beyond the settee was an area that had been divided from the rest of the studio by black velvet curtains. Sadie wondered vaguely what purpose this might serve. Was it a second sleeping area? This seemed unlikely, since Damien had no flatmate and—as far as Sadie was aware—had never been intimate enough with anyone to make arrangements for frequent overnight visits necessary. Besides which, if he had been that intimate, one sleeping area might have sufficed.

The folds of black velvet became oddly suggestive to her. This was especially peculiar since, in being close in nature to a blank surface, they revealed nothing at all for her imagination to throw shadows or make associations with. Perhaps whatever had set up this tingle of intrigue within her had nothing to do with what was visible to her eyes. Then a ripple shivered across one of the curtains like a silent glissando. Sadie felt the shiver echoed in her body half a second later. It was only after this that she was entirely conscious of the thought that the ripple could not have been caused by a draught. The studio was sufficiently lacking in insulation that the curtains might stir as a result of air currents, but the ripple had not been the right kind for that. It had looked more like a ripple caused by the swift passage of a pointed object.

As she was thinking this, she noticed a clicking, scraping sound added to the whir of the aeroplanes and the rattle of the aquatapillar. Glancing about, she failed to find its source, which seemed to be moving. Suddenly, she was aware of a vile and penetrating stench.

"Jesus fucking Christ!"

"He can't hurt you."

"What the fuck is it?"

"Don't stamp on him."

"Jesus. Fuck. What is it?"

"That's Philip."

"What?"

"It's okay. It's Philip. Look, he's going away now."

"Jesus. Fuck."

"Did he give you a fright?"

"What do you think?"

"I think he did. Sorry about that. I should have mentioned he was crawling about somewhere."

"Where's it gone?"

"Don't worry. He can't hurt you. Would you like a cup of tea?"

"Tea?"

"Yes."

Sadie looked Damien in the eye. He didn't look away. Neither did he speak.

Then, when the silence had lengthened enough to accommodate almost any meaning, he added, "Or coffee."

"Tea," said Sadie.

The kitchen area, which was not separated in any way from the rest of the studio, was next to the door, in the corner opposite the black velvet curtains. Here, Damien set up a reassuring clatter of wooden drawer and tinkle of teaspoon. Sadie looked on.

"Where did you get that skull?" asked Sadie.

"Nice of you to notice. I was born with it."

"That's not what I mean."

"Well, I didn't steal it from the hospital, if that's what you're thinking."

Sadie thought about how the thing she had just encountered—the thing Damien had called Philip—had seemed to peer up at her from the floor. It had moved crabwise on long and very spindly legs, and had bristled with pincers, but at its centre had been a human skull; a child's skull, she thought. The skull had surely tipped back, as if to get a better view of her. Its eye sockets had been empty and, as the skull tilted, the light in the studio had revealed the crevices at the back of both sockets, crevices which had once allowed communication, via the optic nerves, between the eyeballs and the brain. It was as if these hollow eye sockets were crookedly smiling at her.

Damien settled the lid on the teapot and began to carry it, with a place mat, to the black chest in the sitting area.

"Can we have it here?" Sadie asked, indicating the workbench.

"Yes. If you like."

Damien set down the teapot on the bench and went back to the kitchen area for the other tea things. When these were all arranged on the bench, he began to pour the tea, first for Sadie, then for himself.

"Help yourself to milk and sugar," he said. Then, apparently having remembered something, "Ah!"

He got up and took the vase from the chest, placing it, instead, in the centre of the workbench, tidying some materials to one end of the bench when he had done so.

"How does it work?" Sadie asked.

"You mean Philip?"

"Yes."

"I'm not sure I should say anything before it's patented. More or less like the others, though."

"That smell—why does something mechanical smell like that?"

"I gave him that smell to bring him to life."

"I don't know anything living that smells like that."

"But nothing inanimate smells like that either, does it? I've been trying to find a bridge, and I've started at the end and worked backwards, from inert matter, through decay, to life."

"But it isn't alive, is it?"

"You want me to tell you it isn't. You thought it was alive, didn't you? I bet the stink had something to do with it."

"Not just that."

"No. Not just that. So, the question is, do you want me to prove he's alive or prove he's not alive? I'm not claiming anything either way. Maybe you should decide what you want to prove and disprove first."

"It's not alive, is it? That's why you won't tell me how it works. If you told me it would spoil the illusion."

"That's exactly the point. You must have heard of the Turing test, haven't you? Named after the guy worshipped by legions of the vocationally indignant—left-wing stand-up comedians and all the other paragons of our degraded intellectual life. You know how that test works? A computer just needs to convince someone for five minutes, or thirty per cent convince them, that it is human, and this qualifies it as a 'thinking machine'. That is precisely where our civilisation is at and no one dare gainsay it. So, if the illusion of intelligence is *ipso facto* intelligence, then it stands to reason that the illusion of life must be life. Illusion is life, or life is illusion. Either way.

"You see, I've been getting to the heart of things here."

"You're still implying that the skull thing is alive."

"You insist on taking it that way, and I'm not going to argue. That's not the point. You know one of the arguments against the existence of the soul? The argument comes in the form of a kind of rhetorical question: At what point in evolution did souls appear? You see, there's a dilemma. Do animals have souls? If not, why not? Do plants have souls? If not, why not? Do single-celled organisms have souls? If not, why not? You could even take this as far back as inanimate matter, at which point the whole aspect of the question changes. But, as usual, people steer away from the real questions—they only want to enforce their usual agenda. What usually happens is that they don't think about the matter of matter, and use the fact of a dilemma to force the conclusion there is no soul because there was no point of entry for it.

"Well, why can't we use the same tactics for intelligence, or for life itself? Some people do, of course, but they refuse to face the consequences of their tactics. All I am asking is that you consider those consequences. Maybe when you came in, the first thing you saw moving was the model aeroplanes. You're familiar with these. You have a concept of them. They are toys—inanimate objects manufactured by humans and not living things. Then I showed you the shrox in motion, and you accepted it, because you had seen the aeroplanes and thought it was something similar, that is, mechanical. You conceptualised it. However, because it is composed of organic parts and mimics organic movement while at the same time having an unfamiliar form, you felt some unease about it. Then there was Philip, who you don't know how to explain mechanically, so you are wondering if life has entered in at this point, though you cannot actually believe it. But you should be able to console yourself that technology is capable of all manner of things today, and that what is hard to believe is simply my access to the necessary technology. But it's here, anyway, that the contradiction begins to show. Everything is mechanical, including life, but you cannot believe something mechanical has come to life. This is essentially because you don't believe in life. And this, in turn, is because you deny life. And, of course, Philip isn't the end of the chain. We are. From the aeroplanes to the shrox to Philip to us, at what point do you think life has entered in? If you think it's between Philip and us, you realise it's you, not me, who has explaining to do. The question is not what Philip is, but what we are."

Sadie became aware that she was listening more than talking, and with this awareness came the decision to continue in this way for the time being. It seemed important to concentrate on taking in information and not giving it out, as if in a mode of energy conservation. She also found herself glancing about the studio whenever she could easily break eye contact with Damien, but it seemed she was not subtle enough for this to escape Damien's notice.

"You're still worried about him, aren't you?" said Damien. "He's completely harmless. Anyway, you'll smell him before you see him. If you can't smell him, he's probably not near."

"You said you'd given him that smell."

"That's right."

"How?"

"It's actually cockroaches. I discovered that they give off a distinctive smell when they're dead."

"It's the worst thing I've ever smelt."

Damien nodded, and his face looked tired and sad.

"Why are you doing all this?" Sadie ventured. "It's not art, is it?"

Damien smiled broadly for a moment. "Maybe it's just questioning what the boundaries of art are, and all that . . ." He could not find a concluding word sufficiently expressive of his derision and sighed instead. "But you're right. I haven't done this with the hope of impressing the management at the Tate Modern. I just want to understand and to be understood."

"Damien," said Sadie, taking her phone from her bag and consulting the screen, "I have to go soon."

"Really?" He looked at her with sober attention. "I thought you had longer."

"I did. But to be honest, this isn't working out, is it?"

"Working out?" Damien frowned, seeming to contemplate the words by repeating them. "Okay. If you really want to leave me and Philip like this."

"Yes. I think I do."

"Wait. I don't think it's a good idea for you to leave while there are misunderstandings between us. What's wrong?"

"I don't appreciate mind games."

"What mind games?" There was a tone of impatience in Damien's voice now. "I'm talking to you about my work. My life's work."

He shook his head and sighed.

"The problem is I always make too big a deal of things. But I suppose I have to make a big deal about revealing my true self. If it were something quick and flat then . . ."

He couldn't finish the sentence.

"There has always been a tension between us," he said softly and quietly. "That is why you are the right person to know the truth. I can feel it now. Can't you? We have to work it out."

"I don't have to work anything out with you. Work it out for yourself!"

And Sadie rose from her chair.

"Wait!" Damien remembered a letter he had sent her long ago. "I'm sorry. I shouldn't have sprung everything on you like this. I should have explained before you came, but I didn't know how. If you go now, with the wrong idea in your head of what's happening here, then I'm afraid we'll never put things right. At least accept my apologies and give me the benefit of the doubt. I mean, I don't even know what you're thinking."

Sadie paused, and Damien took advantage of this.

"I can see you want to go, but at least give me five minutes. There's something I want to tell you."

Sadie sat down again and Damien nodded as if in agreement with this concession to their friendship.

"Have you noticed the flowers?" Damien asked.

"What about them?"

"They're chrysanthemums, like the kind you gave me when you visited me in Nunhead that time. See how these petals at the edge hang away from the rest of the cluster." Damien ran his thumb and forefinger along the curve of one of the petals. "This kind is called an irregular incurve chrysanthemum, but you maybe knew that."

"No, I didn't."

"Would you like some more tea?"

Sadie sighed. "Okay."

Damien took the cosy and lid off the pot and looked inside.

"Just enough, I think," he said, and poured first for Sadie then for himself.

"Help yourself to milk," he said.

"So what were you going to tell me?" asked Sadie, pouring a dash of milk into her tea.

"Well, you're going to go in a minute, and I just wanted to tell you something that you can think about when you're gone so that your last impression of our meeting isn't just Philip. I can't defend against an accusation of mind games, because anything I say against it will seem to confirm it, so I won't try. In a sense, you're right, in that this is all about our minds. I'm even glad you said that. Anyway, I'll tell you what I'm going to tell you, and you'll go away and realise that there was a misunderstanding because I've been in this environment, working on this stuff, for years, without telling anyone, and you arrived without knowing anything about it and it was just impossible for me to bring you up to speed without making you feel . . . a bit sick."

Sadie put down the cup from which she had been sipping.

"So what's the thing you're going to tell me?"

"Okay, it's this. A few days ago I had a dream about you. I just want to tell you the dream. It started with David dying—David from the poetry course, I mean. I don't know how he died. It was a distant event in the dream. Distant, but significant. I knew the instant it happened, by a kind of telepathy. It was like seeing a mushroom cloud rise up, after a momentary flash, on the other side of the world.

"By the way," Damien interrupted himself here and raised his teacup to his lips, then lowered it again slightly, apparently because he had not finished his sentence (Sadie took another sip from hers), "in a dream, symbolically, everything is you—that is, the dreamer. So, this isn't really about David dying at all, of course. In this case, it's some part of me. I got such a funereal feeling from the dream that I had to ask myself exactly what had died. I came to the conclusion it was threefold. Libido as a social expectation, cynicism, and something else. In fact, the third thing was what the first two have in common—easy sociability."

"None of those things sound like you."

"But that makes sense, because in the dream David is on the other side of the world. His death is a big event because his influence was invisible. Anyway, I won't keep giving interpretations, I'll just tell you the rest of it straight. So . . ." Damien raised his cup, then lowered it again to the table, "in the dream this death is something that can't be ignored. It changes everything. You know—the end of the world as we know it. It's as if I'm wounded and I have to react in some way. I react instinctively, but also ritualistically. Do you see what I mean? Apparently Confucius thought a person was made up of the basic stuff of character with a layer of ritual. In the dream I go into a mode where the deepest part of me is in absolute harmony with what is apparently an ancient ritual. I'm floating backwards and forwards, levitating about thirty feet from the floor, in and out of a gigantic doorway. The inside area is too large for me to see it all, like an immense cathedral, and the outside is a corridor, also on an impressive scale, but obviously more enclosed. I'm hunched over as I levitate, and I'm chanting something—I don't remember what—and in my hands I'm holding a thick rope that hangs rights to the ground. Every time I levitate backwards out into the corridor, something on the end of the rope, like a kind of bell, makes a rattling, jangling sound. I can't explain it exactly, but this whole ritual is something like being in a coma. I'm conscious, but I'm locked into an automatic process now. I can't stop by an act of will. It either has to stop naturally or be stopped from outside.

"The other thing is, you're in the cathedral. It's not just you, actually. There's also a girl called Emma who I once met."

"But it can't be me, anyway."

"What do you mean?"

"Because everything in the dream is you."

"Ah, well, in this case it is you. I can tell. And you and Emma are sitting on the bare floor of the cathedral talking to each other. Emma doesn't understand what I'm doing, but, from what I can hear, it seems like you have some idea of what's going on. Eventually, you persuade her to go out into the corridor with you, where you arrange a huge, luxurious, padded silk mattress diagonally across the floor, so that one of its corners is bent vertically up the wall. I look down at the mattress, and I see that part of its embroidery has come out in such relief it's like it's blossoming. But I can't quite tell what the blossom is. It could be a chrysanthemum, or it could be a spool of worms.

"Anyway, the point is, you knew exactly what to do, and because of the influence of the mattress, I can feel myself slowly sinking. And that's as much as I can remember."

"Is that what you wanted to tell me?" Sadie felt her words thick and slow in her mouth.

"Yes. That and the answer to your question."

"What question?"

"I did steal the skull, but not from the hospital. I stole it from its grave. I've given it too much of a build-up, as usual. People in the medical profession are always doing things with corpses, after all. But I can see you're not surprised. I'm glad. Do you mind if I touch your face?"

Damien looked at her intently and quietly.

Sadie felt extremely peculiar.

She felt as if a heavy, heavy silt had settled in the bottom of an ocean inside her, miles deep. Her eyes closed and seemed, for a while, to stick shut. They flicked open again.

"No."

She thought she had said "no", but her tongue was sticking in her mouth, too, and maybe she had only made a sound, or maybe she'd made no sound at all.

"Okay," said Damien, and nodded.

His voice sounded like that of a dentist, thought Sadie.

Slowly, but with apparent calm, Damien reached out towards her eyes. She felt herself humming in her throat. The fingertips touched her eyelids, gently, and closed them.

They stayed closed.

When she opened her eyes, a little queasily, she found that the darkness inside her head was also outside. The outside darkness was colder than the inside, but, though its chill made her shiver a little, it was also comforting, like a blanket covering her.

In the darkness there was also light, and sound.

On something, she was not sure what, there fell a patch of light, and a single bird—was it a swallow?—flapped its sharp, tapered wings as if the light were liquid and it was swimming. There was something magical about its movement, as if it were only-just and trippingly achieving something impossible. The smoothness of its movements was paradoxical; it flickered. There were tiny heartbeats of nothingness between each wingbeat. Its flight was cyclical, like a waltz, but like a waltz that begins again always a moment before completing its pattern.

The sound at first loomed up before Sadie's mind like sheer cliffs of crystal—impressive but unfamiliar. Then the motion from note to note unlocked a little box of memory. As the meaning she remembered trod the rising and falling stairways of the crystalline cliffs, she was slightly saddened to find them become less impressive. However, a sense of vastness remained, within a focus that felt like it might lose balance at any moment.

Somewhere over the rainbow . . .

At first, to Sadie's confused senses, it had seemed that the song and the flickering bird were one, but soon she realised this was not the case.

In fact, the two things moved to different rhythms. When she saw this, Sadie also understood that the bird was flying in a silence so complete it was a separate world.

"Where . . . ?"

Her voice felt untried in her mouth.

The bird was stuck, she thought. It looked like it was flying, but it was caught by an invisible thread, like a butterfly in a web.

"You're behind the curtain," said a voice.

She had not known anyone was there, and the darkness began to resolve, a little unsteadily, into a solid and specific room, at least in her conception; she still couldn't see much more than the darkness itself.

"You . . . drugged me."

"That's true. I really didn't want to, but I must admit I thought it might be necessary. So, I prepared something in advance. I was hoping everything would fall into place without it. But it didn't. I think maybe it had to be like this."

As she became accustomed to her environment, Sadie realised there was something on her head, like a helmet, and even something resting heavily on her nose. Her vision wasn't quite right. There were lenses in front of her eyes. Instinctively, she raised her arm to grasp whatever it was that gripped her skull so uncomfortably; or rather, she thought she had raised her arm, but then she realised that no hand was grasping at her scalp as she had intended. Her arms remained motionless on the supports of the chair in which she sat. Her relationship to her body was not currently that which she took for granted.

"What are you going to do?"

She still was not sure she had spoken aloud, but Damien seemed to hear her.

"I'm not going to hurt you. You really ought to know that. It was because you didn't trust me in the first place that I had to do this.

"I'll undo the straps in a minute. I only used them because I was afraid you'd wake up screaming or something. I suppose I just have to accept the fact you might never trust me again. I committed myself to this and I have to steer all the way through it. If you hate me, that's probably even for the best. What's important is the truth. That's why I'm doing this. If you hate me, then all I have left is to lash myself to the mast of truth and hope I get through this. I really don't want you to hate me. You don't know how deeply it cuts me. But anyway, I have an operation to perform, so I must keep my concentration and a steady hand."

"Operation?"

"Sorry. That was an unfortunate metaphor. I'll try and explain everything as we go along. It's difficult to say it all in one go. It's very frustrating."

Sadie felt a gurgle in her throat that she understood, after a moment, to be laughter, though what kind of laughter she was not sure. It seemed quite possible to her that Damien might do anything. The only thing that was certain was that, despite the touch of irony that crept in and out of his voice, he had never been more serious in her presence. She began to think of scalpels and for a moment an unbearable terror twisted under her skin, like maggots, but this terror tired her so thoroughly, so quickly, that in another moment what she most wanted was to sleep, and she could not make the thought of scalpels a reason to struggle.

The song came to an end and started again. Sadie noticed that the image of the bird had doubled in some way. Then there was a movement near her eyes and filters dropped down in front of the lenses already in place.

"How's that?" asked Damien. "Is the bird three-dimensional?"

Sadie nodded weakly.

Then Damien began to change the lenses behind the filters.

"I'm looking for the clearest, most holographic effect," said Damien. "The bird should really look like it's flying on the spot, in mid-air."

He made adjustments to the projection, too, while asking Sadie questions.

"What's this for?" Sadie managed to ask in return after she had nodded to another question.

"This? All this?"

Damien stood in front of her now for the first time since she had awoken. Two beams of projected light met on his torso, where two birds, no longer three-dimensional, continued their flight. His head, above the level of the beams, remained in darkness.

Sadie guessed he had gestured to indicate the whole environment, and nodded. "Yes. All this."

"All this is . . . It's for you, actually. You gave me your poems, and I'm giving you this. Do you remember—you must remember—that you said it was impossible to be dead and alive at the same time, and I said it was possible?"

"Damien . . . Let it go. Let it go."

"Let it go? But that's just the thing, you see. That's what you have to understand. I don't let it go. You do. You let it go, and you leave it for me, and I have to deal with it, have to . . . to clean up the global pollution of your inconsistency. You say things, and you don't take responsibility for them, but you don't like it when anyone talks back. I've had this my whole life. Mouths opening and closing, opening and closing, and 'letting go' all their stupid ideas into the air in perfect self-satisfaction without any regard for whether what they say correlates with anything else they say, or anything they think or anything they do, or a sustainable human morality. And then the heads with the talking mouths just turn up their noses and turn around to leave, leaving me with their contradictions and no right to reply. I could strangle . . .

"But I'm not going to do that. It's not about anger. I'm angry, it's true, but it's not about that. You appeal to transcendence whilst simultaneously denying it. Contradiction! Someone has to deal with this. Someone has to start closing the gap between what people say and what they do. Even between what they say and what they say."

"When? When did I appeal to transcendence?" Sadie was not quite sure her tongue and lips had shaped the last three words, but Damien either heard them or anticipated them, because she had barely finished the question when he said:

"All the time. All the fucking time. You think I've made a list of examples? Well, I haven't. But pretty much . . . pretty much every other sentence, you're making some fucking appeal to transcendence.

"Okay. You want to know. So, I'll point it out. Next time you make an appeal to transcendence, I'll let you know."

"Let me know, then."

"Did you just say, 'Let me know, then'?"

It seemed, after all, her speech was not very clear.

She nodded.

Damien inhaled with a tone of impatience, but nonetheless paused before speaking again. When he did speak it was in a softened voice, but one not free of bitterness.

"So, for a start, 'let' assumes free will, which is impossible without transcendence, 'me' assumes personal identity, which is impossible without transcendence, and, maybe most of all, the act of knowing is impossible without transcendence. Like I said, every other sentence—at a conservative estimate. I know you could argue it's just built into the language with an example like that, but your opinions, too—not just your received vocabulary and idioms—make the same appeals to transcendence. I'll leave it at that for now. We should get on with the operation. Not a surgical operation. I'm not sure what else to call it."

"What is it?"

"Have you heard of Metzinger?"

She shook her head.

"He can artificially induce out of body experiences. I'm going to be using similar techniques. The point is, we're behind the curtain now. There are no secrets. You can see the workings. But that won't make a difference. Or rather, the difference it'll make is that we get the naked truth."

Damien fell silent. His face was still obscured by gloom and it was unclear whether he had finished his explanation or was just thinking about what he was going to say next.

Finally, his voice came again, its tone a strange balance of weariness and decision.

"This is the sorting that evens things out," he said.

He moved closer and bent forward. At first, Sadie did not know what he was doing. Her vision was not functioning as it normally did and it was difficult for her to judge distance, so that she was taken up, for some seconds, with trying to understand her spatial relation to Damien. Having got a roughly intelligible idea of this, her mind was free to gather that he was now undoing the straps that had fastened her arms to the supports of the chair. When this unfastening was accomplished, he stood back again. Then he resumed his former position, at the edge of her field of vision, to the left. He seemed to be tapping at a laptop. The lack of glow suggested he had adjusted the screen in some way to minimise the emission of light.

It occurred to Sadie that she could try and move again. She remembered how the silt of sensation had settled in some deep, dim region far below her before she had lost consciousness. Volition seemed to have sunk with it to that abyssal seabed. How did she normally make her limbs move? Without thinking, and without knowing how. Now they would not move, whether she thought or not. She was no longer in unison with her body.

"You drugged me," she said. "I can't move."

Damien shifted closer towards the centre of her vision again.

"I'm sorry," he said. "It's true, I drugged you, but that was only to keep you here. I've thought about it in the meantime, and I decided I should leave things up to fate, and also to your free will. That's why I undid the straps."

"I can't move."

"Maybe it's nothing to do with the drugs," said Damien. "Maybe what's keeping you in place now is logic. Those are the tightest bonds of all. Logic, or karma. It's the same thing, really. I've been studying it very closely."

Apparently assured of the truth of his own words, Damien concluded there and shifted again to the left.

The music changed. There was no singing now, only an orchestra, the notes of the instruments gathering in delicate anticipation then slipping into the pulsing momentum of a whirling, floating euphoria. Sadie sensed Damien was busy. At intervals, he adjusted her lenses, swung mirrors out in front of her on metal arms, asked her questions. She wondered if it could be true that her paralysis was not caused by drugs, that it was, as Damien suggested, a mental or spiritual paralysis. He could have given her any kind of injection while she was unconscious. He talked about revealing the truth, but, nonetheless, he could be practising deception. How was it she could move her head and her mouth? Local paralysis? She could not remember, but that sounded like a legitimate phrase.

No, she was confused. She was missing something. There was another factor. The creature she had seen must be somewhere. It had crawled away into invisibility—into an invisibility that now bound her, negated her strength, made her limbs void. She could not move until she knew where or what it was. It was like being trapped in a spider's web. There was a subtle game to be played to win freedom. Perhaps Damien was right—truth would win. To struggle was to use her strength against herself. Was it that she was afraid of the creature? Surely, there was something else. There had to be. Did she believe what Damien was saying? Was that the something else? But if she believed him, why didn't she just say so? If that was what he wanted, surely he would stop, and she would be free?

But he did not stop, and for reasons that remained unclear to her—though there were plenty of good excuses to choose from—she was not free.

Damien was beginning to work the effects he had been preparing. With an empty, ghostly version of the lurch experienced on a fairground ride, Sadie saw her own seated body move away from the place where her point of view remained. She stared at herself on the other side of the dark space, then seemed to look back at herself from the other side.

"It's an illusion," said Damien. "That's why you can't see me when you should."

Something was suddenly folded away—a mirror, or a projected beam—and Sadie's point of view seemed to snap back into its original position.

"Here's another illusion," said Damien, "an old one. Similar principle to the bluebird image from the zoopraxiscope you saw earlier. In fact, you might already know it. It's based on a children's toy. You have a wooden disc, with two holes at the sides to run string through so you can spin it. On one side of the disc is a painted bird and on the other a painted cage. The bird and the cage are separate. But all you have to do is spin the disc and the bird is captured in the cage. Here's what the electronic version of that looks like."

Where the flying bluebird had been before there was now projected the image of a canary on a disc. The disc began to revolve, slowly, on a horizontal axis. When it had revolved one hundred and eighty degrees, the reverse side was revealed, bearing, as Damien had said, the image of a bird cage. The disc continued to revolve, the revolutions becoming gradually faster.

To the side, Damien seemed to be singing, or, more accurately, chanting, under his breath, something unrelated rhythmically and melodically to the background music.

"I put my finger in the woodpecker's hole. The woodpecker said, 'God bless my soul! Take it out! Take it out! Take it out! Re-move it!'"

The projected disc was now spinning so fast that it appeared stationary, except that there was a flickering of the two images—bird and birdcage. It was an almost-solid flicker, like that of a fluorescent light. The cage, as if by magic, was solidifying around the bird. The gaps of nothing in the flicker, like the gaps between the bars, were too small for the bird to escape through them.

Damien clicked some control and the spinning disc began to slow again, emptying the cage and freeing the bird. Then, both bird and cage disappeared.

"Curl it up! Curl it up! Curl it up! Re-tract it!"

Sadie sensed in Damien's movements and voice a mix of confidence and expectant curiosity. He no longer seemed in a mood to talk, but attended to the operation, as he had called it. He passed in front of her now, from her left to her right, and a new light came on, from something projecting a new beam, or two new beams in one image. It was an insect of some kind—a cockroach. It must have been resting on something in principle like the top of an overhead projector, as a pen nib also appeared, poking at the cockroach, which was apparently dead, and Sadie guessed Damien was attempting to position it correctly. He adjusted, also, the size and focus of the projection. After a process of nudging, tweaking and so on, an inert cockroach, showing signs of incipient decay, was suspended vertically in the air before her, perhaps two feet in length from the tip of its abdomen to the termination of its head.

Damien passed in front of her again, this time from right to left. He tapped at a keyboard. The cockroach disappeared, and in its place was an image of Sadie—head, shoulders and torso. Damien had apparently adjusted the image so that the helmet and strange glasses that were visible earlier had disappeared, presumably photoshopped away.

Then this image disappeared and the cockroach appeared again. Then the cockroach disappeared and Sadie reappeared. The alternation between the two images accelerated. As Damien had explained, the principle was similar to that of the canary in the cage. The faster the alternation of the images, the more it appeared that the two images existed solidly in the same place at the same time. The flickering became faster and faster—more rapid, Sadie thought, than any strobe she had ever seen.

Then another element was introduced to the process. Sadie's point of view was switched, as before, so that she was looking back at the place where her previous point of view had been located. She saw the projected image of herself from behind now, but two things were particularly strange. From this direction, too, she saw the carapace—not the underside—of the cockroach; she did not see herself sitting where she should be sitting.

And then her point of view snapped back to its former location. And then back to the opposite side of the darkness. This alternation, too, began to accelerate. At a certain point in this acceleration, the most peculiar thing of all took place. Sadie disappeared.

She had not been able to see herself, anyway, while her point of view had been alternating, but now the sense that there was something to which her point of view was necessarily anchored had gone. There was an image of herself, in the centre of the darkness, and there was a view of that image from the outside. Perhaps the view of the image was not separate from the image; it was hard to know. In effect, then, there was only the image.

Something else was happening to the image. Not only was the dead cockroach embedded in the image of Sadie as if in hardened amber, but the two images began to run together. It was as if the intensity of the flickering also produced heat, and the heat was melting the images where their outlines met, so that rivulets of flesh were running along the legs of the cockroach towards their tips and the legs themselves were sending out molten fibres into the human head that seemed to contain them, like a potato sending out shoots into the earth. Nothing else but this existed, and this was not real.

It had to end, but how could it end? Something was terribly wrong. There had to be breathing, but the breathing was disturbed as if its functioning had been injured.

There was an absolutely evil stink that would suffocate everything, even mind. The mind gagged as the gorge rose like an underground river of bubbling lava. The stink. How could you escape it? It came from nowhere; it got everywhere. It was nightmare and sickness.

Something *greater than* was rising, rising to the surface. Something greater than . . . Greater than what?

Than me.

Me.

Me.

She shrieked and, in a convulsion of agony, tore the apparatus from her head. Then she collapsed on her hands and knees in the darkness and began to vomit.

Footsteps passed her. For a moment other light fell on her—light from beyond the stifling, curtained chamber.

"I'll get a bucket," she heard a voice say. She was not paying attention. The spasms were excruciating, as if some bristling, armoured thing were struggling to escape from inside her.

She vomited again and again.

Surely she had emptied herself, but at least she could move now. Stiffly. Unsteadily. Groping and swaying, she got to her feet and turned around.

The stench was an indelible presence, like a stain that permeated deeper than matter. She scratched in frustration at her head, as if this might make a difference, as if she needed to get inside her own skull to turn the stench off. However, this action made no difference at all.

It smelt like . . . What did it smell like? It smelt like some sordid, irredeemable crime, some cruel but quiet murder, that had made of the perpetrator a hopeless idiot.

She had to get out.

The person she had known as Damien had gone this way, through the curtains. It was probably the only way. Then a shiver ran across one of the curtains. She had seen exactly this shiver before. Something unspeakable dropped—as a spider drops itself upon a thread of silk—down the edge of the curtain, and, reaching the floor, pulled the curtain aside from the bottom like the hand of an obliging servant.

It was the thing, the repulsive and nauseous thing. Just as it had done before, it tilted itself back on its spider-crab appendages and raised its hollow eye sockets to her.

She thought her breath would stop and everything would cease, but she heard sounds from beyond the curtain. Taking a gulp of air, she leapt past the foetid arthropod and into the light of the studio where some time before she had been drinking tea. Damien was there, coming towards her, but she pushed him aside. She saw her bag by the chair where she had been sitting. In horror, she realised she had either to stop for it, or leave it.

"Wait," Damien was saying.

She did not want to have to come back. There were probably things she needed in the bag, even to get across London to Justina's flat. She ran and snatched it up, fled to the drape-shrouded door, and struggled with the latch. At last it clicked open, and she escaped. Damien did not seem to be following, but she did not want to stop to make sure.

Damien clicked the door closed after her and walked slowly back to the workbench. He sat down where Sadie had sat and rested his chin in his hands. He gazed as if unseeing, motionless, while a thing with segmented legs scuttled about the floor and the skylight showed night deepening behind the stars.

VIII. With Direct Eyes to Death's Other Kingdom

SADIE did not have to pretend to be ill; all she needed to do was to conceal the nature of the actual illness and its causes. Why did she have to do this? In fact, she couldn't talk about it. She didn't want to. Of course, she had some idea of what had taken place in Damien's studio. She even pieced together certain things after the event. For instance, while she had been unconscious, Justina had texted her to ask what her plans were, and Damien had texted back, pretending to be Sadie, and saying she would be a little late. She only had to look at her phone to discover this. However, there were many things she could not explain.

Had she been hypnotised? She had certainly been drugged. If that helped to explain some things, though, it was only by making what had actually happened an ungraspable mystery. Besides, she had first seen the crawling thing before Damien had even made the tea. And, more than the crawling thing, which was troublesome in itself, it was the last vision, which was more than a vision, and which nothing could induce her to mention to anyone—that was the real heart of all of this.

There was something like a dead vibration—like flies crawling on a corpse, but mechanical flies—and the vibration meant that everything was wrong. When it came close it was not a vibration, but a lucid nausea that was debilitating. When it went far away and became a vibration again, she could do things—walk, read a little, talk a little—but the buzz of it was maddening, like the evillest boredom she had ever known that made her want to crawl on the floor screaming. And then, even when it was far away, there were intermittent wafts of the stink, that could have been from no source or any, and which made her want to weep for shame or frustration or even for the absurdity of everything, as if the entire world had no more substance than the reflection on the surface of an expanding soap bubble about to burst.

The vibration, which seemed to affirm its own permanence, shifted, in this way, closer and farther and closer again while she made her way to Justina's, while she stayed there overnight, telling Justina not to get too close in case it was infectious, and while she made her hellish way back home the following day—upon which she insisted, despite Justina's protestations.

She could barely eat, and she could not always keep down even water.

Jason was solicitous—even more so than usual. Sadie could tell that he suspected her illness was not a normal bug. Of course, he could not possibly guess what it actually was, but from the questions she didn't answer, and those she answered strangely, he must have been aware of a void that it was hard to fill with comforting and familiar thoughts.

Sadie had long had a bed installed in her study. When work demanded different hours for one of them, they would usually sleep apart. If anything, sleeping separately had come to be expected. On the day of her return, too, she had gone to her study to sleep, rather than to the shared bedroom. Jason had lingered at the study door, a look of concern on his face. He extracted from her, again, a promise that she would see the doctor if he made an appointment for her. She gave her promise, and though he looked unsatisfied, he nodded. He asked if she wanted the light off. She did. He said he would see her in the morning, flicked the light switch, and closed the door.

Sadie was not sure whether it was a relief not to have to keep up the pretence another human presence required, or whether such tiresome pretence was the only thing saving her from insanity. Maybe the doctor would find something physically wrong with her that could be fixed. She could hold out till then. Or maybe she was actually going insane—maybe this was what it felt like. What did it mean, to go insane? What bridge did her mind have to cross? She refused to cross it, whatever it was.

In any case, she felt physically ill—tired and aching. Her body could not be insane. It would shut down her consciousness for the sleep she needed. She would sleep and her body would work on healing itself. Her body. Why couldn't it go insane? Was it different to her mind? Maybe Damien was right, but about what? She did not know.

After all, sleep seemed far away, and when she began to wonder whether her body could be insane, something larger than her seemed to whoosh up from depths outside of her physical form, and once again she was so swept away by the tornado of nausea that she felt all she could do was to cling to the bed in the hope that this particular piece of flotsam would take her with it to some final safe place beyond this tempest of perfect insecurity. But then she felt the twisting, bruising upheaval that was the prelude to vomiting, and, almost without volition, she threw the covers from her, staggered to the door across a floor that tilted like a ship's deck, and ran to the bathroom.

There was little left inside for her system to eject, but she retched in jagged pain over the toilet bowl. Even with all the purging it had done in the last twenty-four hours, her body still seemed to consider itself poisoned. The stink had returned, too. It was an entity in itself. It was silent and acrid and articulated directly to the brain, through the olfactory receptors, a sense of deadly, leprous perversion that made the heart unsteady in its will to beat. In the presence of that smell, Sadie each time expected to see long, dark feelers waving slowly and tremulously from behind some once-familiar object somewhere in her field of vision.

Again, the nausea and the stink subsided and, in moving away from the centre of her sensations, became a vibration, like black smoke pouring from a factory stack on the horizon of her awareness, seeming to be contained within a distant outline, but polluting everything.

She was glad she did not seem to have woken Jason. In no hurry, she got to her feet and made her way back to her room. She wondered if she would ever sleep again. There was nothing for her to do but try. The indefinable sense of familiarity, so pervasive as to be subliminal, that had once been part of the texture of her experience of this house during all the forgettable actions of brushing her teeth, walking up and down the stairs, and so on, had now been stripped away, and for all its human artificiality this domestic environment felt as barren as the cratered surface of the Moon. What is there to do on the Moon? How can one sleep when there is nothing to do? Anyway, she had to try.

She pulled the covers back over herself in the darkness, but the warm obscurity of sleep was not summoned by this action as it would normally be. She lay on her back, turned on her side, then lay on her back once more; the positions she assumed had never felt more unnatural, more lacking in repose. Her closed eyes had not sent a signal of rest to her brain and had not shut out the agitations of engagement with the waking world. Instead, the signal they had given seemed to be for the summoning of an interrogative genie from the aridity of her outer and inner lunar landscape—a genie that was its presiding spirit. At first she did not realise what was happening. She was only aware of a bright, ugly desert in her head, and that this was the make-do backdrop for crude, half-finished impulses of nastiness that her brain had been harbouring without support from the conscious will to develop them. There were ridiculous images of spiders pouncing with a lust for violence upon prey, and lunatics splitting skulls with axes—all manner of such anti-fantasies, like the demonstration modes of badly-coded video games whose only purpose was to sicken and shock the moral sensibilities. The images merged with each other and drew apart, merged and drew apart, in a kind of respiration, and as they did so their nature changed. They were becoming a single entity, a conglomeration of shapes and happenings, but the change seemed to be in spirit as well as form. What Sadie saw now was something like a mass of humanity, physically conjoined in body, but conjoined also in their suffering. Shrivelled, starving infants reached out hands towards her from the flanks of this entity; these were fused with those who had suffered violence, or those who, in poverty, had been unable to escape disfiguring disease. None of them were white.

As it became clear to her what the entity was, she began also to sense, with an icy fear, how difficult it would be to exorcise. It was a product of her own mind, or at least, even if she could not exactly claim ownership of it, it was a phantom, made of more or less the same stuff as her own imaginings. She thought she recognised parts of the entity adapted from photographs she had seen showing the casualties of military conflict, of natural disaster and of oppression. Their sources were such external images and the matrix such images had formed over time in her mind. They represented a reality, but they were not the reality. And yet, they were insurmountable. The entity they formed was irresistible. And it was hateful. Utterly hateful. But to realise this was to realise that she was hateful. But, then again, that was not *quite* true, was it? But—true or not—the ball of hatefulness, bouncing back from her to the entity, could not bounce through or shatter its images. It rebounded again. The reality that the images borrowed was strong enough for this, so that dire hatefulness bounced back and forward between the entity and Sadie in an endless wretchedness of degradation.

They were all victims that made the body of the entity, their existence an eternal prosecution of unforgivable crimes. To want to get rid of them was obscene, and was precisely what summoned them, continuously, in reaction, to accuse the guilty. But it was also obscene to Sadie that her mind, on its own or in co-operation with something else, had assembled together a mass of humans who were designated victims.

It's not my fault, she thought. I am not against them. She looked at her life and saw herself as smart, well-informed, her own person. All this had nothing to do with her. Okay, there must be dirty feelings hidden in the creases of my heart somewhere, she thought, but that's not the same as the choices I make in my daily life. But this was not quite true, either. She had co-operated in the making of these images, or they would not be here. She had co-operated in the generation of the obscene concept 'victim'. The truth slipped from her grasp each time she tried to take hold of it, but what remained each time the truth escaped her was this entity. One way or another its existence was a fact; the fact that it existed was obscene; the fact that its existence was obscene was obscene.

And then, by increments, small and large, she became aware of another dimension to this entity. This living, heaving mountain of victimhood had a kind of head, composed of pregnant women who had been cut open, and their unborn children, which were impaled upon bayonets. The pregnant women were caryatids and the baby-impaling bayonets were columns in this temple-head, supporting a cupola of tiered vultures that was something like a cap of office. Whoever or whatever had placed the cap there, it had been placed there in a snide way. It was an open secret that the entity was being used. In making the secret open, the placer of the cap had engineered another layer in the feedback loop of hatefulness. To try to banish the entity by revealing what was already known—that it was being used—would only make it more immovable and more malignant. How eloquent was the mere placing of a cap, when the intent behind it was so evil. Sadie understood the very words it was intended to suggest: "This is what humans do," and then: "This is what humans always come to." A terrible, entrapping twist of implication linked these two statements. Humans would come to this because they were worthless. They were worthless because this was what they did.

"But why is it bad?" Sadie asked in her mind. "If humans are worthless, why does it matter what they do to each other?"

The mountain before her shuddered and gave out a foetid roar of moral rage. She could not answer. She knew she must be implicated. The roar became whispering sneers and insinuations, threading through her understanding, intimately and painfully.

It's bad, she thought. The human race is bad. The universe is bad. But the one judging, wherever or whatever it is, that is the most evil thing of all.

And she heard, at this, a sound of laughter so distinct that she shivered and opened her eyes to the darkness of her room.

I'm playing mind games with the universe, she thought. Well then, I'll stop playing.

She sat up in bed. There was no triumph in her resolution to stop playing. Surely she was not thinking straight. Could the riddle be so difficult? Maybe there was an answer. Maybe she just didn't want to think it.

She threw back the covers, slid her legs over the edge of the bed, and lowered her feet to the floor. Unsure of her balance, she made her way in the dark to the light switch, and, flicking this to the on position and rescuing the room from obscurity, she felt for a moment the reassurance of solid outlines. But this reassurance soon transformed into something else, since solidity was neither certain nor, in itself, comforting. Of course, what she had seen with her eyes closed, it was all rubbish. But she knew that this was her defence, and that the penalty of such a defence was that it applied to everything. That was what 'it wanted'—for everything to be rubbish. For there to be a way past it, there had to be something that was not rubbish.

She walked over to her desk in the corner of the room, as if she might find something there. This was the desk where she marked the work of her students, devised coursework and so on. It was also here, undisturbed, that doodles and spontaneous notes on scrap paper, begun as a means of exercising the rights of solitude, had become more purposeful, demanded and assumed discipline, and had grown from graffiti-esque play to another kind of work. Although much of her work, both professional and personal, was done on the desktop computer, nonetheless, there were enough sheets of paper, both printed and handwritten, around the computer keyboard and monitor, to give the desk the appearance of an angular container with the capacity to hold periods both of idleness and industry within the larger frame of changeless, transparent order.

Sadie sat down in the chair where she usually worked. Strange, the power of convention and of habit; she felt like an imposter sitting here now. She picked up some loose leaves on which were written and typed some of her poems, in rough and in final form. The verses and fragments now appeared empty structures, like scaffolding erected for an abandoned building project. She read some lines aloud:

> Styles of leisure, are our slangy meanings,
> Obscure, subsidised sports, like personal sumo

Then she put the leaves back down on the desk.

Her eyes rested on something that usually she gave so little thought it had almost achieved the invisibility of familiar indifference. It was a cereal bowl that had contained, for a while, a couple of handfuls of traditional Chinese sweets. A friend of Jason had been on a business trip to Beijing and had brought them back as a convenient souvenir—cheap, unimaginative, but somehow authentic. If they were predictable, so was the fact they would be appreciated. In the bowl, there were still some wrappers, which had contained some kind of white, milky substance resembling nougat. Sadie took one of these crumpled wrappers and flattened it out on the surface of the desk. She could not read the Chinese ideograms, though to other brains they signified something. To her the writing was merely jagged colour. Instead, her attention was drawn to a cartoon rabbit, defined against the white background with lines and pointillist shading of blue, red, yellow and black. It wore a jacket, and seemed to occupy an imaginary niche somewhere between Bugs Bunny and the White

Rabbit from *Alice's Adventures in Wonderland*. It didn't look much like a rabbit. This was unremarkable, of course. Children quickly get used to the fact that cartoons often do not resemble the creatures they represent. But to state a fact is not to explain it. The question remained of exactly how the brain identified these lines as a rabbit. Beyond this, there were other questions. How did the brain distinguish the representation of a cartoon rabbit from the representation of a real rabbit, given that neither of them were real rabbits? What was a cartoon rabbit? The brain identified it as if it had the integrity of a discrete species.

But there was something beyond even this that had begun to trouble Sadie. This was not simply a cartoon rabbit, or perhaps, this was not even a cartoon rabbit—it was a fake cartoon rabbit. Other cartoon characters seemed to have the immortality of archetype. There was something recognisable about them that allowed them to be reproduced in multiple human minds. But this creature was from a place somewhere between archetypes. It would surely not successfully reproduce itself in the human mind. It would remain nameless, or as if nameless, even if someone had tried to name it, had declared it officially named. It was, in some sense, the failure of an ideal. Sadie imagined the rabbit being manufactured in some bizarre sweatshop or disreputable laboratory. Those who concocted the blueprint deliberately stole from other cartoon rabbits, but they had some technique for rendering everything they stole as anonymous as possible, as if they were laundering money. Then, once the design was finalised, and all traces that would identify definite origins were removed, it was passed on to the workers, and from the bits and pieces provided them from vast Chinese mountains of scrap, unloaded on China from Britain and other countries, they patched together this happy-malevolent emblem, this hideous unrabbit. It was, in some way, a creature like that in Damien's studio. Sadie wanted to compare it directly with known and named cartoon characters to see if she could pinpoint actual features that defined a qualitative difference between them and this imitation, but a fear grew on her, rippling over her shoulders, at the thought—almost a conviction—that she would not be able to find any signs of clear distinction, and that, subsequently, the fact that all cartoon characters were of the same species as this would become increasingly inescapable and overwhelming. She found that she did not dare turn on her computer to make the comparison she had contemplated.

It's all rubbish. All of it.

That's what she had thought at first—the mountains of rubbish in China. But she had changed the word in her head, to 'scrap', and now the word 'rubbish' had returned, anyway. Why was she thinking with such a silly word? She knew why. The word did not match with what it referred to and this mismatch created a frisson as if an air hole had been poked into reality, allowing her to breathe, if only a little. But could she escape by saying "rubbish", or did it merely postpone her suffocation? She thought and thought, but could find no way through the apparent hole. Instead, the hole became a ring, which expanded or shrank, but always contained her. She thought, "Rubbish!", and the ring expanded, and she had room to step back slightly from whatever she examined, but she was nonetheless stepping back within the ring's stagnant environment. In this sense, reality was certainly elastic, but so what? It would always snap back into place and take her with it. Moreover, it was inside her, tangled in her guts like swallowed chewing gum.

She tried to extract herself from these thoughts that led her ever inwards, a labyrinth that snaggled and tripped. She brought her consciousness back to what she could see—the cartoon rabbit and the other markings on the wrapping paper.

What she had tried to analyse moments before now seemed very plain, though of little interest. She had begun to notice it in the rabbit, but it really pertained to everything she could see, think or otherwise sense. There was no reaching-out-ness to anything. Writing was evidence of human awareness, as were pictures and other artefacts, but whereas once these had reached out to engage her in some mutual decision concerning what the future might be, now it seemed obvious that there was no reaching out and could never be. Four-dimensionality, she had heard this called—if time is the fourth dimension then everything is fixed and nothing can be helped. Curiously, the unmeaning fixedness of everything gave a smeary, warped impression, as if the absolute redundant excess of merely being, the bleeding waste of it all, was finally unmasked.

Something stirred within. Something vast. It was the monster-victim, unvanquished. Yes, it was that, although it was very obvious the monster-victim was just a form being used by something else. But an unvanquished form, and for all its aura of irony, when it crushed it would crush coldly and absolutely. Suddenly Sadie felt an icy contradiction inside her, and the hollowness she had experienced since what had happened at Damien's was sharpened, renewed to a poignancy redolent of some chance apprehension of the complete shamelessness and unaccountability of human power. And as this hollowness sharpened and condensed, there crystallised within it a number of stabbing, thrilling chakras that told her with certainty that something unspeakable and ineluctable was happening to her.

Damien had been right—why had she doubted what was so clear? His frustration was understandable. He had told the plainest truth and it had meant nothing to her, but now it permeated her, meaningful or not. It flowered with all that was unspeakable. She was alive and dead at the same time. How very, very curious.

Perhaps, she thought, she should phone him, since he would be the only one likely to understand. But, after all, was this exactly what he had meant? She cast her mind back, with surprising ease considering it had made so little impression on her when it happened, to the occasion of Damien's first declaring to her that a person might be living and dead at the same time. She perceived at once the difference between what he had intended then and what he had precipitated now. To phone him would be a nightmare. He would never know. That's right . . . that's right—he would never know.

But what, exactly, to do about it all?

She knew what, and yet, how? It was the how that was important, like a lock that only opened when you turned the key with the right series of manipulations.

Rubbish. Rubbish.

The word recurred.

It was like a distant, barely believable light indicating shore where there could be no shore, like a remembered familiar voice from someone who you can never meet again. She could not go towards that light. She could not find the source of that voice. She must do the opposite, must go the way of all-is-lost, must go the whole way and farther.

Accordingly, she picked up a pen from the desk and found a nearly blank sheet of paper from among the others, and began to trace a curving, doubling-back line, like the folds of a cerebral cortex. She had to be precise, and she had to include every detail—all perfectly mapped to scale, so that everything within the boundaries of the elastic circle that imprisoned her was acknowledged and ticked off.

The detail increased through the small hours, progressing towards simple exhaustion. At one point the nausea became overwhelming again, but when Sadie rushed to the bathroom this time, the retching was much diminished in violence. The suspicion of cockroach antennae waving slowly and eerily behind every object that met her eyes grew stronger. Tracing the maze— as if following a pre-existing line—kept her steady. She just had to follow the line to the end.

Some time before dawn, Justina, Sadie's friend, received an unusual phone call.

"Hello?" Justina sounded still closer to sleep than wakefulness, but she had clearly been conscious enough to see Sadie's name on the screen of her phone. "What's wrong? It's, like, four in the morning."

"Nothing."

"What?"

"Nothing's wrong." Sadie intoned the words as if they were a matter of meaningless formality.

"Why are you phoning? Are you okay?"

"Justina, you know . . ."

"Know what?"

"You know when someone dies, everyone says, 'But she'll live on for as long as we remember her', do you think that the person really lives on?"

"Well, I don't know. In a way they do. In memory."

"But is a memory really the person?"

"I suppose it's not."

"No. I don't think it is, either. So why do people care about memories?"

"I don't know. I suppose . . . Do you mean people who are still alive, or . . . Wait, I'm getting confused."

"No, I understand. I mean both. Why do people care about being remembered and why do they care about memories they have?"

"What would there be without memory?"

"Are you saying nothing exists except memory?"

"No, but, like, if you didn't have memory you'd just be a goldfish, you know."

"Yes. I know."

"Sadie, has something happened? Are you okay?"

"Nothing's happened. I can't sleep. Maybe I have a fever."

"Is Jason there?"

"He's asleep. He's in the next room."

"We can talk if you need to talk, but I don't understand why you're phoning. Also, I have to get up for work today."

"Imagine that there's no memory. Imagine that when you die all your own memories are lost, and, not only that, all memories of you—other people's memories of you—are lost. That's what happens anyway, in the end. All memories will be lost. So, keep that in mind, and then, answer this question: Is there anything you want to tell me?"

For a moment there were vocal sounds from Justina between a sigh and a grunt as if she were giving up on sleep and adjusting her position to focus her attention on the unexpected phone call.

"Sadie . . . I think I understand what you're saying. But the weird thing is, if I really think about all memory being lost, I'm not sure there's anything to say. It's like, what do goldfish say to each other? But the point is, we're not goldfish, are we? We remember things, and . . . things we do overlap, and we have children and teach them things. No one has to do everything in a single moment in the spotlight . . . I mean . . . So, why don't you come and stay again and we can talk about it?"

"There's something else I want to know."

"What?"

"Does it make you feel good saying something is bad?"

"What? What do you mean?"

"If something is wrong with the world and you say it's bad, does it make you feel good to say it's bad?"

"I don't know. I suppose that's why people say things are bad. Or maybe they think it will make a difference. They want things to be good."

"Yes. Yes. That's right. They want things to be good. Justina, I'm going to go now. Sorry to wake you up. I don't think I can talk any more."

"Well, okay, but phone me if . . ."

Sadie hung up. She did not phone Justina again.

About fifteen minutes after the phone call was over, she went to the bathroom again. She was not feeling the need to vomit now. She took some tools with her—a screwdriver, a hammer and some wire-cutters. She locked the door behind her, took a pack of safety-razor heads from the bathroom cabinet and began the task of extracting blades from them. Having extracted eight reasonably undamaged blades, she lined these up on the edge of the tub and began to run a bath.

She undressed, and, when the bath was perhaps two thirds
full, she got in. Carefully taking the first of the thin strips of
blade between her thumb and her forefinger, she began to trace
a line on the calf of her left leg—a line that curved and doubled
back like the pattern of a cerebral cortex. It was harder to keep
the line perfect here, because the blade was in danger of bending,
the surface of her leg yielded, and the line ran red, obscuring the
work she had already done, but these difficulties only made her
more determined to do the job well. She navigated by pain.

After a while the blade was useless, and this time she tried
doubling up in the hope that two blades together would rein-
force each other. The nausea was rising again, but the existence
of these fresh scars already acted as an overflow. The nausea could
only rise so high before it flowed out of her altogether, into the
deepening red of the bath water. The stench, too, on the verge
of being maddening, dispersed little by little, like steam through
the crack of a slightly open window.

IX. Eminem vs. Iggy Azalea

THE first coherent thought that Damien had after learning of Sadie's death was: what I could not do with belief, she did without.

He felt, again, her grasp on the metaphorical spine of his brain, through which ran all his spiritual nerves. He felt her tug, and he felt something coming undone.

He could almost believe now that he was merely the sum of myriad parts—he had the sensation that those parts were losing their cohesion. But if they did not disintegrate entirely, perhaps it was because strange things were happening, and their anomalous magnetism kept him together even though the background meaning of his existence seemed so variable and so volatile that it could not possibly justify his constant figure in the foreground.

The first of these strange happenings was the cessation of Philip's vital functions. Two days after Sadie had fled the studio, Philip seized up, his appendages contracting into a ball, as Damien had seen happen with spiders sometimes, when they were killed by heat or toxic spray. He felt a similar mixture of horror and pity, discovering Philip in this condition, as he did when seeing the balled-up spiders, but the feeling was greatly magnified, as if proportionate with Philip's size. Damien found he hardly wanted to touch him, locked into that final crouch at the edge of the area behind the curtain. Nonetheless, he approached, reached out, touched . . . and trembled as an unpleasant tingle swept through him. Thereafter he tried the usual methods to bring

Philip back to animation, as well as some methods that were without precedent, but it was as if Philip had never been more than this stiff sculpture of death. Even before he stopped trying to revive this offspring of his various delvings, he learnt of Sadie's ultimate response to the operation she had undergone and noted a coincidence of timing that made him, first, instinctively despair of reviving Philip, and then produced in him other, stranger emotions. The shrox still convulsed to order, the aquatapillar still looped its looping crawl, but some irreversible change had come over Philip. The word 'death' rose to the surface of his mind, but with regard to Philip, he could no more think it than speak it. That it was unutterable brought to the mortal frame of his body-soul complex some smoke-bitter echo of the true namelessness of all death. Anyway, facts were facts, and one had to live with them as much as die with them.

The second strange happening came a little later than this.

Four days after Sadie's visit and the culmination of a plan of many years, Damien, uneasy at the uncertainty of the outcome, finally summoned the nerve to phone her. Jason answered. The ensuing conversation was uncomfortable for a number of reasons, but Damien was aware of and had to acknowledge in himself one emotion among many that would no doubt have sickened Jason had he known—but he could not know—and that was a sense of relief, a satisfaction that glowed for a few moments like the element of an old light bulb, that the experiment had made an undoubted difference and the return to daily humdrum evasions had been averted. After this glow faded, however, he felt like someone who had lost his fingerhold on a rock face.

Jason, clearly determined to learn all he could while events were still fresh, questioned Damien persistently and closely on what had happened when Sadie had visited. Sadie's own account of things, minimal as it had been, must have worked in Damien's favour here. He told Jason they had talked, as they usually did, and that Sadie had begun to feel ill, and left. Damien was sufficiently shaken by the news of Sadie's death that his testimony might easily have sounded bewildered and sincere, instead of what it was—bewildered and dissembling.

Recognising that Jason was exerting himself now in order to minimise chances that he would need to associate with Damien further in the future, Damien adopted a similar strategy and enquired where he might send a funeral wreath. With one follow-up e-mail, he had enough information to locate the grave once it was occupied.

When he found it, on a Saturday afternoon, the grave was sufficiently fresh that the headstone had not yet been erected. The presence of his white and yellow chrysanthemum wreath had provided definite confirmation that this was the little patch of earth that was his destination, though it was a destination from which he must walk away again after having stood, impotently, for a greater or shorter duration. He re-read the condolence card he had signed.

Despite the unusually deep interest he had taken in graves and human burial for so long, this was a new experience for him. To visit such a fresh grave, formally plotted in an established ground, and for the remains held in the grave to belong to a person connected to his own life, and for that to be such a young person and for her image in his mind to be so recent and fresh itself as to be alive, and, on top of all this, to know himself implicated in her death, or at least to have little doubt of such implication: all this was quite extraordinarily new and unforeseen.

The freshness of the grave reminded him of what he already knew more intimately than others: that where one may dig to inter one may also dig to disinter; that what had been buried may be unburied. By contrast, he was also aware of something painfully novel: that what was so recently alive, what so newly dead, could not be returned from the latter enigma to the former.

There was a way of wallowing in the difference between the two enigmas. Standing at the foot of this grave, to which he had such a unique relationship, Damien thought of that way; he contemplated it seriously and concretely enough that he shuddered physically with a mixture of excitement, disgust and other emotions seldom experienced simultaneously. That cold body would probably still be in a condition such that the person who had moved and shaped it in life was recognisable in the existing features, haunting that landscape of flesh as if she might return, and though the marks of final ruin would be impossible to ignore, they would be at such a stage that the defects might be more than compensated for by a sense of death's invincible grandeur. What Sadie had called him, he might yet become, with the excuse that she had predicted it.

For some time, Damien's mind was full of images, released from a secret storehouse to erupt with a prolific vigour he had never suspected, and which astonished him so completely that he could not even be appalled. How long, he wondered, had these restless images been bound and hidden in their subterranean dungeon, waiting for a moment that might never have arrived, to burst loose?

He felt himself almost physically degenerate, as if the visions that rioted within him like bats in a cavern might hook themselves so deeply into the tissues of his existence that they could effect genetic changes. He saw himself kneeling to ravish in an ultimate triumph that was also the deepest and most degrading defeat.

The vision was tied in the final knot of a spasm that shot through Damien's abdomen to his groin—an ecstasy that twisted itself into the sharp finish of despair.

Suddenly his mind was clear, and standing in that clarity like a glacier was the thought, once more, that Sadie, without belief, had gone to the extreme before which he, with belief, had vacillated.

This was why the ground was between them now.

Then came an agonising resurgence of the desire that he did not wish to own, and with it a haunting anxiety that more might be known by Google satellites and more traced by cabals of internet industry lynchpins and security forces than he could precisely imagine or live with whilst retaining his sanity, and that someone, somewhere might already have made links between the desecrated grave of Philip Draper and Damien's relationship with Sadie. Damien felt himself teetering on a razor's edge between self-concretising certainty that this was true and an almost hysterical incredulity, not sure which way he would fall. In this giddiness, the one thing of which he felt sure was that reality itself had been artificially degraded by someone, somewhere, and it was his most urgent task to outwit them. Well, then, he thought in a sudden transport of fury, I will give them something worth spying on—what they expect and more. Google will have, under its global magnifying glass, my transcendent abandonment of humanity as I achieve sexual union with the corpse of a dead friend. In a world such as ours, to go all the way we are incited to go by the agent provocateurs, and further—this is the only sanity.

But then something happened—if 'happened' was the word—that made a difference. Everything was seen now, by the impermeable digital eye that promised immortality under surveillance. Surely—surely—Sadie, too, saw everything. In fact, she saw more. She was permeable and saw permeable things, such as the thoughts and desires that had been running through Damien's mind. He felt her knowing breathe through his mind like a cool and soundless wind. She knew. She knew absolutely. He had no doubt that she knew, and this was infinitely preferable to the ghastly travesty of knowing that was the omniscience of the digital eye.

Apprehending now that ghostly, undimensioned, greater thing—greater than the world that spans the horizons of all-there-is—in which Sadie had become a moth-like stir, Damien felt the contrast between this world of measurements and recordings, and that world, and knew that it was only this contrast, which a person might live without glimpsing, by which it was possible to grasp what the word 'truth' might mean. He felt a flutter within him as from some outer benevolence—the benevolence of this contrast. With it, there percolated into his soul an utterly unexpected sense of frank and gentle intimacy. The contrast guaranteed the truth, the subtle truth, larger than the universe, of the finest feathery tracing of the flutter.

He knew, certainly, which side he was on, and submission to the friendly spirit shrouded in awe was without resentment. He knelt, indeed, as he had so recently seen himself kneel in his mind. He bowed himself to the ground and kissed the soil skirting the grave where she was laid in the bed of mortal decay and of eternity.

He stood, rather giddily, recollected himself, and, realising there was no reason for him to linger, left with the haste of someone for whom there is only business, without ceremony, and private, hunger-driven business at that.

He travelled back to Candle Street, on the Tube in an echoing vacancy of mind from which the usual checkpoints between differentiated realities seemed to have been removed. In his studio, as evening settled silty grey in the light, Damien ate a bowl of cereal with milk and a slice of bread with butter and cheese. He felt no need or desire to do anything else, but, when he had finished his brief meal, simply sat in the thickening gloom, only moving from his seat once to turn on the space heater and wrap a blanket round his shoulders.

Eventually, he climbed the ladder to the platform beneath the skylight on which lay his bedding.

Perhaps it was because he had not used any artificial light that day—he did not know—but there was a sense of continuity between his waking and sleeping world, as if he had taken his day with him up the ladder to bed, and, conversely, as if sleep had spread into the day preceding it with the darkness that was its element.

He had a dream. It was not, as usual, all that could be salvaged of a shattered epic of untranslatable otherness, but seemed whole in itself, with the wholeness, in the port of his sleep, of a visiting ship. It was also distinguished from his usual dreams in the sense of where it was visiting *from*. From the waking world, it seemed, but not the waking world as he thought, even in sleep, that he remembered it.

It seemed he was summoned to Sadie's graveside again, now, as he slept—as it were, in real time. He was not quite sure, as he approached it in the darkness, whether this was the real grave in the sense of a consensus reality on which members of the public could intrude, or whether it was more like an exclusive essence of reality locked into a private setting that no other living humans knew the password to unlock. In any case, the grave appeared different to how it had been in the daytime. It was illuminated—it was hard to say whether from within or without. Damien would have said from without, except that there was no obvious external source of light. Also, there was now a headstone. Despite his interest in graves and monumental masonry, Damien could not say what kind of stone it was, except that it was pencil grey, seemed newly hewn, and gave the impression of a texture somewhere between polished and unpolished. He felt his feet on the ground as he moved closer to examine it, and the night air seemed cold and wide enough to suggest he was in open, unprotected reality, and yet, a kind of spice danced in the extremities of his nervous sensations that made him question, in some vague, pocketed way, the literalness of his impression of being awake.

On the surface of the headstone, he saw only two words:

Sadie Bean

The absence of dates and of epitaph told Damien—as good as telepathically—that the Sadie commemorated here had no fixed relations to time, was not bookended by birth and death. In fact, as he looked closer, it seemed to him that the two words had not been cut into the rock, but had appeared there naturally, as might an eddy in a river, or the stripes on the wing-case of a beetle.

He reached out and traced the indented lines with his fingertips. The stone was faintly warm. As his fingers traced each letter in turn, the impression grew on him, shading to quiet certainty, that this warmth was not some residue of the warmth of the day, which had been scant, but a living, internal warmth. His fingertip reached the termination of the final 'n'. He withdrew his hand and then spread his palm, with outstretched fingers, against the stone's flat surface. A tingle seemed to communicate between the stone and the flesh and bones of his hand. Gentle though the feeling was, it seemed enormous in implication, and a wish caught in his heart that he might crouch here with the tingle of contentless communication forever.

As he watched, the tingle erasing all trace of impatience from his expectant observation, parts of the headstone above the writing began to crater and plume, like the surface of a pond hit by slow motion raindrops. Gradually, these swellings and undulations took shape as flowers. The stone was blossoming in petals and calyces of grey—delicate, strong, expressive. Now Damien drew his hand away and stood to watch the continuing transformation.

The stone took on a peculiar tumescence, and a number of local swellings, like teats or pimples, appeared. At first Damien was unsure what these were, and they fascinated him. The fascination was a blend of that exerted by the sexual, and that exerted by physical symptoms of disease. But just as the tension between the mystery of these swellings and their fascination was becoming unbearable, they split like pods—split just enough for the spikes they had contained to spring out with the liquid ripeness of the pressure behind them. Then Damien understood what they were—they were cactus thorns. They wept where they had pierced through the grey skin of the stone. The thorns, curving slightly, tapered to fine, attractive points. The blooms that had first sprouted from the stone nestled between their swollen tubercles. As he had felt drawn to the stone itself, so he now felt drawn towards this panoply of bristling spikes, but he was also wary. Slowly, he reached out to run his fingers along the curve of one of these thorns, when suddenly he felt a fierce heat and a deep, poisonous pang in his wrist, and he realised that he had been pierced. Somehow, he had not seen the thorn, a little lower than the one for which he had reached, that had gone so deeply, so quickly, into his flesh, its absolute rigidity startling inside the soft tissues of his arm. He had drawn back in an instant at the sting and the fright of it. The whole thing had been so momentary, it seemed it could barely have touched him, and yet he was wounded. He suspected, too, that a toxin had been released in his bloodstream, and he wondered if it was deadly. He knelt upon the ground and watched as fluid poured from the wound in his wrist—not blood, it seemed, but some stinking, corrupted fluid of black pus and the grey iridescence of oily pollution. It poured for minutes, while the wound widened with its flow, so that he wondered how he could ever have contained such filth.

At last it seemed that he had been emptied, as the flow of filth slowed and no more issued forth. A weepy residue still clung to the edges of the wound so that his feeling of emptiness was tinged with a slight sense of unbalance and a lingering queasiness; his being was still gravitating towards the wound. However, this was only something like the shock and bad taste of effective medicine. He had been lanced like a boil; the bad stuff had gone, and now he had merely to recover.

He stared at the wound, which was perhaps the most fascinating thing he had ever seen, and in this way, slowly, his sense of balance was restored.

When he looked up from his wound, he saw that Sadie was standing behind the headstone. He stared at her for a long time. Somehow, seeing her was the most unexpected thing in the world, as if someone had just told him the ending to the story of the universe and he considered and calculated but, minute after minute, sheer and seamless, he could honestly find no fault with it. There were questions, though. After all, a sense of strangeness created the impression of unending variability in all things.

"There's a species of flower," said Sadie, "that blooms once every thousand years." She gestured with simplicity towards the headstone, and Damien recognised her usual short-cuts of body language bypassing ceremony and stereotype. "This is it," she said.

And this made clear to Damien, in multi-dimensional ways, how something so strange could be so real, or something so real so strange.

Sadie was wearing a white blouse, and she now rolled up the left sleeve to expose her upper arm. There was revealed here a patch of greeny-blue fuzz. The exact nature of this fuzz was perplexingly unclear. It might have been mould, except that it was too bristly. It might have been body hair, if not for a number of factors. At least, if it was body hair, it was of a kind that looked alien to the person from which it grew.

Sadie now rolled up her right sleeve and exposed a smaller patch of the same fuzz on her forearm. She unbuttoned her blouse, removing it entirely, and more patches became visible.

Damien's initial repulsion was modulated to detached curiosity. It was hard to say what the agent of the modulation might have been. Perhaps the final end of the revulsion was already present within it, and needed only favourable conditions to fulfil what, if not indefinitely postponed, was inevitable. The detachment was an intermediate stage. Sadie wished for him to examine the patches of fuzz, and he did, growing confident within the unspoken but clearly displayed invitation. There was a sweetness in this detachment like a glowing agnosticism—not knowing merely because that is a condition of particularity, though that particularity would not itself exist without a foundation of knowing. As he examined, his understanding of the nature of the fuzz became more focused. This fuzz, he now realised, had been part of Sadie for as long as he had known her. But it had been invisible until now. That is, even if he had seen her previously with her blouse off—and he never had—he would not have seen this fuzz. But there had always been, for Damien, parts of Sadie that were unfeminine or disagreeable or he did not know what. In fact, that was it—he did not know what. It was not that Sadie was his opposite in these patches, it was that she was entirely other, and resistant to all the ways he had for taking the world in. They had always rankled with him obscurely.

He realised he had to touch them. He was apprehensive, doubting he could do it, doubting, somehow, that he was equal to it, that he could respond in the appropriate way. Nonetheless, unworthy or unsuitable as he might be, he reached out and laid his palm closely but gently over the first revealed patch of fuzz—the large one—on her upper left arm.

It was now that Damien felt what had been detachment reach a tipping point and spill into attachment, attraction, entanglement. The very revulsion he had felt, since he first knew Sadie, at the then-invisible patches—if only he had known it—had been a promise. It was, above all, the patches that had signified to Damien a shared destiny with Sadie. Now, that promise, that destiny, was to be fulfilled.

He felt something sink from his hand into her arm. It was as though a two pound coin, stuck to the ceiling with fresh bubble gum, had slowly been stretching the gum until a sudden acceleration when the gum was pulled into long, elastic threads. It was with just such a stretching motion that something descended from Damien into Sadie. In the same way, though the direction was opposite, something extended itself from Sadie into Damien.

For a moment, out of bewildered curiosity, he tried pulling his hand away from her arm. He was surprised and not surprised when he saw a mass of gooey threads stretching between the palm of his hand and Sadie's upper arm, confirming that there was a literal aspect to the sensations he was experiencing. He pressed his hand back in place and submitted himself to those sensations.

What had once been revulsion thawed. The ice of disgust and despair was unlocked, its essence liquefied into a paradoxically thrilling peace.

Damien looked at Sadie's face, and knew he was seeing it as it was for the first time. Its hidden quarters all stood open. What might have seemed an alien and intolerable cubism to him before had unfolded into completeness and perfection.

Now Damien felt Sadie's hand on his flank, beneath his right armpit. She had never touched him there before. She touched him gently and his flesh twitched and quivered as if she had discovered the sensitivity of an old injury. Her touch had a purpose. She was about to kneel and guided him to do the same, so that she knelt behind the headstone, and he in front of it. She circled his wrists with her thumbs and forefingers and moved his hands. His right hand was torn away from the sticky communication of her upper arm again. There was a chill of separation with this motion, but what had extended from each into the other sank within, as if the elastic, gummy threads had finally stretched to breaking point, and the burden of this entanglement, released from suspension, dissolved in liquid sweetness, starred with effervescence like twinned nebulae of quantum entanglement in their two bodies.

Sadie positioned his hands upon her shoulders, then placed her hands upon his shoulders. All her movements were shaped by some practical end that Damien could not yet understand, and her touch spoke this fact to him in clear accents. However, the brusqueness of pragmatism was softened by the subtle but consistent implication in movement, touch and everything else, that the end of all this practicality was a vastly tender one.

Sadie's grip tightened on his shoulders. So tightly did her fingers clutch him that it was even a little painful. It was as if her fingers were biting him. Through his clothing, they gave a tactile sensation as of teeth. Fingers and teeth are both made of bone, after all. The sharp, straight edges of this sensation, blunted a little here and there, and the pressure of it, were a matter of business lined inseparably with intimacy. Since her fingers curled over his shoulders, he could not see them, but the feel of them digging into his flesh conjured up the image of her bitten fingernails, and this image, in turn, seemed to contain the whole of Sadie's spirit. He could see the pressure she was applying make a band of reddish pink in the centre of each fingernail, with pinkish white below and above it. The white of her nails and cuticles seemed to emanate a breeze that lent all surrounding things the sentimental purity of a pencil drawing in a girl's comic book. But the nails also gleamed with the hardness of perfect realism.

She pulled. The jerk was sudden and violent. Had this been a dream, surely this would have woken Damien. Sadie did not seem simply to be pulling Damien towards her; she was also pulling herself towards him.

The spiny headstone was between them, and by the power of Sadie's sudden wrench, they were, in one go, both impaled upon its many thorns.

The pain brought tears to Damien's eyes. He had been punctured in many places. Sadie's eyes merely widened as if she were absorbing the pain like an unusual source of nutrition to which her digestive system had accustomed itself. The pain was such that for a number of moments, in which his mind journeyed across an austere canyon landscape of the meaning of mortality and his relationship to it, Damien was convinced that he was now to die, that all things, as far as he could ever know them, were to disintegrate here. This conviction first magnified, then almost neutralised his agony with a compound of unbearable sadness and confusion. But time passed, and he and Sadie still lived, and a hope grew that the certainty of death had been merely a phase and an illusion. There was nothing to indicate this with finality, but the hope, wavering sometimes, continued to grow. In the meantime, blood from both Sadie and Damien, like water from pipes burst in an explosion, washed in thin waves down the headstone and pooled on the ground, and the thorns on which Damien was impaled seemed to curve and contract inside him, forming fish-hook barbs from which it was impossible to extricate himself. And, as some thorns contracted, others extended, seeking with agonising sharpness an exit on the other side of his body.

Gradually, he understood what was happening, and each phase of his understanding was a little and a limited thing compared to the succeeding phase into which it unfolded. Sadie had told him that there was a flower that bloomed once in a thousand years. Her silence thereafter had not been haughty. No other words had been necessary. The rest was a demonstration and a fulfilment of their meaning.

Damien realised he could no longer move his hands from Sadie's shoulders. His fingers were sinking into her flesh like roots into soil, and hers were sinking into his. As he watched, a stone bud thrust up between his fingers on her right shoulder and opened into a many-petalled flower. There followed a piercing pain in his jaw. Something was pushing its way through and expanding in wonderful growth beyond all the limits of meaning. Then he felt something happening to his torso, which pressed unevenly against the now-uneven headstone. It was not only the stone that was sending its thorny, flowering shoots into him; his flesh was sending tendrils into the stone, where they softly weevilled living passages, juicily communed, and made innovative mergings of organic and inorganic. This process of synthesis, assimilation and budding, blossoming invention would continue, Damien knew, until the flower that they were—Sadie, headstone and he—quivered in the myriad, dilated perfection of full bloom. In the meantime, something had dawned in his gut. The riddle in the outer appearance of the impossible had been solved and it was revealed in its essence as the forge-glow of the nakedly real. The idiosyncratic was the universal, and some unspeakable beneficence stood pre-ordained in the shivering stillness of stony heat on the horizon of being, as the gleaming end that was the cause of all and the intelligence by which every blemish shall at last be read as an etched letter of overflowing glory.

Where Damien's hands were merging with Sadie's shoulders, like ruins in a verdant landscape, he continued to feel the urtication of repulsion, ever distilling itself, as in a crucible of heat and pressure, into blistering joy. Where his mossy fingers joined her flesh, he saw leaking rivulets that ran down her arms, rusty as with iron deposits, and spitting and popping with heat. From the look of this fluid, and the smell, he could not tell whether it was semen or saliva. Perhaps it was some other thing with a related nature, serving consumption or production or both.

The shoots from the headstone were transforming. They grew thicker, sprouted thorns of their own, curved and curled with a crueller luxuriance. The lacerations of joy multiplied, and Damien screamed with the barbs that unwove his flesh even as they wove a stranger fabric to include and extend him. Sadie smiled, faint, mellow, almost sardonic, and did not scream. At some point Damien noted that they were tightly overgrown by a self-organising wickerwork of stone brambles. Some shoots revolved, forming a gory circuit of communication between them. Dog roses bloomed on them, white with tiny yellow stamens, their petals rimmed with scarlet pink. They gave off a honeyed fragrance as subtle as the unmistakeable, unplaceable essence of personality.

Damien felt the flush of a functioning liver intact within him. It was, he knew with marvellous intelligence, Sadie's liver. There was no longer anything to fear, from evil or from good.

Damien awoke from this dream conscious of a glint from a steel blade of well-being inside him.

Two or three times in his life he had woken from a dream the reality of which had been so persuasive that he had needed a little time and effort to adjust to the idea that the world he had woken into was the real one. This was just such a dream. Or perhaps it belonged to a new category of its own, since on this occasion, Damien was unable to make the adjustment entirely. There remained a part of him that was convinced of the greater reality of that he had woken from. It was as if Sadie's liver remained inside him. For some time after he sat up under the skylight of his studio, rubbing his eyes and temples and gazing at the folds of his duvet and sheets in the daylight whose self-existence was both normality and the spell of pretended normality, Damien was captivated by the incandescent certainty that if he arranged for a sample to be taken from his liver and analysed, it would be found to have a different genetic fingerprint to the rest of him. He contemplated how this might be done, a kind of ecstasy floating his thoughts as ashes float on the updraught of a fire. But when it occurred to him that, after all, a test might show the liver to be of the same genetic origin as the rest of his body, the chill of doubt grew, and he decided to pre-empt disappointment by concluding in advance that such a test would uncover nothing unusual, and giving up on a preposterous idea.

He thought this decision might be the blow that slew the authority of the dream and returned him wholly to the jurisdiction of the world in which he now found himself conscious, but this was not the case. Some flickering sense remained that the liver was really Sadie's, the dream a touchstone of reality. In any case, the certainty he had experienced in the dream was a memory rather than a present fact. It had lost its compelling completeness. There was now an inside and an outside. The taste of the certainty lingered, which was exactly the taste of the imagination, and inside the certainty, the taste was an irrefutable argument whose logic was fertility and whose fertility was logic. There was no need of faith. Outside the sphere of certainty, though the taste was remembered, the very fact of an outside meant that faith was needed to enter certainty again, and the fact that faith was needed became in itself a source of doubt. And yet, even beyond inside and outside, questions of faith and certainty, all such phases and demarcations, there was a golden coronal haze—barely perceptible but all the more invincible for that—without source or limit, that in its mellow, elusive way affirmed indeed the certainty, and the inside and outside and faith and doubt as portions of the certainty. There seemed a smile in this haze, and a whisper. Damien could almost thread into words what they expressed. And those words that were almost the expression were as follows: The purpose in this glow is that on the one hand one must know the glow is true, but on the other it is the supremely sweet goodness of the glow, itself to prevent belief in it within the ongoing project of soaring spires and laughing intrigues and jagged demolition that we call 'for now'; and this is how it must be.

After Sadie's death, and the strange things that followed it as if they were the efflorescence of some truth hidden, enfolded, within the calyces of the event, Damien tried re-reading a number of texts of a mystical complexion in the hope that his recent experiences had put him in direct communion with the core of those texts, and that, conversely, the texts would provide a framework through which those experiences might develop, revealing their relation to his mundane existence and so guiding him back to the world that he might live there more fully than before. But the first texts that came to hand he found to be trash. In particular, the discourses of Jiddu Krishnamurti were nothing but ashes whirling on a wind of confusion. The older, more cryptic texts—the ones known as sacred—at least retained some mystery for him, but most of what had been written on the spirit in the last few centuries—at least in the texts he had identified as representative—appeared to be a rubbish heap of disguised self-aggrandisement, a whole haberdashery of hokum mixing the lowest philistinism of thuggish pedagoguery with a soapy affectation of moral challenge. The imposture of such texts was so blatant that it surprised him he had ever wasted time submitting his inner self to its interrogation. Any stranger at a bus stop was more likely to offer him spiritual insight than the likes of these, these Tony Parsonses, these Steve Norquists.

It was not even necessarily that what these people said was untrue, though he sensed some pernicious untruths mixed in with the truth in order to hook the unwary. It was more as if a certain type of person had set out to teach people the art of respiration or sleep. What was worse, when their disciples discovered they were, indeed, able to breathe or to sleep, the self-appointed teachers would slyly declare, "You did it all by yourself. I can't take any credit." Since no other type of person on Earth refuses praise for another person's breathing, the implication of modesty and integrity in these protestations was clear. On this particular score, U.G. Krishnamurti, the so-called anti-guru, was just as bad as Jiddu Krishnamurti. In some ways, in fact, he was worse, his version being: "Only scoundrels will teach you how to breathe. Therefore, even though I am the only human who ever stumbled on the secret of breathing, I will not tell you what it is. Go away! Leave me alone! But, of course, you can keep filming me while I tell you to go away. Why should I mind? I don't care about anything. Yes, you can keep filming."

They disgusted him. The few who didn't disgust him, always eventually came back to the refrain—as Emerson did—that one had to trust one's own inner spirit, not kneel to someone else's.

And so he stood without a guide, and spiritual certainty, having made the mere world irrelevant, departed from that world like a careless cloud, leaving Damien alone with its promise. The very promise with which it left him made him feel the futility of all action, all thought, all being. He was superfluous. Whatever the universe might or might not require, Damien could not prevent it if he tried.

As he had been abandoned, so he abandoned the texts of a mystical complexion. His task, as a superfluous being, was somehow to enter the superfluous world, and somehow to occupy that world with his life.

The depression that had convinced his doctor and his manager to allow him time off work was gone, and he was glad of the chance to fill his time with work again. Tiredness and rest had become matters of indifference to him. Despair had been the paradoxical engine driving him; it had been removed. Another paradox replaced it: Inside he was becalmed, as a boat with limp sails, and there was only vast stillness and shoreless vacuity; outside there was new ease of motion, as he acted always in accordance with the forces acting on him. This, apparently, was the perfection revealed when resistance was eliminated. But if this were perfection, Damien felt himself growing sick of it, without even knowing reason to complain. Surely, he thought, the only thing that would improve this unnecessary perfection was the complete undoing of existence itself.

Over the weeks following the dream, this perfection was distilling discontent, and the discontent slowly gathered and settled into an actual form, mysterious and particular. When the last particle of this discontent had vanished into the seamlessness of its place and the particular form into which it had been distilled was quietly, softly, finally completed, Damien turned to a blank page in the notepad he had used for recording his thoughts during all his researches, and began to write what he intended as an open letter to the universe.

The letter ran as follows:

> How can we realise the seriousness of the situation without immediately giving up in despair? On the one hand, if we realise the truth, we are paralyzed with horror, and do nothing. On the other, without the truth, we squander our lives in grotesque frivolity, and do nothing.
>
> I am something like a murderer, and that 'something like' is the problem. I have not received a sufficient shock to sober up. On the other hand, the promises I receive of salvation are too convenient for me to believe in that I may earnestly submit my days to their otherworldly supervision.
>
> Is the world ending? Perhaps not. Perhaps it is nothing but hysteria of the kind to which the human race, having abandoned philosophy, and with no genuine leadership, is now so very prone. To which, I suppose, it has always been prone.
>
> But let us think for a moment that the world truly is ending. The great advantage of this situation is that it brings our boredom to the surface. Ordinarily, our boredom lies deep within, and is numb and controlling. When it is brought to the surface it begins to ache with the most excruciating pain, and there is a sensation of something crack-

ing open. We could lose everything. Our boredom protects us from and drives us towards this loss. To put it another way, the boredom that prevented us living could save our lives. As it comes closer to the surface and the ache threatens to crack us open, the boredom, deterred by the barrier of pain, might sink again. We are relieved, and we are doomed. But it is just possible—we feel it—that the boredom keeps rising, the ache keeps increasing, and we crack right open and lose everything. Then we will know a different kind of relief—a greater relief. Our boredom will finally have freed us from boredom—freed us to live.

The end of the world might provide exactly the right kind of pressure to make this happen.

It is true that the end of the world might only be the realisation of all our fears, and of what we could not even imagine in order to fear it. To say as much is to say there is nothing to learn or gain by it, and to say there is nothing to learn or gain by it is to say that there is no use in talking about it, except perhaps as something to be prevented.

There is another possibility that would prevent boredom from liberating us, and that is simply if things don't quite get bad enough. After all, millions have been imprisoned, tortured and unjustly killed in the past, apparently without any widespread liberation through boredom as a result. The world situation could keep on getting worse and worse without ever reaching a redemptive crisis. And since we can't rely on any such crisis, and since the end that is only nightmare is best prevented, the remaining question that must be answered is how do we induce the liberation-from-boredom-through-boredom without the external pressure brought to bear by the right kind of end-of-the-world?

The answer, as far as I can see, is this: we need a public language in which we can talk of spiritual needs seriously and unpretentiously. A restoration of one or all of the world religions won't work. Their language is too denominational and too bound to scripture without acknowledgement of context.

Leafing through the *Analects*, I find, in book XX, these words:

> If the Empire should be reduced to dire straits
> The honours bestowed on thee by Heaven
> will be terminated for ever.

This is an allusion to the Mandate of Heaven—that the emperor could only rule by divine sanction, and the collapse of his rule was evidence of the displeasure of Heaven and the withdrawal of the Mandate. By what authority does anyone rule now? The will of the people? What people, and how is the value of their will known? If people really believed in democracy, there would be a referendum not only on the European Union, but on every single issue, but no government would allow matters to be decided in that way. So, instead of the serious conversation we need to be having, for which the Mandate of Heaven would allow us room, we have lies about democracy, and our conversation is limited to trivialities.

Perhaps I can give an example. A while back, naked photographs of the actress Jennifer Lawrence, which she had sent to her boyfriend, were intercepted in the cloud and were leaked on the internet. I read an article urging people not to look at or download the photographs since they were not consensually leaked, since Jennifer was not an object, and since she owned her body. But here we have an unacknowledged dualism, denied elsewhere. How can Jennifer own her body unless there is a Jennifer apart from her body? What I am calling 'the Mandate of Heaven' would allow us to talk seriously about this dualism, so that we could give the real reasons why it is wrong to abuse a person in such a way. The reason—she has a soul. But this subject, which is the only subject from which any serious conversation can derive, is taboo for the left. On the one hand they tell us that women should not be treated like objects, and on the other they subscribe—out of mere hatred of religion—to the materialist philosophy, shamefully given shelter by the representatives of science, that is determined to make us believe all humans are objects (never mind the fact that objects would be unable to believe anything, either way). And so, denying themselves access to the source of seriousness, their cause stultifies, and in lieu of seriousness they become militant.

On this score, Buddhism and its affiliated cosmologies have betrayed us. Since they deny the efficacy of thought and speech, they do not allow us to have the candid conversations about the soul we need to have, but they enforce "lack of all conviction" on the best. There is hypocrisy here, too, because the appointed masters have license to think and so to speak, and, since no one else has license, the principles by which they acquired this license are not transparent to the lay person. And so we have a poisonous elitism. Or perhaps it is better to say we have a dilemma. It is true that a serious conversation requires standards that some might think undemocratic, and the esotericism of traditions such as Buddhism is perhaps one formula for safeguarding such standards. But it means limiting the serious conversation to a very few, and who can be sure that this is not, finally, a system of corruption and disempowerment? Says Wittgenstein, "Whereof one cannot speak, thereof one must be silent." But it is that of which one cannot speak that is the only serious conversation, and in banishing the serious conversation, and laying silence upon all those who would have it, the elitist mystics have condemned us to a world where the noisy, the inconsequential and the destructive, for lack of opposition, occupy the centre of all things and drag us down into the doom of ultimate stupidity.

There is a question here as to what stupidity means. Stupidity is understandable, or it would not occur. There will always be excuses, or even compelling reasons, for it. But, among the choices that might be made, it represents the more detrimental choices. In the film *Annie Hall*, the Woody Allen character expresses surprise and indignation on hearing of the existence of awards for rock music. "They give awards for that kind of music? They do nothing but give out awards. I can't believe it! 'Greatest Fascist Dictator: Adolf Hitler!'" Whether or not you agree with his assessment of rock music, his criticism comes close to providing a definition of stupidity. We have many choices, all of which, whatever else they might also bring, are defensible on some level. Stupidity does not only forgive, but rewards the wrong choices. Of course, Woody Allen is a lover of jazz music, itself once considered degenerate, and this is perhaps an apt indicator of the difficulties and subtleties of the slippery incline towards chronic stupidity.

It might even be argued that stupidity is inevitable. The Industrial Revolution, which has brought us to such a point in our pursuit of particular forms of the good, that we might already have set in motion an irreversible chain of events that will annihilate, or else decimate, the human species, will be defended by some as the natural unfolding of human potential and the necessary result of historical forces. Their argument will be reinforced by the dependence people now feel upon the internet, iPhones, cars, electric light and so on. And if we go back further, the shift from a hunter-gatherer society to an agricultural society allowed the accumulation of material wealth, a complex hierarchy based on this, and the diverse specialisation that is a defining feature of present human civilisation, in which, as long as a social role is valued, it will allow a person access to food, shelter, and other such necessities and advantages, that he or she had had no direct role in producing. In other words, not only did the move to an agricultural society lay the foundations of the Industrial Revolution, but it set the pattern for the dilemmas that became acute for us with the Industrial Revolution. In short, there is a dilemma at the heart of human identity itself. It was first summoned from dormancy by the move to an agricultural way of life and has become acute in the modern era as a result of the Industrial Revolution and the Enlightenment. The dilemma is simple and familiar to all: the more we try to shape the world to the end of human fulfilment, the more we seem to be in danger of destroying humanity, both as an abstract quality and concretely, as a species. Perhaps, indeed, that is too simple a formulation. At least we can say this formulation of the dilemma is widely recognised and deeply felt.

Another way of putting this is that the human world is an ever more complex, ever more precarious balance of mutual spiritual blackmail between a proliferation of opposed forces. Somehow, the keys to our greatest weaknesses always fall into the hands of our enemies, and there is stalemate only because, meanwhile, the keys to their weaknesses have fallen into our hands. The stalemate is not entirely static. Things tip like a see-saw—a multi-lateral see-saw— and there are many disastrous spillages and rash moves. But somehow, so far, tilting this way and that way with breathtaking swerves and lurches, and even while incurring incidental damage and suffering on a scale that makes the mind whirl, the balance has been maintained sufficiently that there has not been utter collapse. Some people even find a time and place to relax, and some to prosper, in the midst of this great teetering and tottering. What we call the freedoms of the Western world, even such freedoms as rights for gays and lesbians, are safe-guarded by ruthless economic monopoly and the lion's share of nuclear weaponry. So our morals are compromised, and our enemy has custody of this weakness in some secret, spiritual way that always translates, in the world, into the language of a peculiar tactical and moral advantage. But, on their side, while they think our freedoms a moral cesspit, they rely on our weaponry, our trade, even our political ideas. And so we, correspondingly, have custody of their weakness.

The injunction to love one's enemy is sometimes seen as promising the triumph of a transcendently generous spirit over the stalemate of reason, but loving one's enemy is perfectly consonant with reason, or, rather, hating them is a form of unreason. I'm thinking now of how the spirit of the dilemma that became acute with the Industrial Revolution has manifested itself since the 1960s (in echoes of various historical revolutions). If one identifies oneself as a member of the counter-culture, and prizes that identity above all else, it's perfectly clear that one owes a great debt to the culture to which one runs counter. If one believes that rebellion is good, then it is perfectly clear that the privilege of being good is a gift from the authority against which one rebels. The enemy has given the rebel his very soul—of course he should love his enemy. But he cannot do this, and here is where the disease sets in. Authority tells us what is right. Authority is bad. Rebellion is good. It is right to rebel. And so, we come full circle, and rebellion, telling us what is right, is authority. At this point rebellion should tell the truth, discard the rebel badge, and simply make the natural transformation, to authority. Or else it can tell the truth, rebel against itself, and implode. But what usually happens is that it lies, pretending it has no authority, but insisting it is right, and so the lies spread, infecting everything. Rebellion becomes eternal, and thus devoted to an eternal lie.

Laurie Penny, online feminist, decrees that "all men benefit from sexism" and does not have to support the statement with a molecule of evidence. We have entered into a kind of Gnosticism, with the righteousness of rebellion guaranteeing certain conclusions in advance, so that even the implied miracle of knowing the circumstance of every single man on the planet does not appear to cause the least embarrassment to the sloganeer, whose certainty is even such that it will brook no dissent. Since rebellion is eternal, and rebellion is good, we cannot ask whether equality has been achieved. Equality must never be admitted to have been achieved. Her statement is given as a universal and eternal truth and research is irrelevant. It is part of the eternal rebellion, which requires eternal oppression, and therefore it must be true, and any who question it must be oppressors, and bad.

In short, once rebellion becomes the basis of one's identity, it contradicts itself. The battle fought under this flag of self-contradiction has brought a choking smog to the intellectual life of the modern world, and from there the pollution has, by unobserved increments, come to taint every aspect of modern existence.

And this brings me back to stupidity and pop music.

Controversies are bruited abroad with hysterical force and, being essentially empty, require constant replacement with shriller and more degraded versions of the same. Somewhere in this cacophony of echoes, last year, I came upon the apparent controversy between white rapper Eminem and the younger, female artist, Iggy Azalea. I hesitated over what word to use to designate the latter, and settled on 'artist'. There is much I could say about this use of the word. I don't have much understanding of the genre, but even I know that the term 'rapper' can only be applied to Iggy Azalea as part of the fawning doublespeak argot of television presenters, who misappropriate all vital meanings in order to advance the cause of ignorance. 'Singer' was also clearly inappropriate in this case, and even the word 'entertainer' suggested an honourable guild and a more profound mode of creative expression than that in which Iggy Azalea operates. And so I was forced to use 'artist', another item in the current doublespeak lexicon, on the one hand denoting Olympian cultural achievement in music (it's always music), but in fact only applied to degenerate egoists who would be considered imbeciles by their colleagues in any other workplace and any other line of work. It is a use of the word 'artist' that reminds me of Woody Allen's derision of the idea of awards for rock music.

Anyway, the nub of the controversy was this. In a freestyle rap section on the track 'Vegas', Eminem appears to be imagining a scenario in which he rapes Iggy Azalea. The words, "You don't wanna blow that rape whistle on me" appear at some point, as well as the command (presumably not a request) that Iggy "suck[s] my fucking dick while I take a shit".

Iggy "hit back", to use the cut-and-paste language of the media, with a tweet in which she said she was "tired of the old men threatening young women thing" and "into the young women making lots of $$s thing".

Now that I write this down, it all seems trivial and exhausted. No doubt, it is. And yet there are riches to be had in pumping such stories up with the steroids of provocation and prurience, and auctioning them in a spectacular market of scandal to an apparently dazzled public.

I mean 'spectacular' in the literal sense rather than the hyperbolic sense in which it is generally used—as descriptive rather than implying a positive judgement. Nonetheless, something about this particular item in the sale of scandals must have intrigued me and made me think that there was something to consider, after all, in the spectacle. Since my dream of Sadie, I have suddenly remembered the brief Eminem versus Iggy Azalea feud, and the memory has been accompanied by an unaccountable feeling of poignant tenderness and melancholy, as if some ancient and legendary love affair were suddenly renewed in the deepest, most responsive recesses of my ancient and juvenile heart, and its agony and longing echoed in me with fresher life than ever before, so that I can see the broken heart of existence now even in the sports pages at the backs of daily newspapers.

Of course, the feminist movement is not primarily responsible for the cultural debacle that has taken place as a result of the demolition of all cultural standards, but it has joined in with the general looting and pillaging in a way that has ultimately been to its own disadvantage. That Eminem, whose renown rests on a finely honed skill in reciting illiterate doggerel at great speed and interleaving crude braggadocio with scatological playground taunts, his targets chosen according to the caprices of personal vendetta rather than an even vaguely informed sense of justice—that such a person should receive international awards and be fêted as a cultural figure, is surely a result of standards being razed to the ground in the name of equality (and those most vocal for equality almost always seem to wish to make things level by dragging down rather than lifting up). We know very well that Eminem's ascendancy to stardom is facilitated and even artificially buoyed by the prohibition on judgement—"*Il est interdit d'interdire.*" To dismiss Eminem as being uneducated and talentless would be viewed as elitist.

Maybe it's worth dividing education from talent here. Eminem has talent. By talent I mean the ability to apply oneself with dexterity (manual or otherwise) and imagination to a particular endeavour. Without education, however, it is hard to judge the worth of what one applies oneself to, or to have much notion of the real possibilities of talent. The mention of education in this context is likely to make people recoil in automatic distaste. They will think of school exams and associate this, in turn, with a sense of shackled uniformity. But by 'education' I do not mean something with any necessary connection to our schools, whose standards are among the many standards of our time to have been sabotaged in the name of egalitarianism. In its true sense, education will not create uniformity, but liberate from it. In any case, to criticise the education of someone like Eminem usually means to invite the knee-jerk defence, "What's wrong with Eminem?" The question behind this question is, "Why shouldn't Eminem take a place in the universe along with everything else?" And though the shorter version of the question—the surface question—is so well worn it is like a rut in the road of colloquial speech, we resort to it because embedded in the lip of that rut is a fragment of flint that still sparks a little wisdom from passing wheels. The wisdom is of a mystical cast—the gentler and more anonymous side of wisdom. Holy shit! This exclamation is a faint echo in the west of the knowledge of masters in the east that the Dao is not less present in excrement than in the highest empyrean. Or, to name names, there is Emerson again, telling us, for instance, that, "The poorest experience is rich enough for all the purposes of expressing thought."

There is Blake, too, who tells us that, seen with purified eyes, all things are infinite. Why shouldn't we see eternity in Eminem as we might—Blake tells us—in a grain of sand?

This is compelling, but the same problems seem to arise here as always arise when we say in a moment of hope and inspiration, "Anything goes!" Let us grant that anything goes—nonetheless, anything, as has been often observed, is not everything. With everything, there is no need to choose. With anything, we must. And then, if anything goes, my disdain towards Eminem goes with equal force of validity as Eminem himself.

But let me be clear, my 'disdain' in this case was for the sake of argument. I, too, would cleave to Eminem with a kind of cosmic fondness. It is true that there is a wild, feel-good liberation, like the first rush in the brain of a new drug, to saying yes, without reservation, and to embracing Eminem. That most excellent feeling is of rendering everything level and good by being co-conspirators in weakness, like diseased angels frisking and lolling together in the tangle of soiled bedsheets. After all, the dungeon cells of Hell are illuminated by the light of Heaven; but this is because, like the Moon, they have no light of their own. And still, when people express a preference for moonlight over daylight, we understand them all too well.

Let me ask the question that, after years of wallowing in the vice and disease of a moonlit dungeon, I cannot help but ask: If anything goes, why did we choose Eminem? Didn't the vastness of 'anything' contain anything better? Oh, and in the art world, which today harbours the most sibilantly hissing fiends among all the sophists and apologists, the view is represented by the established, repetitive lineage from Duchamp to Beuys and beyond, for whom 'anything can be art'. What seductive permissiveness! Why is it that this 'anything' of egalitarianism gravitates always to lower and lower regions? If *anything*, sooner or later, we must ask why, in the lines about Iggy Azalea, Eminem didn't have her actually eating his shit while her younger brother sucked his dick. And then, why not be raping her freshly killed corpse? And then why not keep her in a dungeon first and rape the corpses of the babies sired upon her? Why not? What's wrong with Eminem? Holy shit!

So the problems of equality are the problems of anything goes. Equality allowed Eminem, and it is in the name of equality that Iggy Azalea fights back, equality fighting equality in a degraded rout.

Eminem is the rebel, but he will be trumped and trounced, perhaps, by the rebellion of feminism, by the enemy needed to ensure his valued identity as a rebel. But he won't quite be vanquished, even if trounced. To ensure its own righteousness, feminism also needs enemies like Eminem. Although they will not admit it, they must bring him back from any exile into which they send him. How else will they ensure the eternity of their rebellion?

There's a problem here, of course. I mean, in my analysis. I am taking Iggy Azalea and her exchange with Eminem as representative of feminism, and perhaps this is a lazy identification. But there is a constant shell game played with these terms to avoid responsibility and to take credit. Feminism represents all women, we'll be told, but not all women represent feminism. Let's not get lost in the shell game. The pattern exists, whatever we call it.

When someone says, "This is not science", or "This is not feminism", it seems that they mean—or should mean—"This is not how science should be", or "This is not how feminism should be", though it might be what passes for such things in the world. It is important to make such a distinction. It is also important to ask, "Is there something in feminism that prevents it from becoming what it should be?" This is the question that apologists dodge when they say, "This is not feminism."

Let's look at Iggy's tweet again. An Eminem track called 'Vegas' is leaked, containing what appears to be a dis directed at Iggy Azalea in which the word 'rape' is used. Everyone from Hollywoodlife. com to the *Guardian* seizes upon the salacious bit of clickbait that Eminem has so generously provided them, with the obligatory edginess of the true professional. Of course, subtly or unsubtly, they weight their unproofread articles morally in favour of Iggy's witless riposte, so that they can profit doubly—first, from giving people a cheap serving of scandal over which to drool, and second, from posing as bastions of righteousness by allowing the spasm of Pavlovian indignation to pass through the mechanisms of their public organs of expression. And at the end of this absurd operation, this is what is dangled in front of us as the moral of the piece:

> i'm tired of the old men threatening young
> women thing and into the young women
> making lots of $$s thing. zzzz

By contrast Eminem's 'Guts Over Fear'—just for example—shows, at least, some self-knowledge. In one verse there is even an analysis of the way creativity feeds on conflict, often enough necessitating cruelty. Eminem recognises that he has used his rage, and therefore his enemies, for his own creative purposes. He is even afraid his identity depends upon this rage, that without it the lights will flicker out in that place he is both ashamed and proud of, which is his symbolic home: the trailer park.

The tweet from Iggy Azalea shows no such self-knowledge. The old men are not credited with the part they have in her identity as enemies. She is simply "tired of" them. The messages ends on Z's. She is asleep—even in her triumph. But take away her enemy in this case, and what are you left with? ". . . the young women making lots of $$s thing." There is, of course, nothing wrong with young women making money—certainly not more than anyone else. But is this the height of human aspiration now? I wonder how many people this message reaches, how many human heads it dangles over as if it were the brightest of guiding stars. And what is Iggy getting $ for, exactly? Karaoke rap and the usual photoshopped soft-porn-as-empowerment in the videos. To do justice, I suppose I should try to see infinity in Iggy, as I am able to in Eminem, but there is something so wrong, so unmusical and uncreative, about all her productions that I can't bring myself to try this wrenching experiment, which seems like the analogue for a bad drug if ever there was one, and will have to leave the attempt to others. At least Eminem has the dawning light of self-knowledge on his side, and there is hope in that.

But to remain impartial, I should say, neither side wins. The pendulum swings between Eminem and Iggy, or whatever yin and yang are the chosen representatives of our culture at present, and as it swings it descends. There is thesis and there is antithesis, but there is no synthesis, only this oscillation descending into Hell, because we have staked our identities on rebellion and rejected the higher principle by which oscillation would rise.

The liberal hates the racist for hating this ethnic group or that. All that matters is that we know who is good and who bad, and that we are the former and they are the latter, and so we descend in endless judgement, endless revenge.

I judge those who judge, and thereby have my revenge on the vengeful. I descend, too, inescapably.

The descent, in its treacherous way, is easy, the ascent, ten thousand times more difficult.

I am something like a murderer. That 'something like' is an evasion. If I am a murderer, I must find out exactly what kind of murderer I am. There simply is no short cut out of Hell, and if we do not climb, we descend.

There is something I must do before I can do anything of value. I must climb out of this pit, inch by torturous inch, up the sheer, unyielding rock face of the truth.

At least I caught a ray of light that shattered on the lip of the pit so far above. I am afraid there is no choice now but to try and reach it.

X. In the Midst of Life

DAMIEN looked again at the dedication in the front of the slim paperback volume of verse, written in Sadie's never-to-be-repeated script, the poise and everydayness of which suggested inexhaustibility, as if there might be endlessly generated samples of this handwriting, with endlessly variable, but still characteristic messages, each traceable to one, idiosyncratic source, each unique. The dedication read:

> To, Damien:
> You can say you knew me before I was famous.
> Don't get jealous and I won't disown you. Deal?
> Sadie B. xx

Damien held the pages up to the morning light that near invisibly flooded all that was visible. In the calm, uncountable rays from the skylight, his vision was so clear that he seemed to see every ordinary thing with pristine completeness. He saw the texture of the paper, wavy with wood-pulp craters. He flicked the pages. On these thin wafers of crisp, off-white, organic material, some shadow of the genetic coding of eternity had been precisely captured in lines of printed ink. A snatch of phrasing glimpsed here and there set off associations in Damien's mind like birds startled suddenly from a tree. He thought again what a miraculous thing typography was. There was no concretely fixed form for any single letter, but a font was a style that made itself both visible and invisible by fixing a kind of cross-section of the eternal forms of the letters—font, of course, because it was a spring, an ungraspable nothingness of fecund style.

His attention was snagged for a moment or two, as if on the fishhook barbs of the serifs, by the following lines:

> Compatible with every system,
> As long as the systems are the same.

That was from a poem called 'Happiness'. 'Happiness' was on a verso page. On the recto page opposite was a poem he had noticed before, called 'Concrete', which he judged to be a companion piece to the poem preceding it.

The poem began with a couple of irregular stanzas, seemingly serving the role of curtain-raisers for the poem's stage. The first stanza ran:

> We know what we're here for now.
> It's obvious: concrete.
> It makes all things possible.
> It makes all things new.

Then his eye dropped to the penultimate verse:

> There is no substance more like happiness than
>   concrete,
> Taming every grid-mapped street to sameness,
> Removing nature from beneath our feet,
> And every bus-stop electronic poster blushes that
>   we're blameless, blameless.

It was strange, he thought as he read these lines, how alike he and Sadie really were, and strange that he had never noticed it before. It seemed obvious now that there had been a shared background to the conversation that was their relationship. While she had been alive, he had thought of her as opaque in her difference to him. Maybe all differences are overestimated. But then he thought of how "sameness" in the poem was a half-rhyme to "taming", and he grew distressed at the very pleasantness of the sameness, as if in danger of drowning and dissolving in syrup.

"Blameless, blameless," he recited to himself. They sounded like the words of a betrayal, but he could not think what the betrayal might be.

Instead, he thought again of Sadie. He still kept her last messages on his mobile phone. How were those messages different now that she was dead than they were to when she was alive? They were signs of life when first received, and he could reply to them and expect more. What, really, had changed? Something had, but it remained a kind of puzzle to the brain. The volume of poetry was the same puzzle on a larger scale, or at a slower speed. The poems had passed from one pair of living hands to another—they had a source. Where was that source? He could almost feel the life of it, as if he were trying to pick a lock, knowing it was possible, but also that it was not possible for *him*. Time now stood between himself and Sadie like an airlock. Many things remained in the range of his now, but she had slipped out of it. One day, he would slip out of it, too. What it was like to slip out of one's own now was perhaps the greatest mystery of human life. She could not, he thought, be less real, less alive, than he, though how real and alive that was he did not know; it was just that she was at a remove from him now. It was as if she had passed him her book of poems via the pass-through tray of a bank counter. When the tray was open on her side, for her to drop the book in, it was closed on his; when it was open on his side, for him to pick the book up, it was closed on hers.

However, he would have to lay aside this incredible object and go to work. He was in danger of being late if he lingered much longer this morning. The book would remain in its particular pocket of time and space, which would intersect with his occasionally. And all the little pocketed details of the universe would *tick tick tick* like time-bombs of significance, none of which have ever yet exploded in the mind of a human being, and whose final explosion in synchronicity might be heaven or hell.

He consoled himself with the disciplined rituals that prepared him to leave the flat and efface himself in a way that work still made a sheer necessity.

At the hospital, he just about managed to float on his duties without losing control and sinking. Experienced now, he felt a certain confidence even in the midst of constant pressure, so that he could respond to the world automatically with one part of himself, and wait passively with another.

Early in the afternoon, as the fatigue that shifted from one place to another within the confines of his circadian rhythm was making a comeback, and settling beneath his eyes like leaden bruises, Damien was attending to a patient by the name of Fergus Kinghan. Fergus had recently been moved from intensive care to a small private room off the general ward. He had first been admitted after stepping off the kerb in front of a car. If the car had not swerved at the last moment, it seemed he might not have survived. As it was, he had broken bones in his right leg, his left arm and shoulder, as well as broken ribs, and various other injuries, external and internal. He had been placed, for the time being, in isolation from the general ward because he was vulnerable to infection. Damien's job was to wash him, help him go to the toilet, brush his teeth, take his pulse and so on.

Fergus was scarred, bruised and shattered. His bandages appeared to be holding him together, like medical Sellotape. As he was tending to Fergus, Damien had the impression that the mixture of severe injury and medical attention had rendered Fergus a human archaeological dig. There were strata between the surface level of life and the deep, underground reservoirs of death, and all these strata had been made visible in Fergus at once.

Fergus remained largely silent throughout, occasionally indicating that he felt pain and answering questions in monosyllables. After Damien had taken his pulse, however, he spoke without prompting in a tone that suggested everything else had been a formality suffered with restrained impatience, and this at last was the informal and the essential thing.

"I wish I was dead . . . I wish I had died."

Damien was struck by the self-correction in the change of tense. He discerned with a distinctness at first puzzling to him that Fergus was seizing a perhaps-only chance to present a hopeless petition. Then he understood.

"You did it on purpose?"

Fergus nodded and the small, private room was, at this, suffused with a secret that crept burningly close to the skin like a particularly unpleasant fart trapped inside clothing.

It seemed obvious that Fergus had told no one else. It was almost impossible to translate this hot, intimate stench into an official situation. At least, once translated, its essence would be lost. Damien felt himself stepping silently to the side of his role of nurse on duty.

"Why?"

Fergus's eyes flicked up to meet Damien's. It seemed he had sensed something in Damien's tone—an unexpected permission—and now wished to verify that same something in his eyes. He appeared to confirm what he had looked for, to identify it as an opportunity, and his gaze focused with anger.

"Does it matter? Look at me. I should have died."

His words were released in a white-hot hiss, exactly as if steam had been allowed to escape after pressure had built up.

There was blame in the words. Damien was aware that, in some way, the blame might attach to him. This was one possibility among many. More by a sudden sense of unwieldiness than by skill, as if he were made of heavy blocks, Damien felt himself evading the blame.

"You might be surprised what you can recover from."

The words were calm—so calm it was not clear whether they were meant as an admonishment or a reassurance.

"This world is made for fucking optimists," continued Fergus. His words still had something of the momentum of escaping steam, but the pressure that had expelled his previous words had already dropped a little as he made his meaning clearer. Still, he articulated his meaning with the perfect marriage of tone and diction that occurs sometimes with the knowledge that one's moment has come and one's lines must be delivered, like the loosing of well-notched arrows. "No money, you can't afford therapy. No therapy, you can't hold down a job. Mental health is for the rich. All these fucking optimists—they run everything, changing the world to suit other optimists like them. If you're not an optimist, you're just weak—nothing. They squeeze the rest of us out—the ones who just wanted to live our lives. We can't. We can't do it any-more. They can keep their filthy fucking world. They've won."

"And if you win, you'll become one of them—is that what you mean?"

"I don't want to win. I just want to . . . to live."

Damien nodded at what constituted a confession.

"I don't want to win; I don't want to lose. I don't want Heaven; I don't want Hell. I just want to live."

A sense of comfort spread from the disclosure of this truth-behind-the-truth.

"But I can't," Fergus resumed. "Because of the optimists. They've got the monopoly now. If you live and you're not one of them, you're automatically a loser. You have to beg everything from them and they call you a hypocrite when you do. They still want you to hang around, though. They need losers to know they're winners. What's the point? I wish I had died."

Damien nodded again.

"Well . . . you won't have to do anything for a while. This is no-man's-land. No losers or winners here."

Somehow Fergus's moment had passed. That was it. Only he and Fergus had witnessed it.

Before leaving the private room, Damien paused a moment to look out of the single window. They were high enough that he got some sense of the concrete neverendingness of London. The roofs and façades floated in the afternoon as if paving the sky. Damien remembered, then, the girl who had walked on her hands that morning three or four years ago along the edge of the roof above the Factory courtyard. A strange feeling reared up in him at this memory. It was like the feeling left to him after waking from the dream of Sadie's grave, but also, somehow, different.

After work, Damien travelled home on the Tube, changing at Bank for the DLR. On the first leg of his journey, on the Northern Line, exhausted, he gave himself up to the seat he filled, and his usual nervous cogitation on what must be done—next and in general—fell away, allowing something with the involuntary fluidity of a dream state to rise to the surface and take its place. His mind was filled with Fergus. There had been something un-resolved about their exchange, and, though he was still awake and lucid, it seemed it was the part of him that dreamed that had identified the exchange as also being important. In the world of dream, this was the front-page news, and the newspaper of dream appealed to Damien now as more poignant and genuine than the printed news belonging to the noisy world of so-called waking, where humans clustered in the safety of shallow commonality.

The pages of the dream-edited newspaper spread themselves before him and as he sank into the text he began to gain some understanding of the burning issue that was exposed there for examination. Fergus had already asked him the essential, the *simple* question, and he had not answered it. The question was, what is the point? The dreampaper posed that question again, as its sensational headline, beneath which were pictures of Fergus struck by a car, Fergus unconscious in intensive care, and Fergus conscious but still battered in the private room. This was not merely a question pertaining to the individual known as Fergus Kinghan. This was the *Dream-News of the World*.

Of course, Damien had answers—that to ask for the point was to miss the point, for instance. That 'the point' was life, and therefore the word 'point' itself was a mistake, since to isolate any single speck of life as meaningful was to deprive it of context and therefore meaning. Yes, he had that kind of answer. But this did not satisfy the question that had been asked. What the question reduced down to was, why? Why should Fergus live? Why had he been born? Wasn't it unreasonable to expect him to go on fighting a struggle that must end in defeat without even knowing the answer to that question? Why try to persuade him that he must live?

He could exchange the word 'life' for the word 'God', thereby indicating that life was not a closed system, but included a transcendent aspect, but however true this might be, it would mean nothing to someone who was not already galvanised by an experience of God. If Damien was honest, he was not exactly galvanised himself. His recent experience had left him with a feeling of redundancy that he found reflected in many time-honoured mystical texts—the feeling that creation needed God, but God did not need creation. If so, why place any moral obligations on the unnecessary creatures of an unnecessary creation? The obligation to live at all, for instance?

Damien just remembered to get off the train at Bank to walk to the embarkation point for the DLR, but even as he walked, the dream-thoughts persisted, lapping in his consciousness like a rising tide. A Lewisham-bound train was already at the DLR platform. The doors were open. He stepped through and found an empty seat.

It came back to him that Fergus had singled out optimists as the enemy. Who did he mean? Identifying the right enemy was one of the great problems of life, and Fergus had clearly done his best. Still, part of his defeat was that 'the optimists' was open to interpretation. Damien had some idea who he had meant, and he also had his own idea about who 'the optimists' were. He guessed from what Fergus had said that their ideas would overlap, but that they would not be identical. That overlap would most conspicuously include the corporate leaders, the people of vision and enterprise—the Zuckerbergs and Bezoses. The basic scum of the Earth. But he suspected that he and Fergus would also share a horror of the transhumanists—the grinning geeks who would be gods, the invincible Americans, tone-deaf to the useless, melancholy beauty that sighs in the human spirit, the slick egotists who planned to eliminate death and all its subsidiary consolations. He further suspected that Fergus would reject the principle behind Damien's abhorrence of these people. The principle was simple. The optimist who did not believe in an objective good—which was to say, God—was a fiend, since the good about which he was optimistic would always be a subjective and a selfish good. But the truth was that most people were simply muddle-headed, believing they were one thing, but acting according to the principles of some other thing. It was just unfortunate the muddle-headedness allowed the real fiends to prosper.

And the upshot was that people like Fergus felt themselves to be helpless victims and were not even quite sure who had done precisely what unspeakable thing to them. Why should anyone have to play for time, when it was only time that could be played for? People like Fergus were only ahead of the curve in having despaired of such a game, surely? People strained against the fatal tendency of time like salmon leaping upstream, but who really knew why? It seemed that the greatest mystery of existence was the unparalleled preciousness of what could only be lost. In fact, the entire medical profession, of which Damien was a part, was predicated on the idea that what will inevitably pass is nonetheless infinitely precious, and it was they who were the great upholders of this playing for time, even though most of the members of that profession with whom Damien was acquainted did not believe in an objective good. By Damien's principle, they, too, were fiends. Perhaps Fergus would understand that, after all.

Was there really no reason to perpetuate this life, even with an objective good granted? Damien thought of Sadie and of her swansong volume of poetry. That had been bequeathed him as if by the pass-through tray between life and death. Fergus was like a package that had been forced through the same tray, once from life to death, then from death back to life. The tray afforded only a constricted space for such transference, and Fergus had been damaged in this motion. But what if the transition from life to death and from death to life were painless and without effort? What if it were as simple as flicking a switch? Easy come, easy go. What would people choose then, assuming they could compare experiences of life and death?

But as Damien contemplated such easy transitions, something else crept into his thoughts. It was the untransmittable secret at the heart of Fergus's complaint. The burning stench of the secret was also a shadow that, amorphous though it was, appeared eternally non-biodegradable. Mere ease might not be sufficient to defuse it. In all likelihood, Fergus would recover despite himself. Then, in order to survive, he would have to suppress or abandon his current viewpoint. Or he would champion it hypocritically, and it would be entertained by others hypocritically, or ignored. Why hypocritically? Because if one took sides with life, one should live, and if one took sides with death, one should die. Fergus wanted to take sides with death and still live, at least in order to perpetuate his self-defeating complaint about life. But that was it—that was his kinship with Fergus! He was the very opposite of this. He wanted to take sides with life, and die. But whatever lived, lived; whatever died, died. This was an outrage, though it was a logical necessity. And so the indestructible stench.

Everything is, or nothing is. The universe crystallised inside Damien's mind so that no motion was possible; no thought was, either. Then the crystal universe shattered into a vaporous void.

From the void emerged the image from before, of a pass-through tray in a bank's counter. The tray was open on the side of life and closed on the side of death; then it was open on the side of death and closed on the side of life. As this back-and-forth transmitted its binary code, the image changed. It became rooftops. A girl was walking on her hands across them, nearer and then farther away, as if in doing so she were shifting tiles in a sliding puzzle.

Balance. Balance. Balance.

He repeated the word in his mind as he disembarked from the DLR, descended the stairs to the Brakeburn Street exit, passed through the ticket gate and the pedestrian tunnel beneath the railway bridge, and felt the tired ease of a worker almost home as he walked the short way back to his studio. He repeated the word as if afraid he might fall over even now, on the firm, level ground.

When he got back to the studio, he climbed up and out onto the roof. It had been a while since he had done this. He noticed that he enjoyed the feel of there being nothing above his head but the air and the clouds. Of course, there were other things above him, in all probability—clusters of satellites so that people could be instructed where to drive their cars by automated voices. He didn't want to think about that at the moment, though. He looked out over the courtyard and the rooftop opposite as the evening continued in all the symptoms of its slow decline towards night.

No human activity of any note, however, took place in Damien's field of vision. The question that Fergus had posed for him, like check in a game of chess, remained unresolved. It seemed that the world would get along very well without people.

He climbed back down inside, shivering a little from the pure feeling of chill on his skin.

Idly, he sat at what had once been his workbench and flipped open his laptop. He seldom received personal e-mail these days, but he checked a message forum where he occasionally posted long polemics that people generally ignored, or to which they responded by picking out some incidental detail as if it were his essential thesis. Somehow, he could never bring them round even to seeing the point he was trying to make, so that whether they accepted or rejected it was forever unknown.

The title of a recently active message thread caught his eye. It was, "Human extinction: how will the human race die out?" This was the same news story that dream had chosen for the front page in the newspaper of Damien's soul. What concerned Fergus Kinghan concerned the whole human race. His question was theirs.

Damien was familiar with the tone in which the question of the message thread's title was asked. On the one hand, it had about it an affected amusement, as if the matter of human extinction were a trivial guessing game and we could all prove how superior we were by playing the game with jaded smiles, or even with a certain amount of devilish glee, before yawning (or, alternatively, for the devilish-glee types, nodding with the satisfaction of untouchable prophets) and moving on to something else, such as quotations from E.M. Cioran. On the other hand, there was the intention of alarm—and a peculiarly self-contradictory alarm. It was like a blow delivered with the exclamation, "Take that!" But to what purpose? The hopelessness was calculated to be so urgent and complete as to brook no denial—the alarm must be raised. But because it was so complete, the hopelessness itself denied, the alarm having been raised, that anything could be done. Both panic and apathy were made mandatory by this alarm. Panic and don't stop panicking—but don't ever dare to hope.

All this Damien knew intimately from perusing these message boards countless times over the years.

He scrolled through the various amused, gleeful, jaded and morally indignant suggestions as to how the human race would, or should, soon, or eventually, come to an unpleasant or longed-for or insignificant end.

After skim-reading some of the comments, he clicked 'play' on an embedded YouTube video. The video was four or five minutes long and appeared to be the third in a series of clips that together formed an interview with a glaciologist who had been doing fieldwork in Antarctica. The glaciologist, a curly-haired man for whom English was apparently not his first language, spoke with the friendly engagement natural to humans when they interact with others towards whom they feel good will—an engagement that is frequently a default of social temperament. However, despite the tone of quotidian cheerfulness this engagement brought to his voice, the burden carried by his words meant that his tone was straining beneath the weight. The Western Antarctic Ice Sheet was melting, he said, faster than anything that had previously been recorded. Because this was unprecedented in human experience, it was hard to predict what would happen, at least in terms of the timescale, but he wished that other scientists would put to one side the rather minimal doubts as to whether the changes taking place were anthropogenic and ongoing. The situation was serious enough and certain enough that to doubt it now was irresponsible rather than responsible. He was frustrated—his voice remained even as he said so—that the message wasn't getting out to people that, really, the place is falling apart before our eyes.

"The place" meant the Western Antarctic Ice Sheet, presumably, but, non-specific as the phrase was, and appearing as it did within the ominous, understated context of the nitty-gritty of climate change, it seemed unmistakably to take on the meaning of planet Earth.

Damien felt the usual unbearable hollowness as he listened to these words—an inarticulable hollowness that he supposed was nonetheless familiar to millions of other human beings hearing these words or words to the same effect. What was the root of this hollowness, the root of the tongue that spoke the fear? Survival. Everything might be lost.

But beneath even this primal essence was Fergus's terrible, but strangely buoyant question: why?

Again: why?

Why must we survive?

And then came a curious counter-question.

Why are we trying to kill ourselves?

Damien felt a strange sensation as he allowed the question to settle in his mind. It was as if he were turning right at a certain junction where he had been conditioned to turn always left. The outline of his conditioning was still trying to turn left—the outline that had been his outline. Actually, there was nothing to prevent him turning right except the peculiar feeling of his two outlines becoming separated and disassociated. As he blurred into a double image, the raw outline that remained his, now shorn of conditioning, underwent a nausea and unbearable discomforting dullness, not unlike withdrawal symptoms. This was the magnetism of the outline of the conditioning, which he had almost jettisoned, but which could return and reassert itself with will-sapping ease, bringing the deep, paralysing comfort that necessitated more and more comfort. He could let that outline return, or he could simply walk away from it—take that right turning, and keep walking into the freedom of the unknown.

Why are we trying to kill ourselves?

Because we are afraid of the freedom of the unknown.

The end of the human race threatens. The uncertainty is as intolerable to us as injustice, and so we try to turn it into a certainty. Mortal, we are bound to die, but we don't know when or how. So we try to steal the certainty of death itself by anticipating it.

We quail at death because it menaces our uniqueness, but trying to snare death in our measurements and predictions, we lose that uniqueness ourselves.

We must allow death to be the unknown, and our uniqueness will breathe in it.

The old orthodoxy hid a subtle and fantastic nebula of truth, as if a bald-surfaced egg had cracked before Damien and he saw hatch from it a celestial bird. We must leave the time and the manner of our death to God, and concern ourselves with living.

And so, the unknown is coming, and, in the meantime, there is life. Some might even assert that such a condition is eternal. In which case, we must decide what kind of eternity it will be, waiting forever on the unknown.

That would be his answer to the question why: Because to choose life is to choose freedom; to choose death is to bind oneself. To know death only as a certainty with which one must compete—this was to lose one's very centre; to accept death as the unknown—this was faith in death and oneself.

It was the difficult choice of freedom that must be made. That was the only answer to the recurring hell of the question why.

Damien saw that his hands were trembling.

The blows were not visible blows easy to reconstruct as drama, but one formidable, syncopated truth after another had tempered Damien in reverse from rigidity towards the tremendous flexibility of freedom. The air of freedom was as chill and sweet as the earliest breezes of spring that, in youth, make the hairs prickle on the nape of your neck.

Could he accept such freedom? What would he do with it?

He trembled and sighed.

After standing in thought for some time with the fingers of his right hand resting lightly on the surface of the workbench that now was only a table, he decided that what he would do with his freedom at this moment was to climb up to the platform where his bedding was, to get under the duvet, and to lie there with his eyes closed. He considered for a moment putting on some background music, but remembering that he would have to climb down from his platform in order to act as disc jockey for himself, adjust the volume and so on, he decided against it. Besides, why did he need the insistent noise of other people? He would simply lie there, under the skylight, while the day faded into night and the tender chill of the air increased to seal the completion of the darkness. He would listen in passive absorption to whatever incidental sounds the environment provided. He could not even bring himself to eat something in order to prevent the hunger that would probably intrude before he slept.

He turned off the light and, in the indoor twilight of the studio, climbed the ladder to the platform.

It was hard to tell, he reflected as he tried to find a comfortable position on the mattress, whether choosing to do the easy thing, or to do nothing, was really the exercise of freedom, or whether it was the result of a fear of freedom. He supposed that even when the way to freedom became apparent and accessible in a person's life, habit will always command the gravity of accumulated thought and action so that a free and unbiased choice of freedom will never be made. He further supposed that this was what was happening to him now—the free choice of slavery to habit—though it was unusual for him to lie inactive like this.

In fact, it was very unusual. He had a sense, as he lay there, of remembering something. That is, nothing in particular besides exactly what life is like. He had narrowed his attention for too long, and invested himself too completely in things that were, after all, mere details. It was as if he had been playing a game for decades, and had only just remembered that the game was a diverting but inconsequential way of passing time within a much larger—indeed, boundless—thing called life. Of course, it would be a shame not to play some game or another while he lived, but even this he no longer cared about very much. He didn't care, either, that his lying here might be a choice of slavery or of defeat. He must have chosen it for a reason, and when he wanted something else he would choose something else, if he had a choice, and if he didn't . . . well, why even complete the thought?

There were voices in the courtyard outside as some of the residents of the Factory began to gather for an evening's drinking and dancing. Rain tapped on the skylight in a tiny, gentle volley—once . . . again . . . once more. He shivered, and thought of the emptiness between the clouds above and the upturned glass of the skylight.

The next evening, after work, Damien intended to do the same thing—lie down on his sleeping platform and close his eyes and listen, and drift. This time, however, he decided he should eat first. He made himself a cup of tea and swigged at it while he grilled cheese on toast. When this was almost ready, he decided he was ravenous and remembered a couple of sausages that were probably still edible. He didn't check the best-before date as he didn't want to know. Then he thought he might as well have some beans, too, and emptied a can into a saucepan.

He ate all this at the workbench with a primitive relish that had not been his for some time. He wasn't even sure if it was only hunger that was behind this gustatory, or more exactly, this gut-placatory satisfaction. He felt almost as if the vast unknownness of being alive and physical were expressing itself in this act of consumption, that it was a form of inspiration, like gazing at a sunset and knowing that the grandeur of the colours might prime you to change your life. He almost could not keep up with himself. He smacked his lips, wiped his mouth with his hand.

Sweeping up the tomato sauce with the last corner of the toast, he finished the meal and immediately stood, seeming to stagger a little as if recovering from the energetic and physiological absorption.

He took his plate and cutlery to the sink.

After rinsing the plate a little, he stood motionless and contemplated.

What time of year was this? More broadly, and more specifically, when was this? When was now? There was something delicious about the sense of evening growing ripe and fresh; even in his studio he was aware of it. The sense of freedom that had awakened in him yesterday still had not gone. This was it again, even though he thought he had capitulated to the slavery of habit and defeat. It was almost like something tugging at him; almost like music. And this despite a depressing failure at work earlier in the day. It was altogether strange.

There were, in the courtyard outside, the faint beginnings of the warm hubbub that would, with the darkening of the sky, become first a pronounced and then almost a raucous merriment, as the Factory's own bar, Carnival, drew the artists down from their studios.

Was it a music night tonight? Or would there be comedy? Although he occasionally peered in at the open door, where the heavy old red curtain that made a kind of entrance hall sometimes drew aside to give a glimpse of the counter, the bottles on shelves lit up in the distinctly bohemian gloom, he had only once or twice actually stepped inside, and he was not familiar with the weekly rhythm of events there. He had been put off by the door fee on nights when there was a live performance of some kind, and the red curtain had made the place seem screened to him, and exclusive, like an establishment to which one needed an introduction, though he knew no such introduction was necessary at Carnival. Or perhaps, anyway, having come to the Factory because he had heard the rumour of its convenience and not because he had friends or associates here, he had felt diffident towards the other inhabitants. Moreover, he had been preoccupied, and was keenly aware of having reasons for secrecy in this abode of the curious. Really, he had had little incentive to enter the bar.

Sensing the evening stir and expand, however, he began to feel it would be intolerable to climb to his sleeping platform. Memories were merely drifting clouds that streaked the sky, and the point was, with the sweet fresh air in your nostrils and the meaningless tingle in your blood, to begin life. Each footstep marked a single point of the present, but life fanned out from this point always in all directions, in the vast theatre of air that we called day or night.

If it is to be enticing, possibility must not be too diffuse. The great theatre of air seems to chorus always a collective anthem celebrating that you might go anywhere. But something must be waiting, or anywhere might as well be nowhere. Damien began to conceive the evening now as a colossal oyster. The layered colours and clouds of the sky were the nacre of the inner shell, and around the grit of Carnival a pearl of possibility was being formed. This was where he must go.

Yet, he did not want to go immediately. He suddenly recalled occasions during his teenage years when he would get ready to go out, and how this act of preparation had been, in and of itself, instinctively rather than consciously, a joy disproportionate to what it supposedly preceded. It had been a means of rehearsing to oneself the dramas of identity and of being alive on a temporal stage. In short, it was the natural link between all the imaginative games of childhood and the entrance on to the stage of young adulthood—the very dressing room of the theatre of life.

There was little he could do by way of such preparation now. He shaved, however, over the basin in the corner, and took more care in choosing a shirt than he had since the earliest days of adulthood. If he had owned a necklace or jewellery, he would have put them on, but his mind had been completely absorbed in other things for years, and there was almost nothing, even in this black museum of a studio, with which he could accessorise.

In any case, the act of shaving and choosing a shirt had been a sufficient ritual to signal to his mind that he was about to make an entrance. He took a little time to straighten the collar of the shirt in the splotchy mirror above the basin, checked he had keys and money, and left.

There was a sense of ease in the fact that Carnival was figuratively on his doorstep. He paid the door charge and was given a rubber stamp on the back of his hand by the door attendant, who sat behind a small and rickety desk on which there stood a burning candle, a box for money, some leaflets and the ink-pad for the stamp. When Damien paid his money, the attendant went back to reading a very yellowed paperback edition of Italo Calvino's—unseasonal—*If on a Winter's Night a Traveller* by the candle's sympathetically yellow light.

Damien stepped through the old red curtain and into the bar itself, as cluttered, almost, as the prop room of a theatre, the central space taken by a mismatched assortment of wooden chairs and tables. Tonight there would be music, it seemed, but it was still a little while before the first band would begin, so the place was not yet crowded. Some of the tables were occupied, and people stood in small groups at the sides of the room. Only two people stood at the bar itself. Damien recognised one or two faces, but there was no one here he knew by name. In such an environment, he might have felt the chill of strangeness that some call reality—though he knew now it was one of the lesser gods—had it not been for the melodious freedom that had guided him here, and the sense it bestowed upon him that he was a visiting alien for whom the strangeness was an opportunity rather than a life sentence. Like all visitors from afar, he did not know the local news, the local rules, the accumulated mutual debts of grief, and so the enigmatic expectancy of life's continuous stir—of surface and unknown substance—kept him fascinated.

He approached the bar counter. He would make this concession to local expectations, but all the while he would be free, merely disguised as one of the inmates of custom. When one of the bar staff noticed him, he pointed to a bottle of continental lager and asked how much it was. The answer surprised him. He had forgotten how expensive drinks were in London. He would have liked to refuse in disgust, not so much because the drink was overpriced as because it was, by weight of conformity, almost mandatory in this society to waste one's money in this unthinking way. But he could afford it and the protest would gain him nothing. He didn't want to care about 'the principle of the thing' tonight.

Taking the bottle and glass he was given, Damien turned to face the room, the movement expressing a sense of prospecting for the opportunities whose promise had brought him. What he saw was merely one here-and-now cranny of a world of indifferent autonomy. He remembered that this process was familiar—the feeling of having just arrived on Earth, and the excitement of the implications, followed by painful disappointment as the true specifics of an anticipated situation are encountered. Nothing here seemed aware that it was supposed to be instrumental in realising his general mood of inspiration in the form of concrete but spiritually expansive events. He was faced with a stifling dilemma. He couldn't see a way of introducing himself into any of the established group dynamics without awkwardness and humiliation, but to go and sit on his own was a defeat, which he would be compelled to disguise to himself by pretending he was patiently waiting for the right moment. Finally, this is what he did, too much aware of his self-deception to be fooled by it, yet unable entirely to dispense with it.

There was a small table near the wall, empty except for a lit candle inserted in the mouth of a bottle. Damien put his drink down here and pulled out, for himself, one of the two stools half tucked beneath it. Once seated, he began to think about his disappointment at work, as if he had come to this candlelit table precisely to contemplate this subject.

The sense of freedom that had come to him with such subtlety and profundity yesterday had stoked in him a desire to work changes in the world around him. The desire had been with him vividly today, so that when he had seen Fergus again it had become urgent in seeking an outlet for expression. With what appeared to Damien to be a certain degree of calculation, Fergus had, in a halting voice whose flatness was given shape only by the tension of its pauses, asked Damien what advice he would give—practical advice—to someone determined to kill himself. What Fergus meant, of course, was that he expected a medical person to know a painless means of suicide. This, Damien reflected, had been latent in the confession of attempted suicide; it had been partly this that had given it that uneasy, secret quality that seemed to constrict the breathing. He wondered if Fergus could smell death on him somehow, if he saw in Damien a secretly sympathetic figure to whom he could make such appeals. He was sure that Fergus had not spoken like this to the doctor in whose charge he had been placed.

Damien took this appeal as a test, but did not know how to meet it. The sense of freedom did not quite retreat, but it found no voice in Fergus's presence. He managed, more curtly than he had intended, to say that it was not his job to facilitate suicide. The freedom, though, was like a tide beating against a wall. If only he had spoken the first word of that freedom, it might have forced a leak in that wall which would have grown under the pressure of the tide, but there seemed to be no gap through which that first word could escape.

What would the first word be?

He didn't know.

So Fergus was left stranded because Damien deferred to Fergus's pessimism on the one hand and his own public duty on the other. The dovetailing of these two things was remarkable.

It was because of that failure with Fergus, thought Damien as he returned from these recollections to his current surroundings; that was why he could not quite meet and embrace, tonight, the beckoning possibilities of this flickering, interactive world.

Damien at first tried to make his drink last throughout the short set of the unremarkable first band, then wondered why he was doing so. He knocked back what remained and went to the bar for another.

When he returned to his seat, they played their final song, and an interval followed, in which Damien's feeling of vacancy redoubled, since this was when others were taking a chance to go outside for cigarettes and chat.

After a while, he saw with relief that this vacancy was about to be filled. A couple of members of the second band were beginning to set up on the minuscule stage.

The band was called The Body Hacks. The bass drum began to thump and the guitarist struck one or two chords that crunched and whined like metal being scrapped. As the soundcheck continued, a flow of people began to brush through the red curtain at the entrance as if they had been waiting for this signal. By the time The Body Hacks were ready to play, the room was so closely packed that a sense of expectancy was brought naturally to ready fullness. Damien was sure he noticed the air itself grow warmer.

The lead singer introduced the band, there was applause, and in the ripeness of the moment the band kicked into their first song.

The playing was tight, and the chord sequences and rhythm changes were sufficient to show that the band had a certain amount of musical acumen and ambition. The singer, like the rest of the band, was in his early to mid-twenties. There was something muscular about his performance. Damien found it less theatrical than like that of a charismatic sportsman. Even then, the singer lacked the grace that athletes often possess. Instead, it was as if he had rolled up his sleeves to muck in and get a job done.

This stance, and the singer's floppy blond hair, not quite shoulder length, combined with the scratchy guitar and boisterous, anthemic melodies, made Damien think of the Madchester scene of the nineties. However, when the singer spoke to the audience and to the rest of the band between songs, it seemed to Damien that he was more likely to have come from Oxfordshire than Manchester. The singer certainly showed skill in working the stage. It was remarkable that he didn't fall off, or show signs of feeling cramped in his performance. Clearly this kind of confidence came from experience. However, Damien could not help noticing that he was able to reference every gesture and every nuance of attitude back to something he had seen before, whether it was footage of an early Rolling Stones concert, a video for one of the singles from The The's *Infected* album, or a TV appearance of Reef playing 'Place Your Hands'. Inwardly, he conceded that the singer had the raw charm of a handsome, red-cheeked lad stealing an apple, but he was also gratified to observe how easily he saw through the heir-apparent mantle the band had assumed. The way they held the stage declared they had 'got it', and that if the audience got it too, they could climb up the same ladder, a few rungs behind. Well, there are worse adventures, Damien thought.

Considering himself to have the measure of the band, Damien found his attention straying to the rest of the environment, which had become at least as interesting to him as the stage, and probably more so. He didn't feel like sitting down anymore. Not caring if he lost his seat, he rose and squeezed between the standing latecomers who demonstrated the strange elasticity of the modest floor space in accommodating so many people—or, if there were not so many, in accommodating people of such interesting character that it very much seemed they were numerous. Just as he broke through the crowd who were facing the stage and into the space between them and the smaller number of people facing the bar, Damien's eye fell on two girls waiting to be served. He had seen both of them before, but one of them was a person of particular significance to him. It was the girl he had seen three or four years ago, walking on her hands at the edge of the Factory roof, and who he had been thinking of only yesterday.

He hesitated a moment, and then walked forward, taking his place at the counter next to the hand-walker's friend. He observed them sidelong, with only a bare modicum of tact. To be suspected of finding young women attractive, well, that might even serve his purpose. At worst, it would still reassure him that they didn't suspect him of anything else.

The girl on his immediate right, the friend of the hand-walker, had an almost shapeless puff of feathery blonde hair. This close, Damien thought he might catch the smell of hairspray or conditioner, but he didn't. The friend had a slightly clucking voice—a youthful, and Damien suspected, proudly cultivated iteration of some regional accent. Was she from the Potteries, he wondered. The mere sound of music, even without words, can be humorous. Listening to this voice, Damien thought of some of the guitar picking of Carl Perkins—limited in range of style and almost amusingly diminutive in presentation, but of such a degree of skill within these confines that simplicity and intricacy become indistinguishable parts of a whole that is charm.

Although Damien had not expected anything else to be of interest when placed in the immediate vicinity of the hand-walking girl, and was therefore intrigued that her friend had stimulated novel imaginings in his mind, still, his attention did not linger much about the friend, but was concentrated on the rooftop acrobat, whose name—someone hailed her before joining the siege of the stage—Damien caught (and pocketed) as Jane.

Jane's voice was both harder and softer than her friend's. It had the hardness he knew in the voices of many middle-class

English women, which, though not cold exactly, made one think of rainy days and fresh faces without make-up. But the softness of the voice, surrounding this iron core, was like burning rose petals.

Her face—the glimpses he caught of it with his slightly averted eyes—troubled him. He knew that this was the same girl he remembered walking on her hands on the rooftop. He had recognised her at that time because she had already been slightly familiar to him, and he had, thereafter, taken notice whenever he had seen her around the Factory. But peering at her face so eagerly and at such close proximity, he found she was quite different to the image of her that he had stored in his head.

Suddenly he remembered Kara, from the long-ago party to which Steve had taken him. Of course, this could not be Kara. Their names were different, and their faces were different. But they seemed to share some essential quality in that both had faces that gave the impression of changing when you examined them, melting away from your attempts to assimilate them into a sense of familiarity. And if both had changeable faces, perhaps their changes might coincide at some point, so that they became the same girl. That was ridiculous, of course. Yet the notion was not dispelled.

Did Kara and Steve remember him, Damien wondered, for a moment distracted by the thought, and suddenly woefully sad. What had become of them? But he would never see them again, and this, in fact, was true of most of the people he had known in his life. He must think of Jane, here and now, and who she might be and what she might mean.

". . . which is quite a good reflection of what's happening with her," Jane was saying. "I want to tell her, like, it's not fucked up, you're not fucked up, it's not crazy. It's all fine."

"Are you going to talk to her?"

"I did, but—"

At this point, one of the bar staff came to them and asked if they were being served. Allowed, by this interruption, to reflect,

Damien realised how excluded he felt, not just now, but every time he heard people talking about people. Whatever happened, it seemed as though he would never be included in the warm drama of concern by which individual identities secured a meaning for each other sometimes referred to as 'love', though often enough it was taken for granted and not referred to at all.

He played Jane's words over in his head, like a child treasuring a found trinket, the owner of which he hopes will not come to reclaim it: " . . . it's not fucked up, you're not fucked up, it's not crazy. It's all fine."

As soon as they had their drinks, the two girls left the bar and pushed their way, with practised insistence, to the front of the audience. Damien felt he had been too slow, and castigated himself again for giving in to hesitation. Still, the evening was a long way from being over. The young man who had served Jane and friend turned to Damien with the almost aggressive attentiveness peculiar to London bar staff, and he ordered another bottle of the same overpriced lager, on which, he thought a little ruefully, it was not so easy to get drunk. Thinking maybe he would strategise and make the next drink a whisky, he took the bottle and accompanying glass and turned back to the warm, crowded room of people everywhere concerned with people.

He kept a watch on Jane and her friend for the rest of the evening. More than once he approached, as they stood at the bar, or during the interval between bands when they went outside to chat and smoke. He learnt from eavesdropping that the other girl's name was Charlotte. However, he knew no one who could introduce him to them, and each time he drew near, he felt his determination wilting in a way that caused him almost dizzying distress.

Damien tried to imagine what would happen if he did speak to Jane and told her all the things that crowded in his mind, apparently under a pressure for release that was brought close to crisis by the special magnetism of her presence. He couldn't. It was not simply that he thought he would be rebuffed, or would make an idiot of himself. Various scenarios did present themselves to him along these and similar lines and, notably, it was easier to imagine something painful or dramatic than to imagine a pleasing outcome. But despite their urgency, these imaginary scenarios did not attain any secure purchase on his mind. They glanced off it, or else seemed to collide with some invisible barrier of credibility and, flattened, slide down it into the chasm of absurdity. The real outcome of such an action remained beyond that barrier, unknowable.

This was what repulsed him when he made an approach—not that the result might be negative, or even that it was unknown, but that it was somehow unknowable. Most actions led to imaginable results; this one, he knew, would not. In fact, this was the great trouble of the world, that no one dared to throw themselves out of the groove that keeps each life on its inconsequential course like the particular gauge of a railway track—out of that groove and into the unimaginable.

The evening wore on and the burden of this problem pressed stonier and heavier on him, but still the withering force field of the unknowable foiled his purpose. It was so potent that even alcohol did nothing to mitigate its influence. Damien was unwilling this time to accept defeat, but nor could he advance one step towards the territory he hoped to capture. There was one action, however, by which he might at least call the situation stalemate, and he decided to take it, or told himself that he decided. He would not let Jane and Charlotte leave the bar without his observing it, and he would follow Jane back to her room. That was all. As long as he knew where she lived, there was hope, and he did not have to decide immediately how to put that hope to use.

They stayed later than he had anticipated. After the last band left the stage, a D.J. set up his equipment in the corner near the bar, some of the tables were pushed to the side, and the floor was given over to dancing. Jane and Charlotte's appetite for dancing almost brought Damien to despair. In no mood to dance himself, and afraid he would lose sight of them if he did so too wholeheartedly, he portioned out his dancing and his rest in miserable strategy, increasingly certain that his intention to trail Jane must be transparent.

At last, the D.J.'s set came to a close. Damien was bitter with impatience. Everyone seemed to be moving with exaggerated slowness, lingering instead of making their way directly to the exit, and, accordingly, he was forced to do worse than linger. He lurked. He loitered. Were they determined to spend the night here? He almost didn't believe it when they stopped talking to their friends, picked up their jackets from a table at the side of the room and, putting arms through sleeves, headed out to the nighted courtyard.

Too tired and agitated to compose himself to subtlety, he followed them. Unsurprisingly, it appeared that they lived in that part of the Factory on the opposite side of the courtyard to his own studio.

Being subtle, anyway, was a bad idea, he realised. They need not know there was anything to be subtle about. So, as they approached the barred gate to the stairway entrance, he hastened to close the gap between them and himself. This was a common enough occurrence. Someone wanted to go in a particular entrance, but didn't have a key to that gate and therefore took the opportunity of slipping in immediately behind someone who did. Such people were almost always obliged. Damien, too, was obliged on this occasion as Charlotte held the gate open for him. He became just another Factory transient, dropping in on a friend who was having a party, perhaps. At any rate, the corridors and stairways here were accustomed to footsteps at all hours from people on various errands.

He followed them as if he would have overtaken them, had he been a little more determined. They, like he, lived on the top floor. Perhaps they shared a studio. In any case, they stopped at, and entered, the same door. Damien brushed past them, as if he knew where he was going. When the door clicked closed, he stepped lightly back and confirmed the number: 331.

That was all he needed to know. He repeated it in his head. That door meant possibility and hope. He had to contemplate it fully. And then he had to act.

✳

The next evening, after work, he contemplated that door while he sat in his studio. Nothing came of this contemplation. Yesterday the door had meant everything, but today he couldn't quite get it to mean anything at all. In his mind he recapitulated, over and over, the process that had been tormenting him for some time. He had been assured, by experience and insight, of the meaning of life, and thus freed. But with the assurance came loss of aspiration, so that guaranteed meaning automatically became meaninglessness, and since meaninglessness was a prison, freedom therefore led automatically to confinement. It was stifling.

Restless with this inner distraction, Damien leafed through some old notebooks and scraps of paper. He found, as he was doing so, something resembling a to-do list on a page torn out of a small spiral-bound jotter. He could not remember quite when he had written it. It was like a beach pebble. The daily tides had smoothed away those features that would identify its place in time most readily. One item on the list, however, retained traces that made it particular and pervious in his memory. The item read:

Write poem 'The Rain'.

Somehow he remembered just enough to be sure that the idea he had had for this poem had been original, subtle and complete within itself. There would be nothing strained about the poem, he had been sure from the conception he had formed; it would be an entirely novel but also profoundly natural way of presenting the otherwise commonplace poetic melancholy associated with rain. But this memory was all feeling, without linguistic detail. The all-important conception itself was gone, and there seemed to be no hope of recalling it so that the poem might really be written. Realising that this poem had slipped from his grasp, because he had failed to make sufficient notes at the time it had been fresh in his mind, Damien experienced a surprisingly pulsatory pang of dismay, like invisible bat wings of regret.

The funny thing was, this list was clearly written before the evening, two days ago, when he had lain upon his mattress and listened to the faint tapping of the rain on the skylight. The rain on that evening had certainly had a memorable effect on him, as if his nervous system were a naked web of tenderness on which the droplets were falling with soothing, refreshing vibration—here, there, in this part and then that, without pattern, but as comforting as the finest symmetry. Surely his experience on that occasion had something in common with the forgotten experience that had prompted him to mark this unusual item on his to-do list. Perhaps he could use the more recent experience as a means of retrieving the lost concept.

He reached for it in thought, like groping in waters whose reflections hid their depths. He felt sure there must be something there. It was as if quick fish brushed his fingertips, but when he snatched after them they were gone.

At last he gave up. For this lifetime, the poem was lost to him.

Yet, he felt he had to write something. He selected one of the notebooks that still had blank pages and uncapped a nearby biro. After some thought, he drafted a few paragraphs:

> One defining function of God must be to ensure that nothing is ever lost, even such a gossamer detail as the poem I would write if only I could remember the concept. But how is this permanent record achieved?
>
> Technologists and transhumanists, with their array of toxic imitations of nature and the divine,

strive merely for indefinite preservation, but that is not the same as permanence. With their putative immortality, each moment once more re-opens the question of whether their efforts will succeed.

God preserves all things by allowing them to pass into the infinity of non-existence. What more perfect storage can there be, from which each retrieval is a rebirth?

So things are best kept by being lost.

If so, why bother to try and capture things at all, for instance, in a poem about rain? Why try to persuade against suicide?

Because without the mortal effort to capture, there can be no loss, and without loss, there is no eternal preservation.

Damien put down the pen as if he had just completed a final act. His mind was empty, and then a thought crossed it. At first he did not even know what the thought was; he simply watched its progress like the trail of a jet plane across an otherwise cloudless sky.

Then he became excited.

He turned to a fresh page in the same notepad, but realised this would not do. He must, he thought, have letter-writing paper somewhere, and envelopes. Of course—there was some stationery left over from his correspondence with Sadie.

He fetched the letter stationery from the drawer where he had left it, in the kaidan-dansu that took up one portion of the wall's jigsaw puzzle, opened the pad on the workbench and set the pen down beside it. The paper was like a blue sky. There was so much to write—how could he fill it?

A sudden excess of nervous energy made it impossible for him to stay in his chair. He got up, paced about. How could he even begin to write the letter that was now being born in his mind as a coalescence of excitement and phrasing? He would have to hold it down in order to fix it to the page. Anyway, he certainly could not let it go as he had, reluctantly, let the rain poem go. This letter was imperative, and therefore he writhed under its impossibility as an ant writhes under a magnifying glass.

He had to harness his agitation, and so he decided to make himself some tea. Turning his movement into a mundane ritual, he could begin to steer it.

Finally, when tea was ready, he brought his pacing to a halt and sat back down. It was no good planning. This was simply one of the things in life that must be done, and nothing outside the doing of it would make a difference.

He wrote his address and the date in the top right-hand corner of the page. Then he wrote two more words. Then he put the pen down again, full of an almost intolerable agitation. But he snatched the pen up again after about twenty seconds and began to write as if the need to be legible were restraining a frantic energy that would otherwise make his words a long, broken scrawl. It was the kind of energy that usually burns out swiftly, but on this occasion, it did not burn out. It kept smouldering steadily for one page after another. Damien became painstakingly lost in the intricacies of letters. Once or twice he got up again from his chair, but now, when he did not write, he was drawn back to it by the magnetism of his unfinished purpose.

Finally, the end approached. He was on his last paragraph. He slowed, with trembling hand, like a marathon runner in sight of the finishing line who suddenly feels he might collapse. Then he managed a signature, distorted, as if he were drunk, and tossed aside his pen. After all, what he had written had only here and there come close to the feeling that had been its motive impulse, but, he judged, it was sufficient.

Now was the time for him to go to studio 331.

He took an envelope, folded his written pages to fit neatly within, inserted the pages, sealed the envelope, and wrote, "To Jane" on the obverse side.

Descending to the ground floor, then exiting into the courtyard, Damien wondered how long it would take before the gate to the entrance in question would be opened to him. Confronted by this obstacle, he realised that he might be forced to stand here for hours if he was to rely on others opening the gate. He looked about. There was a length of timber by the skip that stood in the passage leading to the backstreet exit from the Factory. Using this, he reached between the bars of the gate to press the release button on the other side. It was a very simple trick, and he supposed it must be well known among those who lived in and otherwise haunted the Factory. No other obstacles were left, unless Jane's door was open. He wanted to slip the letter beneath, unseen. This last question, along with the knowledge of the letter's content, were the remaining elements of his nervousness as he made his way up the grimy stairs.

Reaching the top floor and turning into the corridor where studio 331 was located, Damien saw that the door was closed, as he had hoped, and one more element of nervousness was removed, so that the essential matter, unalloyed, began to glow in the singleness of its significance. She would see her name on the envelope. She would wonder who it might be from. She would open it. She would begin to read.

Making sure to soften his footsteps, he approached the door. He crouched. Slowly, he slid the envelope beneath the door's lower edge. Then, quickly, he stood, combining swiftness of stride as best he could with stealth, wondering how long it would be until the letter was discovered.

Dear Jane,

We haven't been introduced and I cannot claim that we have friends or acquaintances in common. I have few enough of those anyway, so would consider it a safe bet that we haven't. In short, you don't know me, but there is a sense in which I know you.

How often do you walk on your hands on the Factory roof? I have seen you do it once. Perhaps there have been other times. I am neither jealous nor demanding. If there have been other times, it is impressive that you have the confidence, and if there has been only one time there is a particular beauty in that for me, since I would have been witness to that unique occasion.

Anyway, that's how I know you. I would like to point out that if I had merely seen you in the corridor or at the bar, I would not say that I knew you, only that I had seen you. There is a difference. Maybe you can appreciate this.

But I shouldn't rely on your being able to appreciate it. I should try and explain.

Who would you most want to tell a secret? Your best friend, maybe. Or maybe a complete stranger who you will never see again. It is probably hardest to tell secrets to people you know only a little and might later know better—those somewhere between best friend and complete stranger. I have a secret I would like to tell you, but I don't consider it to be telling a stranger. On the one hand, I know it is not quite as safe as telling a stranger—especially now you have my address—and my motivation is not for some kind of safe relief, either. On the other hand it is especially you that I want to tell. I can't say exactly that I think you will understand, but if I could tell you that would be as meaningful to me as if I told my best friend—perhaps more so. You might hate me, or be horrified. I really have no way of knowing how you will react. All I know is that you are the right person for my confession.

You have been in my mind a great deal. There is no doubt that you have an important and permanent place there, no matter what you may or may not think about me.

First, you inspired me. The more I think about it, the more it seems to me that it really was due to your influence that I was able to do what I did. This is where things get a bit complicated, I'm afraid. I'm not blaming you. I could have used that inspiration in a different way. You could say that it was your fate, unknown to you until now, to inspire the kind of person I am. Anyway, I did what I did as if I had your permission, and partly for that reason, I cannot bring myself to think that it was a completely evil thing that I did. This is the hardest part to explain. Maybe there is some good even in what I did. I think there is. But that does not excuse me. What I did still requires a confession.

And then, after the consequences of my actions had become clear, you came to my mind again. I can't describe how naturally and unexpectedly—it could not have been my imagination. It seemed clear to me that, even if you did not forgive me, you were the right person to hear my story. Something in you understands what it means to balance on the very edge of things.

I suppose I should try to reassure you that, despite my expectation that you will recoil at what I have to say to you, I mean you no harm. I can't think of any way to persuade you on this point beyond the statement itself: abhorrent as I may be, you have nothing to fear from me. In fact, if you were to report me to the police I would consider it the judgement of fate to which I must bow my head. As I said, you have my address.

I do not think I can add any forms of reassurance that are essentially different to the above.

If you've read this far, you will want to know what I have done. But I want to tell you in person. I have to look into your eyes and tell you.

You might also want to know why—as in, why I want to confess—and even if you don't, for me this is the most important part, and I must think now about how I am going to explain this.

Let me start by saying that I am a nurse. I work in conventional medicine—respectable, you see?—but I believe in what some people call holistic healing. It's possible I am more holistic than others. I think I am, in fact. And maybe some people would even say I am too holistic. I try to start from first principles. All bad faith and errors of reason must be eliminated, as if with surgery. This is philosophy. Rightly understood—for instance, as Kierkegaard understood it—philosophy is medicine. Psychiatrists are meant to be the doctors of the soul, but philosophy is older than psychiatry and should be more foundational to the latter.

I suppose that's all technical. Important, but technical.

The point is, everything is related, and I want to turn all those related things to the good.

So, there is a patient I am caring for at the moment. His name is Fergus Kinghan. He is suicidal. As far as I am aware, I am the only one he has confided in. I hesitate to interfere. I wonder if you understand that? I hesitate, because I don't know if I have the authority, and because there is something irregular about it. I don't mean professionally. But, at the same time that I'm hesitating, there is some burning thing—an imperative—that tells me I must save his life. This is why I hesitate—I must contravene his philosophy, you see? I must surgically remove some errors of reasoning. I am not sure I have the authority for that. Some might think it's against his human rights. I might think that. You know what I mean.

But this burning, to save Fergus's life, is also the burning to save my own life. That is why it is so deep, why it's related to everything, why it makes me understand things I can hardly express.

Do you know this quote?: "Physician, heal thyself!" That's philosophy, you see.

I have tried to talk to Fergus. That is, I have opened my mouth to speak, but I cannot force myself to say the necessary words. The words are not really in me yet, though I seem to know what they might be. I cannot help him while I am still so diseased. I see it with the certainty of a broken bone in an X-ray photograph. I must heal myself first, and you can help me do that if you hear my confession.

What I'm talking about is madness, you understand? You've read this letter, you can see that it's madness. But it's the madness of life itself, the madness we all deny, and which we must embrace to live truly.

Let me tell you a little of my confession here. That way, even if you refuse to hear the rest, there might be the possibility of some healing, for myself and for Fergus.

I am a graverobber.

That is only the beginning of my confession. From that, you might be imagining all kinds of things, but I am quite certain you will not imagine the truth. I'll enclose, with this letter, details of the grave I robbed. You can use them in evidence against me. I hope they will help you to take seriously all I have written here.

Do you want to know one thing I have learned? Perhaps here and there, now and then, there has been such a thing as a living human being, but most of us are in our graves. We dig our graves with lies. Some dig with teaspoons, some with JCBs. And because we are all underground, we keep each other there. We support each other's lies. Imagine the universal consternation if someone claws his way out of the grave and lives! But imagine also a world where that person is allowed to live, not only that, but allowed to pull others up from the earth, so that there are more and more living human beings.

Until that happens all of us will pass our days in secret shame.

That, anyway, is what I am trying to do—to claw my way out of my grave so that I might pull Fergus up. As I said, this is madness, and I admit it might fail in the most bathetic of ways. But I thought it was worth the risk to try it.

I don't know how long Fergus will be at the hospital. Please make your mind up soon. If you will hear my confession, come to my studio. I want to tell you, alone, but I don't even mind if you have a friend waiting outside. I'll include my working hours overleaf. I'm usually home when I'm not working. My phone number is at the bottom of this page if you need it. I think I've said all I can.

Yours,

Damien Chase

That night, Damien barely slept. During his commute the next day he was aware of a very unusual sensation. It was as if a bullet, passing through him at high velocity in the normal manner, had left in its wake a huge, cratered hole, perhaps just above the heart. He felt an unaccustomed throbbing in the tides of his blood, an intensity like that of being squeezed. At the same time, and in contrast, fresh air passed freely through the newly opened and tender aperture. The air told him that, quite exceptionally, he had a hole blown through him and still walked about with balance and energy as if unscathed.

He came close to telling Fergus of how he had robbed a grave, but a sense of absurdity held him back—a potent mechanism whose working he did not understand.

When he returned home he was restless, but forced himself to keep to the studio in case Jane made the decision to come.

He passed the evening alone.

This was what he thought he had expected, yet, when he recalled the content of his letter, what he had put into it and what was surely transparent to the reader, he was almost incredulous.

And what if she did come? All that was required, of course, was that he tell the truth, but what if she didn't believe it? What a strange frustration that would be.

He was putting himself entirely at the mercy of fate, as if he expected the best result for himself this way, but what if fate really did have no mercy? Events could go off on all kinds of jagged tangents.

Perhaps his actions would have no repercussions at all. He was unsure whether this was what he most wanted or what he least wanted. Either way, he was troubled by the knowledge that something might happen, that he did not know what it would be or if it would be, and, if it would, that he did not know how long it would take.

Eventually, he grew tired and was diffused in sleep like a drop of grey ink in water. As shapeless as the inside of a pupa, he dreamt. It was a peculiar dream, stimulating strange areas of emotion in him, like muscles that had gone long without use. In the morning he retained only a few images and ideas in the net of consciousness. Jane had been walking, in the dream, along the corridors of the Factory—endlessly walking, as if she had set out to look for Damien, but had been little concerned with her goal and so had begun to walk without aim. Damien, who seemed to be a disembodied viewpoint, could see her walking, but actually, all he saw was the area from about her midriff to the tops of her legs, as viewed from the front. He was always exactly the same distance from her, like a television tracking shot, so that, although she seemed to put one foot in front of the other, it was as if she did not move; the corridors moved around her.

After some time, it looked as though she was not walking at all, but floating. Moreover, this section of her body, from midriff to upper leg, became her, representing her personhood in the way that a face normally would. It occurred to the passively viewing Damien, who moved backwards, ahead of her, without volition, that this was the area containing her ovaries and vagina, and he seemed to see these features of anatomy like the internal organs of a jellyfish.

She was wearing jeans of a dark blue colour beneath a striped woollen jersey. The jeans were of that kind that stay very dark blue in some places even when quite old, while growing a little faded here and there. In some places such jeans are tight, and in other places they are creased in a badly-fitting way. In other words, they are casual jeans rather than sexy jeans, but, as if because of these jeans, he became more and more aware of the sexual attributes of the person they clad.

Not suddenly, but with a creeping swiftness, first Jane's vulva then her buttocks and anus became intimately present to his mind. He was convinced that he had mapped each real hair and each pore of her skin. Vaguely aware he was dreaming, he thought he would be able to verify the accuracy of this when he awoke.

He was not sexually aroused. It would not have been accurate to say he was revolted, either. Instead he was uncomfortable that his attention was involuntarily forced onto this area. It seemed vaguely unpleasant, like an apple out of which someone else has taken a bite. He also felt the indefinable absurdity of this section of the human body, which is only mitigated by the facts that dwelling on the absurdity is juvenile and that it is an absurdity in which all partake equally. There was a strange claustrophobia to sharing his breathing space, mentally speaking, with this vague unpleasantness and irreducible absurdity. He seemed to suspect that all this somehow said something about him—this vagina, this anus. But he could not remove himself from the intimacy he had now formed with this anatomy. As it continued its floating walk, he felt himself growing more used to it so that the unpleasantness and absurdity faded into a sense of naturalness and comfort, and he wondered why he had ever felt differently.

Eventually the corridor faded and all that remained was the anatomy, encased in jeans and jersey. Then most of this, too, disappeared, leaving behind a fossil in the form of Jane's knickers. These floated now—whether in motion or motionless was impossible to say—against a background of nebulous colour like that visible to the closed eyes of a waking person. These knickers bore the imprint of unpleasantness and absurdity where vulva and anus had been, as if they had thus taken a sample of the distilled essence of human history. To be nostalgic or to be compassionate was to acknowledge the necessity of these twin blossoms of unpleasantness and absurdity. The ascetic might be right in his limited way, but without the kisses of these blossoms, which brought all to life, he would have nothing to be right about.

So Jane's knickers hovered in warm chaos. Lightning began to flicker from the gusset, and the lightning spoke. Damien was aware that he had become a tiny, silhouetted figure kneeling on a colourful nothingness at some position lower than the floating knickers. He listened with bowed head to each thing the flickering lightning chiselled upon the atmosphere, but when he awoke, all of this wisdom, more ancient and profound than the Bible, had shattered into so many pieces that he could not reassemble them into anything meaningful.

Damien felt himself wistful and softened. When next he had to tend to Fergus he remarked that Fergus had survived such a violent physical trauma because his body wanted to live and was doing all it could to heal itself.

"Why?" asked Fergus. "If it wants to live then it's not on my side. Why do I have to live just because my body wants to?"

Damien attempted to dispel the dualism he had unwittingly encouraged in Fergus. He had hoped to make Fergus identify with his body, not declare war against it. However, Damien realised his own attempts to deny Fergus's dualism were leading him into confusion, and he retraced his steps before he could sink into a rhetorical morass.

Fergus, anyway, took this as another opportunity to vocalise the grievances that seemed to eat into him like infected wounds. Damien decided his sally had been hasty and ill-conceived and that the best way to save his position was to become a listener. He learnt a little more of Fergus's motives for his attempted suicide. There were financial factors that had played a significant role, making a disaster out of a situation that would otherwise have been one of endurable though debilitating sadness. There were people higher up who had been firm in safeguarding what to them was pocket change, and the life to which Fergus had been accustomed had been demolished as a result.

It seemed Fergus's life had long been precarious, and he had almost expected something like this—only the worst he had feared was that he would be so cornered by circumstance that he would have no choice but to kill himself. This was worse than that, he said, because he had survived. For the past few years he had worked a number of day jobs while playing bass and writing lyrics for a band, somewhat in the Joy Division mould, called The Holy Family. The band had a number of times been on the verge of being recognised by the music press, but the impossibility of earning money from album sales meant that all the members needed to maintain undemanding day jobs. One by one, they had had to commit to other things, and the band had disintegrated like a spacecraft on a failed mission burning up on re-entry into Earth's atmosphere. Fergus, now out of work too, had experienced mental health issues at this time and, as a result, had broken up with his girlfriend, exacerbating the situation further. It was at precisely this time that he had been notified by the Department of Work and Pensions that they had been overpaying his housing benefit—due to clerical error—for some months, and now they demanded a repayment amounting to over a thousand pounds.

On the one hand, Damien felt that to attempt suicide for financial reasons was absurd, like buying new clothes because you feel hungry. On the other hand, lack of money seemed like the most legitimate reason of all, since poverty had a kind of autonomy to it as a fact of life. Refusing to be abstract, poverty exerted a deleterious influence on all the fundamental variables of the existential mixing desk. Sheer and terrible as an unsterilised blade, when poverty fell upon a person, it severed them from the dignity of problems concerning 'the human condition' and left them to deal with desperate animal pain. Poverty possessed the disruptive power of death itself. Arguments might have seemed academic when the problem in question was the violence inflicted on a human life by poverty. And yet if Damien's arguments were serious enough to tackle suicide generally, why not the despair induced by poverty? If his arguments did not withstand poverty then they were not worth making at all. But still, today, he was not ready to make them.

Friday came, then Saturday.

There was no change in Damien's situation and he wondered whether he had somehow got away without precipitating the kind of crisis he had desired. Limbo is safe, he told himself, but it can't last.

On Saturday morning he set out by train for the southwestern suburb of Isleworth. He had been selling a number of items by eBay, and had included personal delivery for some of them. In this case, it was one of the projectors he had used to create the effects he had on the day of Sadie's final visit. He was glad to be getting rid of this equipment. Handling it, he felt like what he supposed he was: an untried criminal whose crime weakened him like an internal injury. But the day was bright and the air, though chill, had about it the refreshing purity of an unclouded stream that flashes in sunlight.

Damien was happy to find himself in the Quiet Zone of the train he boarded at Waterloo. However, it wasn't long before this mild happiness was marred by a reminder of what he should have remembered—that no one takes any notice of the signs in the Quiet Zone. A few seats away from him a young woman with clacking bracelets began to chat loudly on a mobile phone, only a few minutes after they had pulled out of the station. Across the aisle, a young man in a business suit was watching a film on his laptop. Elsewhere in the carriage people made conversation in voices that seemed to Damien of a gratuitously high volume. The egotism of it all appalled him. They were either oblivious to the other people around them or wished to broadcast the fact of their existence as widely as possible. He only wished the values of the society of which he was an unwilling member were such that he could have had these people thrown off the train, but he knew the Quiet Zone was an ineffectual token of support for something endangered that few people genuinely cared about now. The winning side was the noisy side, and the case for the defence of silence would not be heard. No one would even understand it if it were made.

He tried to concentrate on his book, Henri Bergson's *Time and Free Will*, but had to keep re-reading the same paragraph. Soon after Clapham Junction, he gave up and gazed out of the window at the passing welter of angled rooftops, leisure centres,

dilapidated garden fences, screens of trees, the trackside brickwork
and arched bridges of the approach to Putney, station platforms,
tapering streets leading away from the exits from such platforms,
a silver-shimmered stretch of river, Old Chiswick Cemetery, al-
lotments, and so on.

The transaction at Isleworth was brief and pleasant. He had
a glimpse of the buyer's home—a flat near the river—knowing
it would be his only glimpse. It allowed him a sample of the
warmth of domesticity uncomplicated by any of the pain or difficulty experienced by the occupier in his ordinary human struggle
for survival and meaning.

Damien didn't want to go straight home on such a fine day and
after such a long journey. Besides, he had nothing else planned.
He decided, therefore, to spend the afternoon in Richmond, eating at a café, browsing the shops, wandering.

He walked along the banks of the river, crossed a slender
bridge, then found his way through some narrow streets that took
him to the green, where small groups of people sat on the grass,
some of them eating sandwiches from cardboard packaging, others talking or playing with small children. A path cut across the
green diagonally, and he followed this to the far corner and a road
that led to the High Street, where most of the shops were.

Crossing over, and heading once more in the general direction of the river, he was intrigued to see another side-street on
his left, with the awnings of a pub and a café on one side, and
the glazing of a branch of Tesco on the other, apparently leading
to a courtyard of some kind. A sign informed him that this was
Church Court. Past the passage, in the court itself, Damien saw
what looked like a war memorial—a tiered edifice of stone surmounted by a cross and surrounded by a hexagonal flowerbed. A
sense of stillness drew him down this passage to the court, away
from the noise of the main street. He quickly saw that the memorial stood in the grounds of a church with clear-glass arched
windows and grimy walls of once-red brick, as well as portions

whose walls were a mosaic of flint. Coming to the entrance, he saw a sign in the vestibule: "We are open. Please come in."

The invitation was pleasing to him, as if meant for him personally yet without the off-putting pressure of another person's expectation. Through the windows of the vestibule's inner doors, he saw that the pews were empty and no one else seemed to be present. Grasping the pull-handle on one of these doors, he pulled it open and walked through, immediately sensing the difference between the external and internal atmosphere. The sound of the door closing behind him—the ordinary creak and catch of wood and metal—was almost ticklish in this new air, on the one hand soothing and on the other like the unknown something that suddenly teases the hairs and nerves in the nostril and unleashes a sneeze. There was, indeed, a smell of dust here, and of age. In his younger years, he knew, he would have found it to be the smell of dullness itself, but now it seemed rich in suggestion. If, alongside the usual varieties of incense, such as jasmine and sandalwood, it were possible to find the scent 'dust', this is what it would smell like. If there were decay here, this half-spicy dust seemed to testify, it was not the kind that tended to disease and corruption, but the kind that tended towards peace. The younger self that would have thought the dust a sign of dullness would have found the atmosphere itself mere anti-climax; now it occurred to him that this was precisely the welcome that peace gives. It seems to shrink away to make space for you. He glanced at a board to the left where a number of index cards had been slipped under criss-crossed ribbons. On the cards, in different hands, prayers were written.

It was almost peculiar, he thought, given his other interests, that he so rarely entered a church, but a disappointment of ancient date was buried deeply in him, so that he did not question this peculiarity very closely.

Walking slowly down the aisle between the wooden pews with the prayer cushions hanging from their backs, he looked about himself like a respectful tourist. There were memorials of one kind and another among the stone flags of the floor. The windows, on each side, showed the outer world as if through runnels of silent rain. The panes were warped, as window panes in old buildings sometimes are. The trees and buildings visible through them were bright with the undivided light of the day, but, in their distortion, looked weightless, like rippled reflections, so that it seemed the very substance of the world was revealed as light, the forms it took a diaphanous play.

A little more than halfway to the altar, Damien looked to his right and slipped into the pew. He sat and closed his eyes. His ears were ringing as if he had just escaped an explosion. That, he realised, was the ordinary noise of the world, even in a relatively tranquil suburb. The continual noise seemed nearly to have shattered his hearing. In this stillness, it was obvious. In the same way, the noise of the world continued to echo in his heart. He was safe here. It was a weekend. No one was looking for him and no one knew where he was. Yet the noise continued in his heart, and the pain and the loneliness, restless, as if something must be done to prevent some vague and terrible thing. As his ears had been ravaged, so had his heart.

It was not even that it was silent in here. He could still hear all the sounds from outside. There was the constant drag and bray of car engines, the sound of tyres on tarmac, of a passing police siren, of footsteps and voices and planes to or from nearby Heathrow. In a sense, these sounds were more distinct now—he was freshly aware of them and distinguished them from each other with a clarity as if he had regained his hearing after impairment of some kind. At the same time, they had been made distant and delicate—watercolour sounds. The church made him safe from and intimate with them. Just as the windows warped what was seen through them, the atmosphere of the church warped the sounds. They seemed to warble at the edges, speeding up or slowing down, like a cassette in a faulty tape player. Strangely, in this way, they ceased to be agitation and became peace.

He could sit like this, he thought, all day. In fact, he wished he could live like this, awake in the midst of the gentlest of all dreams. But however long he sat, there seemed to remain, unsoothed-away, in his heart, some nub of the noise and pain he had brought in with him, and this nub told him that sooner or later he would have to get up again and leave, taking his place once more in the endless tilting and sliding of events whose shuffling would eventually eliminate him from the entire process.

With the sense of having found a tonic but not a cure, he finally opened his eyes, stood, and moved lingeringly to the exit.

The path that had brought him a while ago to the church entrance continued, sloping upward, to a main road not far away. On either side of this path there was turf that had obviously once been used as a graveyard. In fact, a number of graves remained. Nearby, on Damien's right, was a raised tomb surrounded by the bars of ornamental black iron fencework. There was an inscription at the foot of the slab. Damien drew closer and a squirrel that had been twitching from one frozen pose to another on the lichened surface of the tomb scampered away between the bars. The inscription read:

WILLIAM HICKEY Gent.
a great Benefactor to the Poor
of this Parifh
DIED MARCH 5, 1728.

Beyond this grave, perhaps twenty feet away, a low brick wall divided this burial ground from what looked like rented residential properties with sash windows and cluttered balconies. Set against the low brick wall were a number of extremely weathered headstones, probably displaced to the edge of the ground at some date after new burials had ceased here—or would it be before? After all his delvings, he still couldn't say. Damien had a sense, suddenly, of the very idea of the grave as something historical, a culture, though widespread, nonetheless specific to certain conditions limited in time and space, and showing signs of declining into obscurity. The population of the planet had passed the seven billion mark this century, he reflected. Where to bury all those people? Yet here were graves still, as much a reality in his life as cars or squirrels or language. How thoroughly beautiful these tombs were, like pine combs dropped from some great, grey tree of faith and death. How lucky he was to be alive while what was declining yet remained.

He walked on, reached the main road, crossed at a pelican crossing, all the while thinking what a beautiful thing a grave is, limited and cultural. But then, he thought, isn't the whole world a grave, all of this, everything I see now? This was certainly true, and he knew it was beautiful.

Damien had a late lunch, or early dinner, at a Richmond café, and made his way without haste back home to the Candle Street studio. Once back, he snacked on cheese and crackers, drank tea, and alternated between reading and daydreaming. It was dark before he knew it. Looking up from *The Abolition of Man*, by C.S. Lewis, he shivered, stood, turned on the space heater at the plug.

He was just stretching and yawning when there came a knock at the door. This was such a rare occurrence that instantly a whole diorama of expectations that had been switched off and laid to one side was brought forth again within him, and activated. He looked to the workbench. After all, he was ready.

With a most delicate nervousness playing about his torso like an aurora, he walked to the door, still hung about by curtains. He did not allow himself to pause, but opened it wide immediately. For a conspicuously long time—a duration negotiated by the gaze of the person at the threshold meeting his—he could not find anything to say. It was Charlotte.

Apparently understanding his difficulty, she raised her hand, in which she held an envelope—opened—that he recognised.

He nodded.

"Come in," he said, and she closed the door behind her, following him through the curtains and into the studio.

"It's hard to know where to start," said Damien, "but I want to tell you about *him*."

And here he pointed to the workbench, on whose surface Philip sat contracted in his bony wickerwork of rigor mortis like a baleful trophy.

A PARTIAL LIST OF SNUGGLY BOOKS

G. ALBERT AURIER *Elsewhere and Other Stories*

S. HENRY BERTHOUD *Misanthropic Tales*

LÉON BLOY *The Tarantulas' Parlor and Other Unkind Tales*

JAMES CHAMPAGNE *Harlem Smoke*

FÉLICIEN CHAMPSAUR *The Latin Orgy*

FÉLICIEN CHAMPSAUR
The Emerald Princess and Other Decadent Fantasies

BRENDAN CONNELL *Clark*

BRENDAN CONNELL *Unofficial History of Pi Wei*

ADOLFO COUVE *When I Think of My Missing Head*

QUENTIN S. CRISP *Graves*

QUENTIN S. CRISP *Rule Dementia!*

LADY DILKE *The Outcast Spirit and Other Stories*

CATHERINE DOUSTEYSSIER-KHOZE *The Beauty of the Death Cap*

BERIT ELLINGSEN *Now We Can See the Moon*

BERIT ELLINGSEN *Vessel and Solsvart*

EDMOND AND JULES DE GONCOURT *Manette Salomon*

GUIDO GOZZANO *Alcina and Other Stories*

RHYS HUGHES *Cloud Farming in Wales*

J.-K. HUYSMANS *Knapsacks*

COLIN INSOLE *Valerie and Other Stories*

JUSTIN ISIS *Pleasant Tales II*

JUSTIN ISIS (editor) *Marked to Die: A Tribute to Mark Samuels*

JUSTIN ISIS AND DANIEL CORRICK (editors)
Drowning in Beauty: The Neo-Decadent Anthology

VICTOR JOLY *The Unknown Collaborator and Other Legendary Tales*

BERNARD LAZARE *The Mirror of Legends*

BERNARD LAZARE *The Torch-Bearers*

MAURICE LEVEL *The Shadow*

JEAN LORRAIN *Errant Vice*

JEAN LORRAIN *Masks in the Tapestry*

JEAN LORRAIN *Nightmares of an Ether-Drinker*

JEAN LORRAIN *The Soul-Drinker and Other Decadent Fantasies*

www.ingramcontent.com/pod-product-compliance
Lightning Source LLC
Chambersburg PA
CBHW050825190726
48286CB00007B/1994